Dead Storage

The Maggie McDonald Mystery series by Mary Feliz

Address to Die For

Scheduled to Death

Dead Storage

Dead Storage

A Maggie McDonald Mystery

Mary Feliz

LYRICAL UNDERGROUND
Kensington Publishing Corp
www.kensingtonbooks.com

LYRICAL UNDERGROUND BOOKS are published by

Kensington Publishing Corp.
119 West 40th Street
New York, NY 10018

All Kensington titles, imprints, and distributed lines are available at special quantity discounts for bulk purchases for sales promotion, premiums, fundraising, educational, or institutional use.

Special book excerpts or customized printings can also be created to fit specific needs. For details, write or phone the office of the Kensington Sales Manager: Kensington Publishing Corp., 119 West 40th Street, New York, NY 10018. Attn. Sales Department. Phone: 1-800-221-2647.

Lyrical Underground and Lyrical Underground logo Reg. US Pat. & TM Off.

First Electronic Edition: July 2017
eISBN-13: 978-1-60183-007-4
eISBN-10: 1-60183-007-6

First Print Edition: July 2017
ISBN-13: 978-1-60183-147-7
ISBN-10: 1-60183-147-1

Printed in the United States of America

*For my families: those I'm related to
and those I relate to, all of whom I love.*

ACKNOWLEDGMENTS

Thank you to everyone at Kensington who helped make all of the Maggie McDonald Mysteries better than I could make them on my own.

Thanks also to everyone who contributed in ways both big and small. You know who you are.

And thanks to Neil Bevans, who helped me with Stephen's legal issues on very short notice. If Maggie, Stephen, Nell, and Rafi cut some legal corners, it's not Neil's fault.

Chapter 1

According to popular wisdom, there are few things more
dangerous than mixing friendship with one's
professional life. But organizing is a personal business
and I tend to make friends with all my clients.

From the Notebook of Maggie McDonald,
Simplicity Itself Organizing Services

Thursday, February 16, Morning

"Maggie, we've got a crisis," Jason had said the last time I'd
talked to him. "I know you insist on working with both halves
of a couple—"

"But I'm also a problem solver. What's up?"

"That spate of tornadoes and flooding in Texas, that's what. I've
been deployed. I can't back out or delay our departure. Those people
are hurting, and it's the first test of my new auxiliary law-enforcement
team. A group of TV journalists is reporting on our project for some
newsmagazine. Our funding and the future of programs like this depend on our success." Jason rattled off the sentences breathlessly,
without giving me a chance to comment or interrupt.

I understood his predicament. He'd been working on establishing
a rapid-response law enforcement team for as long as I'd known him.
The short version of the saga was that the team, with all its supplies,
could swoop into a disaster area and support law enforcement efforts
under local authority. The idea was to prevent looting, keep people
safe, provide skilled guidance to volunteers, and eliminate many of

the problems experienced by civilians, volunteers, and first respon-
ders following Hurricane Katrina and other disasters. Jason's team
and others like it hoped to plug gaps between what FEMA and the
National Guard could provide and what community resources were
designed to accomplish.

"No problem," I said. "We'll start after you get back."

"Stephen's ready to start, like, yesterday, and the demolition is
only two weeks away."

"Ah . . ." I began, stalling for time. "To be successful, any system we
develop will have to include you. If it's going to work long term—"

"Look, Maggie, I've got to go. They're loading our containers on
the cargo plane. Stephen and I talked about priorities and goals last
night. We made a list. I gave him parameters for tossing my stuff, and
I promised not to divorce him if he gives away my favorite baseball
glove. If that works for you, great. If not, take it up with Stephen.
Arrange something—"

The phone cut off. I was left with the decision of whether to begin
or postpone. I spotted several potential problems with Jason's plan.
Among the stumbling blocks was the fact that they might waste time
and money creating a system that would work for Stephen, but not
for Jason. When I'd spoken to Stephen, afterward, he considered my
advice but ultimately decided to go ahead.

"No matter what Jason says, he's going to have trouble making
time for this project, even once he's home again," Stephen said.
"Damn the torpedoes . . ."

That was two days ago. I'd decided Stephen was right. With Jason's
full-time job as a police detective he was never in full control of his own
hours. Stephen was a retired US Marine who worked unpredictable
hours volunteering with veterans and their canine counterparts, creating civilian partnerships. If we were going to have their house ready
to start a major remodel, there was no time to waste.

Today, Stephen and I were meeting to start purging their belongings,
deciding what to save, and fine-tuning our organizational strategy.

I knocked on the front door of their sprawling Victorian near the
Palo Alto border. There was no answer to the bell. No resonant woof
from Stephen's huge mastiff, Munchkin. I peered through the front
window, leaving the print of my nose on the glass. Only dust motes
moved inside.

I sat on the front step and texted Stephen:

My calendar says we're meeting at 8:30 today. Do I have that right?

Stephen was an early riser, so I'd agreed to meet him as soon as I dropped my teen boys at the middle school and high school. He'd promised me coffee and bagels. At the thought of food, my stomach rumbled and my mouth filled with saliva. I was starving and caffeine deprived. My golden retriever, Belle, thumped her tail, whined, and leaned into me, looking up with yearning. Normally, I didn't bring Belle to work with me, but Stephen was a friend of mine, a dog person, and Munchkin was Belle's BFF.

"They'll be back soon," I told her, referring to both Stephen and his seldom-absent canine partner. "I'm sure everything is fine. How often are they ever late?"

Belle made a polite sound in response.

"Right," I said. "Never . . . Well, nearly never."

Extreme and unrelenting punctuality was a fault of Stephen's, an artifact of his time in the military. Some of his friends found it annoying, but I shared the trait and appreciated his timely arrival whenever we got together. I bit my lip, sighed, and squinted into the sun to scan the neighborhood. There was no car in the drive. He must have had a last-minute errand that went longer than he had planned. Unexpected traffic tie-ups were a recurring Silicon Valley problem. With the high-tech economy, growing population, and high-density building projects booming, the area was home to a record number of people. More people meant more cars. A trip to the dentist that took fifteen minutes a month or two earlier could easily take thirty minutes or longer today, even without a rush-hour fender bender creating gridlock. The problem grew worse daily and there was no easy solution.

I looked at my watch. Any minute, I expected to see Stephen and Munchkin loping up the street from one direction or the other. At six-foot-four inches, accompanied by a dog that weighed almost as much as he did, Stephen was hard to miss.

I paced in front of the house. This situation reminded me too much of a client session I'd begun four months earlier, standing on a front porch a few blocks away when my client was late. That morning had culminated in the death of a dear friend. I shivered, drew my fleece coat closer to me, peered at my phone, and dialed Stephen's number.

The phone rang before I could finish punching the buttons.

"Hello?" I said. The phone responded with crackles and pops.

"... police station ... jail ..."

"Hello? Who is this? I'm not going to fall for that trick. My kids are safe in school." I disconnected the call. Our entire town had been plagued with phishing phone calls from crooks pretending to be our children or grandchildren. The calls all followed the same pattern: a distraught young voice claiming to be kin begged for money to be wired immediately. Most people, like me, recognized it for what it was and hung up the phone. But older people, those in the beginning stages of dementia or vulnerable in other ways, grew distraught. A friend of my mom called her daughter nearly every day to be reassured that the children and grandchildren were safe. The scams were criminal, disruptive, and downright cruel.

I shook off my righteous indignation and dialed Stephen again. In the process, I noted that the crooks, whoever they were, were getting crafty. My phone reported that the phishing call originated from the police station in Mountain View, the town that abutted Orchard View's southern border. I made a mental note to tell Jason about the call the next time we spoke. When he wasn't helping flood-ravaged towns in Texas, Jason was an Orchard View detective. He'd know who to notify about calls from people impersonating the police.

My call went to voice mail.

"Stephen?" I said. "I'm here at your house for our meeting and to get started on the front room. I can begin without you, but I'm a little worried. Can you please call and let me know what's up and when you'll get here? If you're in a bind and want to reschedule, that's fine. Just let me know you're okay."

I heard the tension in my voice. I *was* worried. But the best cure for fear was action, so I let Belle into the backyard through a side gate and started unpacking the tools of my trade from my trunk.

I unfolded a collapsible wagon and filled it with portable garment racks for sorting clothing. I added a dozen flattened cardboard boxes for storing anything we decided to keep and move. On top of the pile I added my newest find: a stack of flat-bottomed paper bags generally used in towns that required them for yard clippings. I'd marked them with an assortment of color-coded stick-on labels: garbage, recycling, and donations. The flat bottoms made it easy to set the bags up anywhere and their double-walled sides were stiff enough that the bags stayed open, making loading easy. Anything we wanted to keep would be put on a garment rack or in a box. I asked my clients to touch everything they needed to make decisions about, but to handle each item as few times as possible.

It would be a bit tricky to make decisions about Jason's belongings in his absence, particularly since his team had been asked to avoid making phone calls from the disaster area. When a widespread disaster occurs, communications networks quickly become overwhelmed by public safety officials making emergency calls, and hundreds of thousands of people checking on loved ones. Jason's emergency team was intended to help the situation rather than compound the problem. Hence, they were allowed to send and receive texts, but Jason had asked us to avoid calling and told us not to be concerned if we didn't hear from him. He was going to be very busy, working long, hard days to help the people of Texas restore their lives.

We'd agreed to temporarily store Jason's belongings in the garage for him to sort through after he returned. Part of my job was to organize those items in a way that would streamline the decision-making process.

I rattled the wagon up the front walk and unloaded it so I could get everything up the steep porch steps. If Stephen were here, he could have carried the wagon for me. I glanced up and down the street again, searching for man, dog, or car. Where were they?

I'd arranged my supplies neatly on the porch when I stopped again to glance at my phone for messages. Stephen was now more than half an hour late. Momentum was important to clients who were doing the hard work of sorting through years of belongings. Every time they hit a snag, they were tempted to stop, which made starting again twice as difficult. That was part of my job as a professional organizer: keeping things moving forward and smoothing out the inevitable frustrations.

Belle barked from the backyard. It wasn't a bark I recognized but she sounded alarmed. She scratched at the gate and barked again, louder this time. Something was wrong.

"What's the matter, girl?" I bustled down the steps and around the corner of the porch to the back gate. "Are you lonely? I've got the key, but I'm not sure I want to go inside without Stephen and Jason here. It's not an emergency, after all."

Belle barked again with a sharp tone that sounded remarkably like *Is too!*

I sighed. I'd call Stephen one more time before giving up and going home to tackle some dreaded paperwork. But then I heard something and looked up. I squinted. "Munchkin?"

Belle barked again and I took a few steps toward the distant shape slowly approaching on the sidewalk. It moved somewhat, but not quite, like the big mastiff. But it couldn't be him, could it? If it was, where was Stephen? I could count on one hand the number of times I'd seen one of them without the other.

I broke into a run as soon as my brain sorted out the clues. It *was* Munchkin, but he was limping badly, walking stiffly, and his head drooped. I winced, empathizing with his pain.

I sank to my knees as I reached him, tempted to scoop up the dog in my arms to comfort both of us.

He growled quietly to warn me off, then whimpered, looking up with an expression of pain and a brow that wrinkled more than usual. He whimpered again as he sat, leaning heavily to the right to take weight off his left leg and hip.

"I'm no veterinarian, but something is very wrong with that leg, Munchkin. You poor thing." His fur was dirty and matted with mud, leaves, and an alarming amount of blood. Close up, I could see a deep laceration on his bad leg. Several clumps of hair seeped with the bright crimson of an actively bleeding wound. A dotted line of blood marked the sidewalk behind him.

I looked at the neighbors' houses and listened for sounds that might tell me someone was home . . . a car starting up, a lawnmower, a dryer thumping with damp tennis shoes or clanking as a zipper went round and round. It was dead quiet.

I sat back on my heels. "Okay, boy. Do you think you can make it back to the house? You're going to need some cleaning up, and maybe a veterinarian for some stitches. Yup, that's a certainty, I'm afraid. He can check you over and make sure there's no damage we can't see." My knees creaked as I stood, reminding me that I hadn't been paying enough attention to my stretching and strength-training regimen.

Munchkin groaned as he lumbered to his feet. I patted his shoulder in what I hoped he'd understand was encouragement.

Belle helped, barking from beyond the gate.

Munchkin was a mess and smelled terrible, as if he'd been raiding dumpsters or playing with the undead.

"Where have you been, old boy? And where is Stephen?"

Belle threw herself at Munchkin as we came through the gate. He growled and bared his teeth, warning her to back off, even as he wagged his tail to let her know they were still friends. Belle jumped back, but then whined and crept forward slowly. I pushed her gently back with my foot. "Give him a moment, Belle. He's hurting, but we'll get him sorted out."

Belle responded to the tone of my voice, looking up at my face for reassurance. "Heel!" I said and she gratefully glued her head to my left pant leg, keeping her eyes focused on mine for more instructions.

"Bath first." Stephen had an old washtub he often filled with water for the dogs to drink from and play with. I wasn't sure whether the injured Munchkin could climb into the tub, and cold water from the hose didn't seem like the right thing to inflict on an injured animal. If I were home, I'd use old rags we marked as "dog towels" and kept in the barn and by the back door.

I pulled out my key to the garage and told both dogs to sit, lie down, and stay. Munchkin settled slowly with an enormous sigh. Belle sat, but then squirmed sideways to lean against her friend, looking from me to him for reassurance. They both sank their heads on their front paws and sighed again. I hoped I could live up to their confidence in my ability to salvage the situation.

The garage was unlocked, but dim. I flicked on the light and took in my surroundings. Typical of this part of California, a washer, dryer, and laundry tub were aligned on the wall next to steps going into the kitchen. Above the appliances, rough shelving supported by utilitarian brackets held soap powder, bleach, stain remover, and the odds and ends that tend to accumulate on the flat surfaces of garages and laundry rooms. At the end of one shelf was a teetering tower of mismatched towels that I hoped could be called dog towels. If I was wrong, I'd apologize, but this was an emergency and I doubted Stephen would begrudge even his best linens if Munchkin needed them.

As I passed the laundry tub, I had what I thought was a brilliant idea. If I screwed the end of the garden hose to the laundry tub faucet, I could bathe Munchkin with warm water, which might be more comfortable and soothing for both of us.

As I got everything set up, Belle licked gently at Munchkin's ear, whining.

I filled the galvanized wash tub with warm soapy water, wet one of the towels, and dabbed gently at the worst and smelliest patches of debris on Munchkin's coat. "Were you confined somewhere?" I asked him. "Did you escape? Was there an accident?"

I looked more closely at the injuries I could see, most of which were deep lacerations rather than the pervasive road rash he might have if he'd fallen or jumped from a moving car or truck.

I turned my head as I washed a particularly foul-smelling wad of fur, and then sat back on my heels. "That's not *your* blood, is it?" I dabbed again. While this particular patch of Munchkin's coat was soaked in blood, I could find no abrasion or cut. Could it be Stephen's? Or belong to someone Munchkin had attacked to defend himself or Stephen? I couldn't know. Not without testing.

I slapped my hands on my thighs. "I don't want to destroy any evidence here, guys. I think we're off to see Dr. Davidson."

I gathered up all the smelly wet towels I'd used, along with the dry ones, hoping that there was some way to prevent Munchkin from transferring too much of his blood, filth, and smell to me, Belle, or my car.

I smoothed towels over the car seats and Belle clambered in. Munchkin yelped as I boosted him into the car when his bad leg failed him. I left the windows open and phoned the vet to let him know we were on our way, that we had possible criminal evidence, a dog who needed stitches, and we weren't fit for the waiting room.

Chapter 2

A nineteenth-century Prussian general famously said that
no plan survives first contact with the enemy. I'd go a
step further. While I can't live without a plan, I find all
plans require continuous adaptation. No plan survives
first contact with the real world.

From the Notebook of Maggie McDonald,
Simplicity Itself Organizing Services

Thursday, February 16, Morning

"I assume you're Maggie? I'm Amy," said a young woman in
bright pink scrubs who helped me ease Munchkin from the car.
"Your car is fine right there. Let's get you and both dogs inside
quickly. We've been keeping this door locked because we've had a
few break-ins. Dr. Davidson thinks it's addicts looking for drugs.
Can you imagine? In Orchard View?"

I shook my head, unable to break into Amy's monologue. I held
the dogs' leashes and stood on a nonslip mat inside the big loading
dock doorway. Both dogs leaned against me and whined. I wanted to
join them. We all smelled awful, were worried about Stephen, and
felt miserable.

But our collective misery didn't dim Amy's perkiness. Her blond
curls were meant to be up in a bun, out of the way, but the bun was on
the verge of an explosion as tendrils sprang loose. The curls resem-

bled the ones in an illustration of Goldilocks or Little Bo Peep, but were much more frantically active, much like Amy herself.

"I'm going to take Munchkin straight into an exam room," Amy said. "But I'm thinking you and Belle might want to do a little cleaning up." She didn't wait for a response. "Stay right here until I get back."

Belle pulled at the leash as Amy led Munchkin away, but Munchkin must have felt he was in good hands. He never looked back.

"I need to talk to the vet," I called after her. "Dr. Davidson. I think a violent crime has been committed and all that . . . gunk . . . on Munchkin's coat is evidence. It needs to be collected properly and documented. Please don't give him a bath!"

Amy stopped to open a door at the end of the hallway and turned back to me, smiling as if I'd offered her an ice-cream cone rather than suggested the dog whose leash she was holding was a criminal witness.

"That's fine. I'll pop him in an exam room until Dr. Davidson can see him. No bath until later, I promise. Doc will know what to do. He's been working with the animal crime lab at UC Davis for years."

Amy and Munchkin disappeared as the door closed behind them. Standing in the hallway, I could hear muffled barks, plaintive meows, and the squawking of a few birds. Dr. Calvert Davidson ran a large-animal clinic on weekends on his own property up in the hills. His office in town dealt with smaller companion animals like cats, dogs, rabbits, and birds.

I knelt next to Belle and hugged her despite the rancid smell she'd picked up after rubbing shoulders with Munchkin. She licked my face and I laughed. "Vets are amazing, aren't they? A horse and a bird are as much alike as . . . I don't know, two things that are very different, I guess. A blender and a freight train? How can one vet with one degree have an affinity for treating all those creatures, none of whom can talk?"

Before Belle could respond, Amy was back with a stack of fluffy white towels, the kind you'd expect at a spa, rather than the worn-out, scruffy gray-green towels we used for washing our animals.

Amy caught me looking askance at the towels and laughed again. "This is a brand-new batch. We use white because we can bleach them. They don't stay this fluffy for long, I assure you."

I'd said little since Amy had urged us out of the car and I couldn't think of a proper response now, either. Amy bustled off in the opposite direction and down a nearly identical hallway.

"Follow me," she said. "I'll get you set up."

My phone buzzed in my pocket. I reached for it, hoping it was finally Stephen, but then decided to let it go to voice mail. I didn't want to touch anything, since Munchkin had transferred a considerable amount of his accumulated mud, blood, and other stinking detritus to me.

Amy was about to disappear around a corner and I raced to catch up.

She ushered us into a room that looked much like a locker room, with showers around the edges at varying heights and a line of benches down the middle. Amy put the towels down on a bench, along with a plastic bag and what looked like a small bolt of children's fabric.

She turned the faucet of a shower at the far end that was at people height, and then started up another one lower to the floor. She reached out to test the temperature. "It takes a while to warm up sometimes."

She pulled a sheet of plastic from the bag on the bench and spread it on the floor, safely away from the shower. "If you stand on this while you take off your clothes, we won't lose any of the material that may have come from the crime scene. I can collect it all later, when you're done. I don't know how important the evidence on your clothes might be, or whether it will be accepted by the court, but we'll collect it all and let a judge decide later."

Belle looked up at me, but I didn't move. The idea of being this close to criminal evidence shocked me. I shook my head and shivered. It was ridiculous. It had been my idea to preserve any materials that might point to a crime or criminals, but I'd only been thinking of Munchkin. The evidence on my clothes, my skin, and my dog was a whole different story—a horror story I wanted no part of.

Amy ignored my discomfort or didn't notice. She picked up the fabric bundle. "When you're done, you can pop on these scrubs. And I've got a pair of shoes you can borrow if you need them." I shook my head. I had an extra pair of sneakers in my emergency kit in my car.

"All right, then, I'll leave you to it. Push that green button when you're done, and I'll come back and take you to Munchkin. The shampoo in the dispenser is gentle enough for both you and Belle. I'd recommend you let her get right in there with you."

"How often do you do this?" I asked, thinking she seemed confident in her job, skilled at handling my confusion as the shock set in, and completely unfazed by the violence.

"Hardly ever," Amy said. "Certainly not with dogs. But I was a forensic nurse in a trauma unit before I decided it was too much like being in a combat zone. This is nothing. You're going to be fine. So is Belle, and Munchkin too, I promise."

She opened the door and left me standing in the middle of the locker room holding Belle's leash. Normally, Belle was energized by water and would be racing from faucet to faucet to drink, splash, and shake herself off. Maybe the floor was too slippery for her usual antics or maybe she was picking up on my own discomfort, but she waited patiently while I stripped down and left all my clothing in a pile on the tarp Amy had spread out.

The soap had a lavender herbal scent that I breathed in deeply as I lathered up both Belle and myself. One of the first people I'd met in Orchard View was an herbalist who'd told me that lavender was a great relaxer. She no longer practiced herbal cures, but the woodsy floral scent—or the hot water, or rinsing off the stinky gunk—was definitely helping me feel better.

I'd almost forgotten the earlier horror of finding Munchkin injured when my ringing phone startled me. I lost my balance on the soapy tiled floor and slammed into Belle, knocking us both to the floor as I lunged for my phone.

I didn't recognize the number identifying the call, but I answered it anyway.

"Hello, this is Maggie," I said, grabbing a towel and covering myself up as if I were on FaceTime instead of a phone call.

"It's Jason. Have you been able to get in touch with Stephen? I wanted to let him know I landed here safely and to give him the unit's number in case of an emergency. Communications are going to be spotty. The storm knocked down a bunch of cell towers, and everyone's trying to call in or out to check on loved ones."

"Are you okay? I thought you told us not to call unless it was an emergency."

"I'm fine. The airport is miles from the disaster zone. Everyone's taking one last opportunity to call home from the airport pay phones while we can. But didn't you have a meeting with Stephen this morning? How did it go?"

I chewed my bottom lip, not sure what I should tell Jason about Stephen. *When in doubt, lead with the truth* was one of my guiding principles, but I didn't want to worry Jason unnecessarily. And the truth was, I had no idea what was going on with Stephen.

"Maggie? Are you there?"

I decided to start slowly and add facts as needed.

"I'm here. I haven't been able to get in touch with Stephen either, I'm afraid, and he missed our scheduled appointment time. I'm not sure where he is."

"He didn't call? That's not like him. Where are you now? If I reach him, I'll tell him to call."

"At the vet with Belle and Munchkin."

"Both dogs? Is everything okay?"

And there it was. The question that demanded I come clean or deliberately hide the truth from Jason.

"Um . . ."

"Maggie, what's going on? Is something wrong? Do I need to come home?"

"No!" I said, more vehemently than I'd intended. "You need to be there. This project is your baby. You can't let your team down."

"What aren't you telling me?"

"Not much. I've got Belle and Munchkin here at the vet. I found Munchkin with some cuts. He may need stitches. We should be here a few more minutes and then I'll take him home. Or to my house if Stephen isn't back yet. I'm sure everything is fine." I'd told the truth, but felt a little guilty not sharing with Jason how concerned I was. I could text Jason later when I had more information. Or Stephen could text him.

"Cuts? How did that happen? Was the poor boy in a knife fight? A bar brawl?" Jason laughed, but had no way of knowing how close he'd come to what I feared might be the truth.

"I don't know. That's partly why I brought him to the vet. That and he has a bit of a stiff leg that I want to make sure doesn't need any special treatment. The vet's still looking at him, though, so I can't give you a report. I can fill you in later by text, right?"

"Sure, that'd be great. They're telling us that texts should get through most of the time. Apparently they take up less bandwidth than voice calls. And let me hear what you learn from Stephen, too. Tell him to call me. I gotta go now, though. There's a long line of people trying to use the phone."

"Take care, Jason," I said, but he'd already disconnected.

I dressed quickly and toweled Belle dry. I pushed the green button on the wall to call Amy, but also clicked Belle's leash to her collar and set off down the hall in my bare feet to find Munchkin. My stomach rumbled. It was nearing lunchtime. I was hungry and it was time for me and the dogs to salvage something useful from this crazy day.

Belle and I ran into Dr. Davidson before we got to the examining room. I greeted him and reintroduced myself, since I'd met him only once several months earlier.

"Of course I remember. Newton, right? A giant Russian wolfhound?"

I nodded yes to the doctor's memories. "How is Munchkin?"

The doctor frowned and my mouth went dry. Belle sat and whined.

"He'll be fine," he said, brushing his hair back from his forehead so it stuck up in stiff spikes. "But I want him to stay here tonight. I'd like to sedate him and keep him on intravenous antibiotics. It will let his body focus on healing. When he came in he'd lost a lot of blood and was severely dehydrated. He's lucky you brought him in when you did. Much later and . . ." The doctor cleared his throat, brushed his hair back, and looked at the floor, then the ceiling, and then the corridor behind him. Anywhere but at Belle and me. "He'll do a better job of healing if we can keep his electrolytes balanced and his fluid levels up. We put in a hefty number of sutures and I don't want him pulling them out. I can't put a collar on him right now because it would irritate the stitches on his neck."

My skin prickled and I felt the room begin to spin. I'm not usually squeamish about blood and injuries but from the doctor's assessment I could tell that Munchkin had had a close call. Imagining what might have happened made me feel sick. That horror, coupled with my concern for Stephen, made me sink to the floor to kneel next to Belle. She nudged at my arm until I wrapped it around her and drew her close. "Can we see him?" I asked. "I want to be able to tell Stephen Laird how he's doing. Stephen is Munchkin's person."

"Amy will bring you the paperwork," he said, kneeling in front of both Belle and me. He rubbed Belle behind the ears and under the chin. "Now you," he added, looking into Belle's eyes. "I assume you and Munchkin are chums, right? I think it's best if you don't visit him today. He needs to be kept quiet and I'm guessing that wouldn't be possible with you around, huh?" Belle smiled in agreement. But then, golden retrievers are almost always smiling.

"That goes for you too, I'm afraid, Maggie. But I assure you that there's no reason to think he won't make a full recovery." The doctor's stomach rumbled. He blushed and glanced at his watch. "Oh wow. Past noon. You've had a shock yourself. Would you like to come back to my office and split a sandwich? You're looking a little pale. Amy will bring the paperwork back to us."

Once in his office, I took the sandwich out of politeness, but after forcing down a few bites, along with sips from a can of cola the vet shoved my way, I felt less like I was living on a Tilt-A-Whirl. I wolfed down the rest of the sandwich. In between bites, I glanced at the paperwork and filled out as much as I could—Stephen's name, address, and phone number, along with my own phone number as the emergency contact.

I explained what I could, which wasn't much, about what was going on with Munchkin and his owner. "They're bonded more than any other dog and person I know," I told him. "I'll get Stephen over here as soon as I can. Munchkin will be anxious, I expect."

Dr. Davidson inclined his head sagely while surreptitiously passing Belle treats from behind the desk. "Right now, between the shock he's gone through, the healing he needs to do, and the sedative I'm giving him, anxiety shouldn't be a problem for Munchkin. We'll address that issue if and when we get there."

"Do you have any idea what happened to him?" I asked. "Could you tell from his injuries or all that . . . gunk on his fur?" *Gunk.* A technical term if there ever was one. But I had no idea what was clinging to poor Munchkin's coat. Nor was I sure I wanted to know.

"Chinese food," said Amy, walking through the door with a smoothie in one hand and a clipboard in the other. "If the noodles and duck sauce are anything to go by."

She closed the door with a quick hip check and lifted her chin in Dr. Davidson's direction. "No appointments until 3:00 p.m. I locked the front door, put the phone on messages, and sent Brittany to lunch too. Bashir is taking vitals. I phoned the university lab at Davis and sent a courier up there. They need you to call with the codes before the samples arrive."

Amy turned to address me while pulling out another desk chair with her foot and sinking into it with a sigh. "We had an emergency at five this morning and have been moving like a NASCAR pit crew since then. We don't usually shut the door during the day, but we need a breather and there's an emergency bell if anyone desperately needs us."

"Wow," I said. "I would have thought we were the only ones here."

"That's the impression we try to give all our customers," Amy said, laughing. "Some days it's easier than others. Today wasn't one of those days." She turned her attention back toward Dr. Davidson. "The treatment codes?"

He leaned forward over the desk. He grabbed a piece of scratch paper and scribbled a series of numbers on it before handing the scrap to Amy. He looked at me. "From your story, I take it you have no idea where Munchkin was when this happened."

I shook my head. "I came on a hunch—but I don't have any authority to order a review of the evidence, if that's what you're getting at. Stephen's partner, Jason Mueller, is a cop here in Orchard View and could probably give you all the appropriate requisition codes, or whatever you need, but he's in Texas as part of the emergency response team for all those storms—the flooding and tornados. I can try to reach him, but chances are . . . Maybe his partner Paolo Bianchi could help?" I fumbled for my phone. "I've got his number in here."

The doctor waved his hand. "We don't need anything from you or the police at this point. Amy needs treatment codes to fill all the appropriate administrative boxes on the UC Davis lab forms."

He turned to his assistant. "Amy, I'll phone up to Davis myself. Can you call the Santa Clara County District Attorney's office and see if they know anything about recent crimes involving a dog of Munchkin's description or anything near a Chinese restaurant?"

Amy stood quickly and left, but not before she gave my shoulder a comforting squeeze. Dr. Davidson stood and took the clipboard containing the paperwork from my hand. "I know Jason and Stephen pretty well," he said. "I'm not worried about getting paid. And I'll make sure Davis has whatever they need for the proper chain-of-evidence documentation. I need to get back to work, but I don't want you to worry about *any* of this. Have Stephen phone me when he gets in touch, will you please? We'll take good care of Munchkin. If you can't get hold of Stephen . . . Well, never mind about that. Your instincts are good. There's no doubt in my mind this is a criminal case.

Someone went after that dog with a knife and beat him with a blunt object."

He drew a sharp breath in through his teeth. "I hope Stephen isn't badly hurt. I don't understand how anyone could get close enough to injure Munchkin unless Stephen had already been incapacitated and unable to prevent the attack. I wish he'd get in touch."

It was my turn to reassure the vet. "I'm sure Stephen will call soon. He's resilient. If necessary, Munchkin can stay with my family for as long as he needs to." I gathered up my backpack and Belle's leash, not exactly sure where we'd go from here. It seemed like hours since I'd set off for Stephen's this morning, planning to get a huge chunk of accumulated clutter sorted and organized. But the whole day had fallen apart since then. I said a quick good-bye and thanks to Dr. Davidson and left the building by the same door I'd entered. My car was right where I'd left it.

I let Belle into the back seat. She hopped in promptly, but I gagged and nearly lost the sandwich the vet had so generously shared. An hour or so of baking in the sun had done nothing to improve the smell of the evidence that had transferred from Munchkin to my car seats.

I rolled down the windows, knowing that my next stop should probably be a car wash and detailer. But they were almost certain to ask questions I couldn't answer. And after all the uncertainties of the morning, I wanted to be home. I started the car, hoping that I could at least organize my own whirling thoughts and figure out what my next step would be. If only Stephen would call.

My phone rang before I got home. I pulled to the side of the road to answer it.

"Hello?" I said, but was met by silence. "Hello?" I was about to hang up.

"Maggie, thank goodness I found you. It's Paolo. Do you have time to meet me?"

"Stephen Laird isn't with you by any chance, is he? Jason and I have both been trying to reach him all day. He was a no-show for a meeting we had this morning. It's not like him. Not at all." I started to tell Paolo about my adventures with Munchkin, but my voice broke. I shivered as the impact from the morning's events settled in. I swallowed and began again. "I'm on my way home now. Can you come to dinner?"

"I need to see you right away. Someplace people can't overhear us. The dog park?"

I thought for a minute and looked at the time on the car's dashboard. It was nearly two thirty and school would be letting out soon. I didn't have much time. But Paolo was a friend of the family and Jason's partner at the Orchard View Police Department. If he said he needed to see me, I knew a meeting was essential.

"I'm too far away. What about Starbucks or the bakery in the old train station?"

"The train station would work. Outside, maybe? There won't be many people there at this hour."

"Can you look into whether there've been any accidents? Could Stephen be in the hospital? I don't mean to be a fear monger, but I'm running out of upbeat reasons for him to be out of touch this long."

"We can talk about that over coffee. See you in a few?"

I agreed to meet him, but warned him that we'd have to talk quickly so that I could leave to pick up the kids from school. As I drove across town, I wondered what he had to say that couldn't wait until the dinner hour or be communicated over the phone. Come to think of it, it wasn't like Paolo to disagree with anyone else's suggestions or refuse an invitation to dinner. He was the most nonconfrontational police officer I'd ever met, and he hated to cook for himself.

We arrived at the same time and requested plain old-fashioned brewed coffee to speed the process. Paolo shifted from one foot to another as the barista filled our orders. "You're like a flea on a griddle," I told him as we took our cups to a rapidly cooling patio where our voices were drowned out by passing traffic.

"What's up?" I assumed a light tone to make Paolo more comfortable. I guessed he wanted my advice on how to handle a social situation. If it were about work, Paolo would have talked to Jason, not me. And social nuances were not easy for him to interpret, manage, or understand.

"It's about Stephen." Paolo looked from one side of the patio to the other, shifting in his chair and nervously turning his coffee mug by its handle.

"Stephen? You know where he is?" I leaned back in my chair and smiled. "I'm so glad to hear he's okay."

Paolo held his coffee mug with two hands and lifted it shaking to his lips. He swallowed hard and set the cup down. Opened his mouth to speak and closed it again. Something was wrong. Paolo looked like he'd rather be anywhere than here, even though he'd insisted on meeting me.

"Has something happened? Where is Stephen? Is he hurt?" I normally tried not to fire question after question at Paolo. It confused him and he got stuck trying to decide which question to answer first. He wasn't stupid. He was brilliant, in fact, and a huge asset to the Orchard View Police Department. But his brain didn't work the same way that mine did and my rapid-fire delivery of questions wasn't the best way to get information from him. I tried again.

"Tell me what you need me to know."

Paolo relaxed, but only a bit. He leaned forward and whispered, "Stephen's in jail."

I gasped and bit my lip, forcing myself to ask one follow-up question at a time.

"What do you know?"

"Mostly nothing. He was arrested very early this morning but hasn't talked to the police or anyone else. He was picked up in Mountain View. They can hold him for two days. After that they'll need to charge him and send him to the county jail in San Jose."

Again, I sorted through all the questions I wanted to blurt out and selected the one least likely to derail Paolo's thought processes. "What can I do?"

"Visit him. As soon as possible. You're the only one he'll talk to. The only one who can help."

I frowned and squinted at Paolo, trying to make sense of what I was hearing.

"How do you know all this?"

Paolo made a sound that was halfway between a low-volume scream and a growl. "One of the guys on duty at the jail last night went through the academy with Jason. He recognized Stephen and wanted to let Jason know. He phoned the station. Because Jason's in Texas, the call forwarded to me."

"Why wouldn't Stephen talk to Jason? Or this friend of Jason's at the jail? Or you? Why me?"

"Maggie, please. I don't know. I don't know anything." He cleared his throat and lowered his hands to his sides, shaking them as if trying to loosen all his muscles at once. He looked at a corner of the patio and recited in a monotone as if he was reading from a whiteboard filled with notes. "Mountain View Police picked him up late last night after getting an anonymous tip about a possible murder at a Chinese restaurant called the Golden Dragon. The restaurant owner was discovered dead in the cold-storage room and Stephen was found covered with blood, wiping down tables and chairs. No one else was there."

Paolo stopped, but I leaned forward and raised my eyebrows, encouraging him to continue without saying anything to distract him.

"Once they figured out that Stephen wasn't badly injured, they took him to the station. But he won't answer any of their questions. His fingerprints were found, along with someone else's on a knife in the alley behind the restaurant where there were some puddles of blood and bloody footprints going every which way."

"Were any of them dog footprints?"

Paolo furrowed his brow and stared at me. "How do you know that?"

"Never mind. What does Stephen want? What can I do? Have you called Jason? Someone must have witnessed something. Who called it in? How did they call it in? Did they know someone had been killed or had they overheard a fight? We could tell so much if we knew about the phone call."

Paolo sighed. I knew better than to pelt him or anyone else with my long lists of questions. But they had a tendency to spill out, unbidden, in an overwhelming torrent that put most people on the defensive. "I'm sorry, Paolo. Go on. Please, tell me what you know."

"That's the problem. Stephen will only say that no one should call Jason. They've tried to call him anyway, but calls aren't getting through to the disaster area and no one wants to send bad news in a text. Jason told me not to call him under any circumstances because the phone systems in the flood zone are already so overloaded. The Mountain View Police let me talk to Stephen. I guess they hoped he would tell me what happened, but he just asked me to phone you. He said he'll talk to you, only to you, and *only* if you promise not to speak to Jason."

I pushed my hair back from my forehead and sighed. "This is getting weirder by the minute. Why would he want to talk to me and not Jason? It makes no sense." I shook my head. "But that doesn't matter right now, I guess. How do I see him? How soon can I see him? Does he have a lawyer? Does he need a lawyer? Do I need to get him one?"

"Visiting him will have to wait until 9:00 a.m. tomorrow morning. I don't know the answers to your other questions. This isn't a situation they prepare you for at the police academy."

Chapter 3

The self-storage industry in the United States generates
some $30 billion in annual revenue. Most of us have too
much stuff. Some of us spend more on storage than we
might spend if we discarded everything we own and
re-purchased only what we need.

From the Notebook of Maggie McDonald,
Simplicity Itself Organizing Services

Friday, February 17, Morning

First thing the next morning after dropping David at the high school
and Brian at middle school, I headed to downtown Mountain View.
I inevitably became enmeshed in the heavy traffic crossing the Peninsula
to get to Google, LinkedIn, Facebook, and dozens of other high-tech
companies.

After dodging pedestrians glued to their cell phones, cyclists
wearing earbuds, and drivers who were shaving, applying mascara,
or pretending they weren't texting, I sandwiched myself between two
little white Google self-driving cars. The rounded cars sported silver
rooftop bubbles that held much of their sensing gear, making them
resemble the sugar bowl from my grandmother's fine china tea set.
But I knew I could rely on their driving. They never grew distracted,
angry, or tired, and they always followed the rules of the road.

I relaxed and surrendered to the tedium as we crawled along like
a millipede with hundreds of mismatched segments. I tried to use the
time productively, focusing on what I would say to Stephen. But that

made me worry about what might be involved in visiting the jail. I had no idea how long it would take, what paperwork I'd need to fill out, nor what sort of condition Stephen might be in. Had he been hurt, like Munchkin? Had he received medical attention? How was he coping with being locked up when his ongoing struggle with PTSD forced him to walk miles daily with Munchkin's comforting support?

I'd talked it over with my husband, Max, the night before. He didn't like the idea of me spending time at the jail with Stephen or anyone else. Eventually, we were able to agree that I would make one visit to try to learn what had happened and what kind of help Stephen would need. After that, we'd get someone with more expertise to disentangle Stephen from whatever mess he was caught up in.

I'd watched enough television that I thought I was prepared. To breeze through the metal detectors, I wore my sports bra instead of an underwire and leggings instead of zippered jeans with rivets. I wore clog-type sneakers with no metal eyelets, and a long modest tunic dress. I'd removed my earrings, watch, and wedding ring, and carried only my driver's license, passport, and keys.

Despite a wide array of helpful English and Spanish directional signs displayed throughout the parking lot, I wasn't entirely sure how to get to the jail. Squaring my shoulders and pretending to a confidence I didn't feel, I embraced my ignorance of procedures and asked for help at the main entrance to the police department. Introducing myself to the uniformed desk officer, who sported a French-braided ponytail streaked in teal and magenta, I told her I wasn't sure where I needed to go.

"Good morning, Mrs. McDonald," she said, giving me a warm and welcoming smile. "Paolo Bianchi from Orchard View PD told us you'd be coming in this morning. I think they're all ready for you. Let me call back and check. Have a seat. Would you like some coffee? A local boutique roasting company is treating us to their service this month. It's pretty good—not the normal burned and overaged cop-shop blend."

Flustered by her welcome when I'd expected something much grimmer, I sat on the edge of one of the brightly colored and surprisingly comfortable chairs. Officer French Braid held up one finger and spoke into the mouthpiece loudly enough for me to easily overhear. "Mrs. McDonald is here to see Stephen Laird." She smiled, winked at me, and nodded. "Yes, ma'am, right on time. Do you want to talk to her first, or should I send her on back?"

She made a few more cheerful remarks into the receiver, laughed, replaced the phone in its cradle, and turned back to me. "Detective Joan Smith will be out in a second. Grab some coffee and take it with you. There are go-cups on the left of the machine there."

I'd finished pouring my coffee just as Officer French Braid looked up at the door, smiled, and stood.

"Morning, Joan. Mrs. McDonald, this is Detective Smith. Joan Smith—like Smith and Jones—her whole name screams 'made-up alias,' but it's real, I promise."

Detective Smith crossed the room, smiling. I stood to meet her, though I was still unsettled by the homey friendliness exuded by everything and everyone I'd encountered so far. For some reason I couldn't quite explain, the detective's gentle demeanor made me wary. I feared her manner was a calculated ploy to throw me off guard and trick me into revealing information about Stephen that he'd prefer to keep secret. I tried to shake off my feelings as I suspected they were unwarranted. Chances were they sprang from watching too many cop shows or reading too many murder mysteries.

"Good morning, Mrs. McDonald. We're glad you're here. We're hoping you can answer some questions for us so we can make sure that your friend Mr. Laird gets the care he needs."

"Care? Is he injured? Has he seen a doctor? Should he be in the hospital?" My voice wavered and my hands shook. "You know I'm here at Stephen's request, right? Not as a witness. I have no idea what's going on and I don't think I can help you."

Detective Smith was tall, thin, poised, and pleasant. She held the door for me and smiled.

"Please relax, Mrs. McDonald. May I call you Maggie? I understand that you're here to visit Mr. Laird and we're going to make that happen. We haven't arrested him and he hasn't been charged."

I nodded when she asked if she could call me Maggie. "Paolo Bianchi from the Orchard View Police Department said that Stephen was going to be transferred to the county jail in San Jose and that I needed to get down here fast. Was he wrong about that?"

Joan bit her lip. "The district attorney is looking into the possibility of charging him with obstructing a police investigation and any one of a number of other offenses up to and including murder." I gasped, but

Joan leaned toward me and whispered, "Between you and me, I think it's unlikely that he'll find a judge to sign off on any of it."

She straightened and spoke more firmly. "Look, I know you'll feel better once you see and can talk to Stephen. Let's get you two together and I'll follow up with you later. Sound like a plan?"

I nodded again. My mouth was dry and I could think of nothing to say. I wasn't equipped with the vocabulary required for visiting a friend being held at the police station—whether he was under arrest or not.

Joan led me into a small room, maybe ten feet by twelve. Though it was softly lit and held a sofa, a coffee table, and two cushioned armchairs, no one would mistake it for a living room. I took a seat and experienced the same sense of foreboding and restlessness that I felt as a child in the principal's office or waiting for an uncomfortable dental procedure. I reminded myself that I was here for Stephen, because he'd asked me to be and because I was his friend. But my legs and shoulders tensed as I fought the urge to run.

On one wall was a large whiteboard with incompletely erased markings in four colors. Opposite that was a window framed by curtains and covered with mini-blinds. It looked suspiciously like the mirrored windows I was familiar with from TV and movies, and I was tempted to investigate it more closely and tap on the glass.

"Make yourself comfortable. Is there anything you need?" Joan asked. I shook my head, but then I leaned forward, tilting my body toward the fake window and then at a discrete camera painted the same tasteful cream as the walls and ceiling.

"Will this be a private meeting with Stephen?"

"I'll get him for you," she said, dodging my question.

A chill settled over me as I reminded myself that although Joan was being considerate, she wasn't here to offer me tea and cookies or anything else, no matter what she said or how she acted. She was here to investigate what Paolo had said was a homicide. And she was legally entitled to lie to me and to Stephen.

I put my coffee cup on the table with quavering hands and waited for Stephen to appear. I'm not sure I'd ever felt so helpless.

Detective Smith returned quickly with Stephen, but he wasn't the Stephen I knew. My friend Stephen was always neatly dressed with a trimmed beard and a smooth bald head. He didn't wear aftershave, and I'd never noticed that he smelled of anything in particular. If I'd been forced to guess, I'd have said he smelled wholesome, like soap and shampoo, mixed with something homey, like cinnamon and snickerdoodle cookies.

This Stephen smelled of fear and looked as though he'd been run through a car wash. His beard seemed to have grown at least a half-inch in every direction and had bits of what could only be described as crud embedded in it. His jeans were streaked with dirt, and his rumpled shirt was stained and untucked. I'd always assumed he was bald, but he apparently shaved his head because tufts of hair had sprouted from his skull like a dandelion gone to seed. I frowned and narrowed my eyes, thinking that he looked as miserable as Munchkin had when he'd limped up to Stephen's front door yesterday morning.

My expression must have been fierce, because Stephen recoiled. "I'm sorry, Maggie," he said. "I'm really sorry." He sat on the sofa with his head in his hands and I rushed from the chair to sit beside him.

"I don't know what you're sorry for," I said. "This is a terrible mistake. We'll get it sorted out."

Detective Smith cleared her throat. "When you're ready, push that green button on the wall."

Stephen whipped his head toward the door, his eyes wide and his nostrils flaring.

"It's okay," she said. "The door's not locked. If you push the button someone will come and help you with whatever you need or guide you to wherever you want to go."

As soon as she'd gone, Stephen leaped up to test the door. His movements were jerky and his head moved as if on a swivel, checking every corner of the room for monsters, listening devices, or something worse.

Finally, he took his seat on the sofa again. I took his hand. He jerked away, but then grabbed hold of my arm with both hands and held on like a toddler afraid of being lost in a shopping center.

"Maggie, thank you for coming. I'm so sorry."

"Start at the beginning, Stephen. You have nothing to apologize for. You needed me and asked me to come, so I came. If I can help, I will. That's what friends do. But I have no idea what's happening. Are you hurt?"

I looked him over with the scrutiny I would give either one of my boys if they'd appeared as rumpled and terrified as Stephen did. The fact that he was a decorated marine and a grown man twice my size made no difference to me. He was in trouble and he thought I might be able to help.

He opened his mouth to speak, cleared his throat, and came out with a sob. A tear escaped the corner of his eye.

I waited. "Take your time."

He cleared his throat again, then glanced quickly at the blind-covered glass. "I don't know who's listening," he said in a croaking whisper, turning away from the window and bending his head toward my shoulder. "Look at my right ear if you need to talk. I don't want them to read our lips."

If I hadn't been consumed with apprehension myself, I might have found Stephen's uncharacteristic paranoia amusing. He was normally straightforward and informal without any hint of pretense, fear, or drama.

"Have you seen Munchkin?" he asked.

I relaxed my shoulders and smiled, happy to have been asked a question I could answer. "Yes, he came home yesterday morning. He was a little worse for wear, but he's fine." I lowered my voice and looked toward his right ear, angling my head away from the mirrored window as instructed. "I took him to the vet to get patched up. Dr. Davidson is collecting evidence, just in case."

"He's going to be okay?"

I nodded. "Some stitches, antibiotics, intravenous fluids, and a good rest will set him right. He's under light sedation now to keep him quiet so he can heal, but I'll pick him up this afternoon and look after him at my house. He'll be fine." I patted Stephen's shoulder. "But what about you?"

"It's a long story and I need your help."

"I have time."

Stephen glanced up at the window, slumped, and shook his head. He reached inside his rumpled shirt and pulled out a sheaf of papers, folded tightly to the size of a small index card.

He handed the packet to me, surreptitiously, hiding his movements by turning his back to the window. He gestured that I should put it away, inside my clothes.

"Not in your pocket," he said as I moved to put it in the back pocket of my jeans—forgetting that I'd specifically chosen to wear leggings to the jail. "Inside, where they can't say it 'accidently' fell out. Put it in your bra or something." He blushed a little at the mention of my underwear. We were good friends, but not underwear-mentioning friends, at least not until today.

I did as he asked and then turned back with my eyebrows raised in question. "What on earth?"

"Read it later. It's all in there."

"But what do you need me to *do*? Can I call Jason for you? Get you a lawyer? Get you out of here?"

He shook his head vehemently. "Not Jason. Don't call Jason. Not one word. If you call him, he'll come home. And he needs to succeed with his efforts in Texas. He's been setting up this deployment team since he was on medical leave. He's managed it and expanded it throughout Santa Clara County until it included firefighters, paramedics, chaplains, social workers, and every other kind of disaster-response assistance. It's what he wants to do now, full time. This Texas trip is their first and they're being followed by a group of journalists. Funding renewal for the program will depend upon how well the team performs. He's got everything riding on this. He has to prove it will work."

I looked at him, skeptical. Surely Jason would want to know Stephen was in trouble. Surely he *needed* to know. And while the trip was important to Jason, I knew how thoroughly he'd trained his team. He'd often said that a well-trained unit should be able to operate without a commander. I doubted that anything was more important to Jason than Stephen's health, happiness, and well-being. Chances were that Jason wouldn't even have to leave his post to make a huge difference in Stephen's current situation. One phone call, one word to the Mountain View Police from Jason's chief in Orchard View, and MVPD would cut Stephen loose. I had no doubt.

But Stephen clenched his jaw. "Promise me. Trust me. I have good reason to want to keep Jason out of this for now. Besides, he'll be so focused on helping people in the disaster zone and managing his team that he won't notice I haven't texted. Not for a few days at least."

"Seriously? He won't even check in?"

Stephen shook his head. "Not for days. He's going to focus on his mission and assume that we'll catch up when he returns. If his plans change or there's an emergency, of course he'll get in touch. This is a short mission, anyway. His team is expected to be there for only two weeks, to carry some of the load until the local public services can get the problems under control. Communication will be tough enough for those injured or displaced by the disaster. They don't need a bunch of helpers swooping in and clogging up the phone lines."

I nodded, but Stephen must have seen my reservations telegraphed through my facial expression or body language.

"Look, Maggie, you know Jason. He's going to put everyone else's needs ahead of his own, and ahead of mine. It's not that he doesn't care about me. He does. And he trusts that I'll get in touch if I need to. It's one of the things you learn in the military, I think. Every couple has different communication needs and standards. This is what works for us."

"But he already phoned from the airport, concerned that he wasn't able to reach you and that I'd not heard from you either. He knows that you missed our meeting yesterday and that Munchkin came home without you. He promised he would call again and asked me to text when I heard from you."

Stephen sighed and lowered his head. "I can't control what you or Jason do, Maggie. If he's going to phone, he'll phone. And you'll have to decide what you're going to tell him. But I'm asking you to rely on my judgment and keep my situation to yourself for as long as possible." He looked up with a hopeful expression.

I let out a long, slow breath. "I do trust you. I'll give it my best shot. At least for now. I hope you're right and that he'll get so caught up in what he's doing that he won't call for a few days at least."

Stephen took my hands in his much larger ones and held them captive. "A few days is all I think we'll need. Thanks, Maggie. I know you're much better at uncovering secrets than keeping them."

"So what's next?"

"Read those papers. If you have questions after that, we can talk." He stared at my face until he became convinced I would do as he asked.

"You know that they want to book you in at the county jail on some charge of obstruction?"

Stephen breathed out hard and I gritted my teeth so as not to grimace from the smell of his breath. He slumped again, with his head in his hands, but his legs shook, apparently out of his control until he placed his hands on them and exerted pressure to hold them still.

"Either that or murder . . . or maybe a psychiatric hold," he said, not bothering to hide his face from the mirror.

"But—"

"But nothing. They can keep me for forty-eight hours before they need to put the evidence in front of a judge. That takes us into the weekend, so that gives them more time to try to make a case . . ."

Stephen's voice trailed off and I sighed in frustration. It seemed so pointless. A good lawyer or even a bad one would surely be able to get him out of here. Stephen moved forward toward the edge of the sofa. "It's all in the notes, Maggie. Read them. They'll answer most of your questions. Trust me."

"Of course I trust you, Stephen," I said. "But right now I don't understand you. Not one bit."

He looked at me, shrugged, and smiled much like one of my kids—slightly sheepish, slightly mischievous, but completely sure of himself. I tried another tack.

"Okay, I'll leave it for now. I'll read your note and I'll do the best I can to cover for you with Jason. He's fine, by the way. Arrived safely. More weather is coming in, though . . ."

My voice trailed off as I considered what on earth I could tell Jason if he called. Something that would tamp down his fears without revealing Stephen's secrets. I was stumped. Deciding to address that problem later, I pushed back my hair and straightened my shoulders, which were carrying all the strain of the day's events and threatening to bring on a wicked headache.

"But what about you?" I asked, going back to one of my first questions. "If you're going to be here for the weekend, won't you need . . . I don't know . . . clothes? A toothbrush? Medication?"

I let my voice trail off. Stephen and I were friends and he'd shared his struggle with PTSD with me. I knew that he walked miles at night when he couldn't sleep and that while Munchkin was not officially a service dog, his companionship helped Stephen cope. Munchkin had his own PTSD-type issues and they were dependent on each other. Without his dog's soothing company, confined in a small space without exercise, I wasn't sure how Stephen was going to hang on to his hard-won mental health.

But he shook his head at the suggestion of medication. "I never had any luck with drugs, prescription or otherwise, and had a terrible reaction to one of them. I've done well with exercise and Munchkin and working with the dogs and soldiers at the VA."

"Don't be a hero. If you need meds, you need meds. Especially given the stress of whatever it is that you've laid out in your note."

"I'm not being a hero," he said with a dismissive snort. "I'm the first to encourage guys to look into prescription drugs to prevent them from self-medicating with other dangerous stuff. But the meds don't work for me."

I brushed off my leggings as if they were covered with dust. They weren't, but I needed to do *something*, since I was so helpless in any of my efforts to rescue my friend.

"Look, Maggie, I know you need to do something. Read the note. I'll be fine. I'm meditating and writing and I'll keep myself on the right side of sane. If you take care of the things in there," he said, lifting his chin in the general direction of my chest and the hidden papers, "I won't have to tough it out for long."

Chapter 4

Clutter costs time and money. Even if you aren't renting extra storage, if you've got so much stuff that you don't know what you have or where it is, or you can't find it when you need it, it's nearly the same as having nothing at all.

From the Notebook of Maggie McDonald,
Simplicity Itself Organizing Services

Friday, February 17, Morning

After leading me to her office, Detective Smith invited me to sit, but I remained standing. I wasn't going to answer any questions or show her the papers Stephen had given me. I wanted to leave as quickly as possible. To smell fresh air, hug my family and Belle, and get Munchkin out of his enforced confinement.

She offered to freshen my coffee, but I shook my head and looked at the clock—a loud industrial one remarkably like the schoolroom clocks I'd grown up with.

"I need to leave," I said. "I have an appointment. Thank you for your help." I took a step toward the door, but then turned back to Detective Smith. "Stephen Laird does not belong in jail. I don't have any information that could help your investigation. I don't know anything more now than I did when I came in."

I wondered if that was one of the reasons Stephen had written everything down. Until I read his note, I could honestly tell the officers that I knew nothing about what he was doing here or what had happened last night that left Munchkin seriously injured and Stephen in the hands of the police. But maybe Detective Smith knew something that would help me. I forced myself to ignore my urge to flee and put my hand on the back of one of her visitor's chairs.

As if she could read my mind, the detective smiled and gestured toward the chair again. "Please, sit. If you can stay for a few minutes, I'll tell you everything we know at this point."

I wasn't sure I wanted to hear what she had to say. I felt as though I were balanced on a tightrope over a churning chasm of molten lava. But my balance was bad, and I knew I'd fall at some point. I might as well choose the moment myself. I closed my eyes, stepped off the tightrope, fell into the chair, and waited.

Detective Smith sat down slowly behind the desk, took a sip of her coffee, then leaned forward on her elbows with her hands steepled, tapping her fingertips against each other.

She sighed. "You've probably figured out that we were eavesdropping on your conversation with Mr. Laird. I know that he handed you something and I wish you'd let us see it."

I stiffened and prepared to leave, but the detective waved her hand in the air, motioning to me that I should both calm down and stay seated. "I know, I know. You're not going to give me anything today. I could tell from your body language that both you and Mr. Laird are, for some unfathomable reason, resigned to his spending the holiday weekend in jail."

I gasped, shocked to hear her say the words out loud—words I'd tried to avoid uttering, even to myself. She ignored me, or pretended to.

"Here's what we know. Last night, at 12:34 a.m., we received an anonymous tip from a burner phone, saying that there had been a break-in at the Golden Dragon Chinese Restaurant and someone was dead. The caller described a man who matched the description of Mr. Laird. I think you'll agree he's distinctive looking."

When I didn't respond, the detective continued. "The anonymous citizen said he'd heard sounds of a fight and a gunshot. We went to the scene and found the restaurant's back door unlocked. Our officers found the owner, Mr. Xiang, dead in his cold-storage locker, apparently from a gunshot wound. The medical examiner reports he had defensive knife wounds and extensive bruising from a brutal beating.

Blood covered the floor and four sets of footprints led away from the body. Three headed toward the back door, out into the alley, and away from the restaurant. The fourth set belonged to your friend Mr. Laird. We found him at the scene, wiping down tables, obliterating evidence. Time of death judgments are notoriously imprecise, even for the most experienced medical examiners, but the refrigeration in the food storage room makes estimations particularly difficult."

I leaned forward and blurted out questions as quickly as they occurred to me. "But what evidence was there? Could you learn anything from the gunshot wound? Like how close the shooter was or how tall? What kind of gun was used? What sort of a knife caused the lacerations? A kitchen knife or a street knife? Did Stephen have any gunshot residue on his hands or clothing? What about blood spatter? He didn't have any blood that I could see on his clothing, and he was still wearing his shoes, so you didn't take them for evidence. Did he have knife wounds? What about the footprints? Don't you do something like, I don't know, recreate the choreography of the scene so you can tell where all the suspects were and what they were doing? Did you find a gun? Was there any chance that Mr. Xiang could have shot himself? Surely it's possible that the fight the caller referred to could have been Stephen trying to talk Mr. Xiang out of committing suicide?"

I took a breath and leaned back in my chair, exhausted and frustrated.

Detective Smith gave me a half-smile. "Are you finished? Those are all good questions and we're working on them. Mr. Laird hasn't said a word about any of this. If one of our officers hadn't recognized him, we might not even know his name."

"He didn't have ID?" I knew that Stephen always carried his phone and wallet with him when he walked at night, and he was known to offer change and dinner money to homeless people who were in trouble. And Jason, at Christmastime, had made ID tags for all of us to attach to our running shoes or cycling gear to identify us in case of an emergency. I also knew that Stephen had an ICE app on his cell phone. The critical "in case of emergency" information that police often used to identify next of kin following an accident.

"We later found his empty wallet and cell phone tossed over the fence in back of the restaurant, but by that time we already knew who he was. He made an extra effort to deliberately delay identification, but he must have known we'd find out fairly quickly anyway. Because he's a marine, his prints are in the FBI database. Identifying someone through their fingerprints normally takes hours, but he must have known he couldn't keep his identity a secret for long."

"So why hide it at all?"

"That's what we were hoping you might tell us." When I didn't respond, she added, "And his shoes? He's wearing a pair loaned to him by one of our officers. Mr. Laird's shoes were covered with blood. They are at the county crime lab being tested."

No one had shoes quite like Stephen's. He'd had a too-close encounter with an IED in Afghanistan and had a distinctive gait as a result of his injuries. There would be no mistaking his footprints.

"I'm sorry," I said, shaking my head. "I don't know the answers to any of your questions. I wish I did."

"That's all right, Mrs. McDonald." She shook my hand and gave me her business card. "If you remember anything you think might help over the next few days, please let us know. We're on the same side here. Our tech experts are working now to unlock his phone and see whether there are photos or contact information that will provide us with other details about what happened."

I wasn't sure about us being on the same side, but Stephen certainly wouldn't have agreed with her. I didn't want to make her my enemy, so I politely thanked her for her help, for letting me see Stephen, and for her service to the community.

As I left the building, Officer French Braid called out, "Have a nice day" from behind her desk and I waved to her as I let the door swing shut behind me. I raced to the car, not wanting to waste any time before reading Stephen's note. I removed the scratchy pack of papers from my bra after looking carefully around the parking lot for anyone who might spot me rummaging in my underwear.

This Maggie McDonald, the one who had friends being held by the police, the one who just blew off questions from a detective and who'd been asked to keep secrets from friends, was someone I scarcely knew. But it looked like we were going to have to get acquainted quickly if I was going to keep my promises to Stephen.

The note was scribbled in pencil in tiny writing on what looked like endpapers torn from a worn mass-market paperback.

Dear Maggie,

Thanks for listening. Let me tell you as much as I can about what I think is going on. If, after you read this, you decide you don't want to get involved, I'll understand.

Rafi Maldonado is a 17-year-old junior at Orchard View High School. He works nights at the Golden Dragon. The restaurant owner, Mr. Xiang, pays him in cash. Rafi was born in the United States, but does not have a birth certificate because he was born at home. His mom was considered an illegal resident and has been deported, though based on what Rafi's grandmother has told me, she may have been able to at least obtain a green card through her marriage to Rafi's father, who is missing. Rafi and his two young half sisters live with his father's mother. The grandmother is a citizen and owns her house. She has social security and a small pension from her late husband. Beyond that, Rafi is the sole provider for the family. He goes to school during the day, taking the minimum coursework required to graduate. Because his mother was deported, he doesn't trust strangers or the government. Therefore, he has no access to public services. Neither do his sisters.

The grandmother claims that Rafi's parents were married, but there is no documentation. His sisters have birth certificates because they were born in the hospital in Mountain View. Rafi's father was serving in the military overseas when Rafi's mom was reported as an illegal alien. The mother and grandmother didn't have access to good legal advice. The military refused to help Rafi's mom because she couldn't prove she was married and she wasn't mentioned in any of the father's official paperwork.

The father vanished after leaving the military and no one knows where he is. Rafi's grandmother took good care of the children when she was younger, but has been in poor health recently. A neighbor helps out, but the situation is spiraling out of control and Rafi is spread thin. He needs his job because he takes leftovers home to his siblings. What leftovers he doesn't take home, he leaves outside the restaurant for the homeless people in the area.

According to Rafi, Mr. Xiang knows he does this and approves but pretends he doesn't know. He wants to have deniability in case leaving food out like that is a problem for the health department or any other government agency.

In fact, someone recently reported them to the health department, saying that leaving the food out has attracted rats. Rafi doesn't think that's true because he makes sure the place is clean and tidy before he goes home at night. Rafi thinks the problem is that the health inspector and whoever reported him thinks of the homeless people as vermin. The official let Mr. Xiang off with a warning and muttered something under his breath about how the only way to get rid of them was to poison them or shoot them. Rafi didn't think he was talking about any actual rats.

Rafi has continued to leave food out, but now has to stay later to clean up the food before he leaves. I found him one night last month dozing on the back stairs of the restaurant, coughing hard and holding his chest. I gave him a lift home, and since then, I've been helping the family out a bit, trying to get a birth certificate for Rafi and working to convince them to connect with social services. I've provided groceries, transportation, and medication.

On Wednesday, I had a late meeting at the VA and stayed to play poker with a group of injured vets. It's a regular gig and I sometimes give other folks a lift home, so I drove my car rather than walking.

But both Munchkin and I were restless so we stopped on the way home to take a walk around Cuesta Park and the nearby neighborhoods, including the alley behind the Golden Dragon. We came upon two scumbags roughing up Rafi outside the restaurant. Munchkin and I intervened but they beat on us too.

I stopped reading and took a breath. I looked up and was surprised to find that it was still light out and that I was still in the police parking lot. I'd become so immersed in Stephen's note that I'd lost track of both time and place. But the idea that Stephen and Munchkin had been beaten knocked me back into the real world. I knew enough about Stephen to know that along with being a marine he was ex-special operations. I imagine he could easily defend himself from the average thug, even if he was outnumbered. I knew that Munchkin would do anything to protect Stephen. But I also knew that Stephen carried no weapons and seldom used force.

I read on.

The men had knives and Rafi at one point mouthed the word gun. I submitted to the beating because I realized that if the men were concentrating on me and Munchkin, they'd leave Rafi alone. I also wanted to get a sense of who they were. Often the best way to do that is to see how a guy fights. These two were strong, but undisciplined and untrained. They were likely low-level gang members, independent operators, or just your basic lowlife opportunists looking for some quick money.

At some point, we all heard sirens and the men ran off. Rafi was badly beaten but refused to stay to help the police or get a ride to the hospital. He insisted on going home to give his sisters the leftover food he'd saved for them. Rafi seemed to recognize the bad guys, but wouldn't tell me anything more. Not that night anyway. There wasn't time.

He thinks they were coming for Mr. Xiang because he's been feeding the homeless. I'm convinced there's more to the story. I can't believe someone would kill another person over something like feeding vagrants. And there's been tension among the businesspeople here, as though they're being stalked and don't feel safe in their own shops after hours. I don't know who we can trust, but I do know that Rafi needs to be protected. The bad guys know he can identify them and are likely to return to finish him off. He also needs protection from the police, at least temporarily. I've been working on getting documentation for him, and believe we'll ultimately be successful, but right now I'm afraid that the first thing the police would see is that he's nearly 18 and without papers. I fear they'd deport him before he could set up any kind of safety net for his grandmother and his sisters.

What I need you to do is to check in on Rafi and his family and make sure they're safe. If you're willing, I'd like you to help Rafi finish the work on his papers so that, after he's fully documented, he can safely go to the police and tell his story. Better yet, he may be able to point to other witnesses who could testify about what happened on Wednesday night so that he can stay out of it.

Here's what I know so far about what happened: Rafi came to work late on Wednesday because his grandmother had fainted at home. A neighbor named Alejandra took the grandmother, Gabriela, to the hospital, where they treated her for dehydration. Rafi stayed at home with the girls until his grandmother and Alejandra returned. The discharge nurse at the hospital was concerned about Gabriela's ability to care for herself but Alejandra assured her she'd look in on the family and help out. Alejandra told Rafi that social services might be stopping by to check on the girls. Rafi is worried that the family will attract too much attention and that the authorities will put his sisters in foster care and deport him.

After Rafi got his sisters and grandmother settled on Wednesday night, he went to work at the Golden Dragon as usual. He found Mr. Xiang in the open doorway of the refrigerated storage room. Rafi tried to help Mr. Xiang and was soon covered with his blood. He heard the thugs breaking into the cash register in the front of the restaurant, saying that they knew there must be gold hidden in the restaurant somewhere. Rafi tried to pull Mr. Xiang into the refrigerated storage unit, secure the door, and call the police. But he couldn't budge the body. He ran, but slipped in the blood. The thugs heard him, chased him, caught him in the alley, and beat him, urging him to tell them the combination to Mr. Xiang's safe. That's when Munchkin and I arrived.

Later, when I asked Rafi what he was going to do, he said his grandmother's younger brother lived outside Sacramento and might take him in. I gave him my car keys and told him to go.

I went back into the restaurant and tried to figure out how to prove Rafi's innocence. But before I could do much of anything, the police arrived, saying that they received an anonymous phone message reporting a "disturbance" at the restaurant. I think the caller must have been a witness. The police have probably already figured out where that tip came from. Since they've got me locked up, I don't know how interested in pur-

suing that lead they'll be. But if you can find the witness I think the whole problem will go away quickly. She could be an older homeless woman I've seen often who wears long skirts and braids and hangs out in Cuesta Park at night. I don't know where she is during the day.

The police brought me in, but I haven't said anything. I want to delay the investigation and keep it focused on me so that Rafi has time to get away and establish his innocence and his citizenship—but he needs help to do that. I'm hoping that you'll be willing to call the phone numbers below. They are the people who've been helping to document Rafi's citizenship and may be close to a solution.

Please don't let Jason know any of this. Jason's sense of responsibility to me and to the police force would put him on a plane back here in an instant, and he has a job to do in Texas. People are depending upon him. Like any husband, he's adept at reading me. I can't lie to him. He'll pull strings to get me out, which will endanger Rafi and his family.

As long as the Mountain View Police believe they have the right guy, they'll leave Rafi alone.

I know Rafi. He'll turn himself in as soon as he knows he won't be deported. The police will be able to investigate thoroughly and I'll be off the hook.

You will help, won't you? Please?

I folded up the papers slowly and thought about what to do. I felt confined in the car and decided to walk around a bit. I opened the door and stood, shaking a little from what I assumed was an adrenaline rush brought on by the enormity of the task Stephen had set for me.

I needed to clear my head, figure out my next steps, and regroup. If I didn't, I knew I'd be useless to anyone, ineffectively chasing shadows as I grew more frantic. I took a few deep breaths, stretched, and set out for the peaceful park behind the library about three blocks away. I checked my watch. It was a little past noon, though I felt I'd been inside the police station all day.

Everything I'd learned to count on in my new hometown had been turned on end. If Stephen Laird could be in jail, nothing I thought I knew about Orchard View, its inhabitants, or the surrounding towns could be true. Stephen's note had a paranoid tone that wasn't like him.

Yet, I was confident that if he sensed that the downtown business owners were uneasy, he was right. Stephen always seemed to know when members of the community needed help. The whole situation needed looking into, but it also seemed far too nebulous to alert the police. For the first time, I realized how lucky our little town of Orchard View was to have Stephen and Munchkin patrolling the streets, getting to know everyone, and providing an early-warning system for when the police might need to step in. Stephen's access to Jason's law enforcement connections and expertise gave Orchard View an opportunity to resolve many problems long before they would ordinarily come to the attention of law enforcement.

But, for now, with Jason away, Stephen in jail, and Munchkin at the vet, I was going to take over that role without being able to ask Jason or Stephen for advice. I wasn't sure I could handle the job, but I had to try.

I squared my shoulders, put my hands on my hips, and took a deep breath, trying to attain the superhero pose. I'd read articles in various popular magazines and online that the stance engendered self-confidence that could help with public speaking and job interviews. It was worth a try.

For now, though, I only needed to accomplish one step. If I could do that, and then the next and the next, I might be able to succeed without scaring myself to death in the process. First, I hoped that Jason would become so wrapped up in his work in Texas that he would be unable to phone me and wouldn't think about how long it had been since he'd heard from Stephen.

I still felt wobbly and shell-shocked from the news of the murder of Mr. Xiang so close to home, and Stephen and Rafi's proximity to the violence. I needed to let the news sink in before I could talk sensibly on the phone to any of the people on Stephen's list, which included Forrest Doucett, a defense lawyer, and Nell Bevans, his associate who was researching Rafi's immigration status and looking into Rafi's father's whereabouts and history to determine benefit eligibility for Rafi and his sisters. And I needed to learn more about Mr. Xiang, why at least one member of the community wanted him dead, and why the men who'd broken into his restaurant suspected he'd hidden gold on the premises.

My stomach growled. I needed food. Comfort food. No one can solve a murder on an empty stomach. While I ate, I'd jot down a plan of attack that would include phone calls to Forrest and Nell. I hoped I'd be able to figure out how I could break this enormous problem into bite-size pieces.

Though the best burger joint in the area was less than a mile from the police station, I walked back to my car and drove to the restaurant, thinking it would save time later to have the car with me. Before I'd gone a single block, I remembered that Paolo must know something, since he was the one who'd told me Stephen was at the police station. I called and left a message telling him I was stopping at Clarke's for a burger and fries. If he called me back quickly, I'd order food for him. If not, he could meet me there.

The smell of the place greeted me before I had time to park the car. For a meat eater and junk-food junkie like me, the smell was heaven. Long-time area residents told me they could smell charbroiled meat in the air here even when the tiny A-frame restaurant was closed. Whether the aroma had seeped into the building's beams over the past seventy years or their clientele had imaginations that had been trained over decades of burger consumption, I didn't know. As my stomach growled again, though, I knew it was the comfort food I needed.

Inside, a few stools snuggled up to a bar that hugged the walls on three sides. But I only knew that because I'd been here before. The room was so packed, I took my place in what I hoped would at some point coalesce into a line and draw me toward the counter where I could place my order. I made up my mind to order enough for Paolo. No way would I get a chance to talk to him if he had to wait in this line. If he didn't show, I'd take the food home where my boys would make quick work of it.

The crowd was made up of burly construction workers, khaki-clad techies, lawyers in suits, and high school kids with backpacks. The press toward the counter never thinned, but there were at least six employees working with practiced moves that delivered meals more quickly than I would have thought possible. My turn came and I ordered two basic burgers that turned out to be thicker and larger than my palm. I grabbed a tray that was filled close to overflowing once I added the fries and drinks.

I made my way back through the crowd without dumping my food on anyone's suit, though I had to laugh when a hand crept out to steal a fry from my tray. A young suit-clad worker yanked his hand back quickly and blushed in chagrin. "Sorry, I . . ."

I shook my head and laughed. "You don't have to explain. They smell irresistible. Go ahead, take some. I don't need them all. Not by a long shot."

Grabbing a fry, the young man chowed down with an audible crunch followed by a moan of delight. "Why do all the things that are bad for us taste so good?"

"Because why else would we eat them?" I answered. "We cannot live by bean sprouts alone."

We were holding up traffic as the line snaked passed a condiment bar and out onto a spacious patio that was well used even in the coldest and windiest days of winter. I staked out room on the end of a nearly full picnic table, brushed off the surface, unwrapped my burger, and dug in. I was hungrier than I'd thought. And the burger hit the spot.

I was ready for a second bite when Paolo arrived. He stood in the doorway to the patio. I assumed he'd cycled over because he was wearing his bike helmet and Lycra cycling kit. He scanned the crowd and squinted. I waved my hand, and he spotted me quickly. He clomped to the table in his bike shoes without removing his helmet, said hello, and then swung his long legs over the bench on the opposite side and sat down. I passed him a paper-wrapped burger, an old-fashioned cardboard dish of fries, and the white fluted cups I'd filled with ketchup and mustard. He dug in without saying a word, consuming half the burger before removing his helmet.

When he surfaced, I filled him in on everything I'd learned so far and showed him Stephen's letter. After he'd had a chance to read it, I told him I intended to honor Stephen's request to not tell the Mountain View Police or Jason what was going on.

"What is he thinking?" Paolo asked. "We could get him out of there right now. He can't be enjoying being in jail, not with . . . I mean . . ."

"It's okay, Paolo. I know about his PTSD. He's one tough marine but looks grim already, and he's been in there less than forty-eight hours. Once they move him to the county jail? I don't know." I shuddered. Santa Clara County Jail was probably better than some in California or elsewhere in the country, but it was overcrowded and a recent investigation suggested it was understaffed and needed improvements in safety, security, and basic health measurements such as the cleanliness of both cells and inmates. It was certainly no place for an innocent man who needed extensive exercise and the company of his dog to manage his mental health.

"But you can't do anything to get him out. Not yet. He's asked me not to tell Jason anything for fear they'll let him go and start concentrating their investigation on Rafi. To protect Rafi, Stephen feels MVPD needs to assume they've already got the right man. Surely that means he doesn't want you or anyone else from Orchard View stepping in to help at this point."

Paolo shook his head. "We have a mutual cooperation agreement with Mountain View. If anyone finds out how much I know about this, how much I'm keeping from my own department and from MVPD . . . there goes any trust I've built up."

"I feel the same way. It goes against my sense of justice to keep an innocent man in jail when the truth would get him released. But Stephen's doing this to make sure that Rafi isn't unfairly accused and has asked me to have faith in him. I'm willing to do that for at least a little while. I'm uncomfortable keeping anything from Jason, but with the communication situation so iffy following the storms, maybe we won't be able to talk much. I am going to text him tonight to let him know that I found Stephen and Munchkin, but I'll avoid offering up any of the details."

I leaned forward and pulled Stephen's letter toward me, pointing out the names of people he'd said could help. "Forrest Doucett I know. I'll call him as soon as we're done here." Forrest had gone to college with my husband, Max, and had helped out other friends of ours in the past. He had a vast network of other consultants available to provide aid to those navigating the legal system, and I was convinced he'd be a huge help. "Do you recognize any of these other names?"

Paolo frowned at the list. "I don't know them, but I'm not surprised. I'm not nearly as plugged into the local law enforcement and veteran's network as Stephen and Jason are, particularly if you veer off into the area of health and human services, child protective services, or immigration." He leaned back and brushed his hair off his forehead. "Every time I think I've got a good handle on being a cop, I find out how much I don't know."

I smiled. "It's like that for all of us, Paolo. Don't worry, there's time." He frowned and looked like he thought I was nuts. But it was a sentiment I wished I could implant in the brain of every teenager and twentysomething. So many of them felt pressure to be at the top of their professions from their first days on the job. And no matter how well they did, they often felt they fell short. But learning is an important part of any job. Employees who strive to consistently learn more are a valuable commodity in any field. "Look, it's probably good that you don't know these names and can't help me. You're in a tricky position as Jason's law enforcement partner and as a sworn officer. But would it compromise your ethics to keep me posted on anything you learn about Stephen's situation? Particularly if they move him to county? I'm all for honoring his request, but if he starts to suffer, I think we need to yank him out of there, no matter what Stephen says he wants. He may feel a loyalty to this Rafi kid, but I don't." I frowned. "At least not yet."

Paolo crumpled up the paper wrappings from his lunch and stood, completing the awkward movements required to extract oneself from a picnic table with attached benches. "I've got to get back to work, but I'm with you both so far. I'll let you know if I hear anything. I'd ask you to keep me informed, too, but I'm not sure how good an idea that is. I don't like this, Maggie, not at all. I much prefer situations that are cut and dried, black and white, hard and fast—"

I cut Paolo off. He had a wide vocabulary and a tendency when nervous to list synonyms for as long as you'd let him. "Can you come to dinner tonight? To catch up on everything else? No shoptalk? Max and the boys haven't seen you in ages."

Paolo blushed and looked down at the crumpled papers in his hand. "I've got a meeting after work." He looked up and smiled. "A date, actually."

I beamed, which was probably an overreaction, since Paolo took a step back and looked toward the exit. Paolo was shy, but I knew he'd taken an interest in a young woman who worked at a small local farm and I hoped he'd asked her out. I clamped my jaw closed on all the questions I wanted to ask. "Have fun. We'll do dinner another time soon."

Paolo left and I gathered up the remains of my own lunch. I tossed my trash in the receptacle, then dashed around the building and back to the parking lot as quickly as I could.

Chapter 5

One best-selling book on decluttering suggests tackling
all of one type of item on a single day. I think a tightly
focused approach works better for most people. Big
organizing projects are scary and exhausting. Breaking
them down into manageable pieces helps you overpower
them.

From the Notebook of Maggie McDonald,
Simplicity Itself Organizing Services

Friday, February 17, Afternoon

Halfway home after getting the kids from their respective schools,
I realized I'd forgotten to pick up Munchkin. Brian and David
put up a token protest when I told them we needed to stop at the vet's
on the way home, but they didn't seem to mind playing with the
adoptable kittens in the waiting room while we waited for the doctor.

"We're here for Munchkin on behalf of his people, Stephen Laird
and Jason Mueller," I said to the receptionist. "Do you need ID?" I
grabbed for my backpack and wallet.

She shook her head. "Dr. Davidson told me you'd be coming in. It
breaks my heart that someone would hurt that poor sweet thing." She
talked about Munchkin as if he were a tiny helpless kitten rather than
a massive creature who outweighed us both. "Have a seat. The doctor will be out in a minute."

Dr. Davidson himself came out rather than sending a technician to
fetch us. He smiled, greeted me, and introduced himself to the boys.

Taking us all back to an exam room, he handed me a white paper bag that rattled with what sounded like plastic pill bottles.

"What are they?" I peered into the bag before handing it to Brian.

"I want him to stay on antibiotics for at least two weeks. Those were nasty wounds. We cleaned them out aggressively while he was under sedation, but please keep a close eye on him. If anything doesn't look or smell right, phone me right away, day or night. I want to stay ahead of any possible infection. He seems run-down and depressed, which isn't ever good for healing."

"He's missing Stephen and Jason," I said.

"And they'll be the best medicine for him. In the meantime, try to keep him quiet and well fed. No tussling with kids or other dogs." He looked pointedly at the boys. "No running for at least three days. Mastiffs can be inherently lazy, and he's no puppy, so that shouldn't be too hard, but I've put some light sedatives in there in case you need him to slow down. Use the smallest dose necessary, as infrequently as possible."

I nodded.

The door behind the doctor opened with a screech as a technician came in with Munchkin on a nylon rope leash. The dog perked up when he saw the boys, who knelt to greet him. His huge tongue licked their faces, nearly covering their heads, and the boys used their hoodies to wipe off the drool. Munchkin lay down with his head on his paws and sighed. The escaping air made his jowls wobble and he looked like the poster dog for depression. I wondered whether being with Belle would cheer him up without revving him up.

"Please call if you need anything or have any questions," the doctor said. "Normally I'd plan on keeping him here another day or two, but I think he needs to be around his friends. I'm no dog psychologist, but . . ."

We both looked at Munchkin and sighed heavily ourselves. "It's hard to be cheerful in the company of such a morose dog," I said, "but we'll do our best. Does he need one of those collars? The cone of shame?"

The boys patted Munchkin and gently rubbed his ears, avoiding the worst of his wounds. The doctor tilted his head. "You've got a golden?"

"Yes, Belle. She was here when I brought Munchkin in."

"Right. I'd be more concerned about her trying to help her friend by licking his wounds. Munchkin hasn't shown much interest in them. That may change, but we can skip the cone for now. If Munchkin starts licking or biting them, I'd recommend you bring him back in case they are infected. If your dog pays too much attention to Munchkin's wounds, you'll have to keep them separated until he heals."

He handed me the leash. "You're all experienced with dogs and know Munchkin well. Do your best, use your judgment, follow the directions on the meds, and let me know if you need help. Any questions?"

I shook my head and thanked him, then we trooped out, taking a few moments to adjust our plan as Brian, David, and Munchkin all tried to go through the door at the same time. The boys deferred to the dog, who led us into the lobby.

The receptionist waved us off, saying that the bill would be worked out later with the owners. We thanked her and left.

Back at the car, Munchkin climbed onto the seat between the boys, with his head bent a bit so he could peer out the window and keep from smashing his skull into the roof every time we hit a bump in the road. I pulled out of the parking lot and onto El Camino Real, which was already congested with rush hour traffic, though it wasn't yet four o'clock. We waited through several cycles of the light at San Antonio Road. The boys were busy with their phones and Munchkin was asleep.

"Mom, don't let me forget to give you some papers I need you to sign," Brian said, derailing my train of thought. "I need to hand them back in on Monday."

"Me, too," said David. "I need you to sign for that MEHAP advanced placement class next year."

"MEHAP?"

"Modern European His—Whoa, dude!"

A panhandler had rushed up to the car and was banging on the rear passenger window.

"Mm—Mm—Mm—" he shouted, stuttering and revealing that he was missing teeth.

David leaned away from the window. Munchkin lunged over David, put his paws on the door handle, and lifted his nose to the partially open window. His wagging tail walloped Brian across the nose.

The light changed. Traffic started to move. The car behind us honked. I swiveled my head between the vehicles in front of us to the man who was now rattling the door handle.

The car behind us honked again.

"David, are you okay? Is the door locked? How close is he? I don't want to run over his foot."

David made an unintelligible sound, his face buried in Munchkin's side as the huge mastiff licked the window, wagging his tail.

The driver behind us leaned on his horn and shouted something I couldn't hear. Other cars behind him honked. In the rearview mirror, I spotted an SUV pulling out from the line of traffic into the bike line, hoping to pass us all before the light changed.

I hoped the old man was safe and I accelerated slowly through the intersection and away from the conflict and confrontation. But as I pulled away, I thought I heard the man say "Munch," I saw him step back, his shoulders slumped and his hands held out in a posture that looked like dejection and disbelief.

"What was that about?" I said to no one in particular. "Have you seen him before?" The boys struggled to settle Munchkin, right themselves, and brush wisps of dog hair from their clothes and the upholstery.

"Calm down, Munch," Brian said, holding the end of the leash. "Lie down. You heard the vet. Who was that guy? Did you know him? He seemed to know you."

"Munchkin liked him," said David. "But how do they know each other? We can ask Stephen, I guess, Mom, can't we? Where is Stephen, anyway? Why did *we* pick up Munchkin?"

I was still rattled from the encounter with the panhandler, so it took a moment for David's questions to sink in. He shared my habit of firing off questions so fast it was impossible to know which one to answer first. I realized that in the after-school rush and confusion, I'd told them we were going to make a quick stop at the vet, but I hadn't yet addressed why we were doing this favor for Stephen. The kids were used to Munchkin by now, of course. And Stephen had helped our family so much in the past that it must have, initially at least, seemed perfectly reasonable for us to be returning the favor by running an errand.

"Mom, what's going on?" David pressed for an answer. "Who was that guy? How did Munchkin get so roughed up, anyway?"

"Can we talk about this when we get home?" I said, glancing in the rearview mirror. "It's complicated and I need to focus on the traffic. Can you check your phone and see if there's an accident somewhere or if there's a faster way to get home?"

Brian began tapping on the screen of his cell to find out, but I could tell that I was only raising more questions by putting off answering the ones David had asked.

How far did my promise not to tell anyone about Stephen extend? Was I going to keep secrets from my own family? Damage my relationship with my teenaged boys? Expect them to confide in me when I kept secrets from them? I bit my lip and wrinkled my forehead. Family first, I thought. Family first. The kids didn't need to know everything, but they deserved to know at least part of Stephen's story. If for no other reason than to keep them from speculating and using their powerful imaginations to create a story that was far worse than what had actually happened. The reality was bad enough.

I took a deep breath, sat up straight, and pushed my back into the cushions of the seat. I signaled for a lane change, checked my blind spot, and turned into the left lane, stopping at yet another red light. I made eye contact with both boys.

"Stephen's in jail," I said. "We'll talk about it when we get home." I didn't want to have this conversation without being able to see the boys' reactions.

When we arrived at the house, Belle seemed to instinctively understand that Munchkin wasn't there to play. In place of her normal enthusiastic bouncing greeting, she lay down on the floor and inched forward on her belly, making a sympathetic whine as she sniffed Munchkin's nose and licked his snout. He returned the greeting.

The boys moved more slowly than usual. They headed straight to the kitchen for a snack, but poured out food for the dogs before attacking tangerines, milk, cookies, and last night's leftovers.

I made myself coffee and was adding milk to it when I realized both boys and both dogs were seated and looking up at me expectantly.

I sighed and joined the boys at the table. "I'm not sure where to begin," I said, half hoping Brian or David might have a suggestion. But they were remarkably silent. Belle moved under the table and put her head in my lap. Munchkin curled up by the back door.

"I told you that Stephen's in jail, and the truth is that I don't know much more than that, not for certain. The rest is mostly speculation.

That and a few things Stephen told me." I took a long sip of coffee and pulled my sweater around me for comfort.

"Mom, what did he do?" Brian whispered. "It's a mistake, right?" "Does Jason know he's there?" David asked. "He doesn't, does he? If he did, Stephen wouldn't be there anymore."

And then Brian hit on the crux of the matter. "What are you going to do?"

"I don't know." I looked at my boys then, each of them, closely. At thirteen and fifteen they were both maturing at a faster rate than either Max or I could keep up with. But it was a roller coaster. When we were willing to give them more responsibility and freedom, they'd do something or say something that told us that parts of them were still small boys. And when we wanted to hug them closely and protect them as we always had, well, that was when they chose to stretch and launch themselves, often fearlessly and without looking, into the adult world. I looked in their eyes, searching for fear. There was none. What I saw was determination, confidence, and an aching desire for justice and the truth.

"Do you want to know everything?" I asked. "The details are a bit rough."

They nodded. Brian scooted his chair closer to the table and leaned forward on his forearms. "Of course we want to know. We *need* to know. Stephen and Jason are our friends. We have to help them."

David uncharacteristically agreed with his brother. "Brian's right. Besides, you know that if the details are interesting, the story will be all over school by tomorrow morning. Do you want us to get the news from you or from the rumor mill?"

I smiled and David smirked. As teenagers so often do, he'd noted one of my favorite rules, saved it up, and hurled it back at me. Max and I urged them to tell us what was going on with them, with their friends, and at school, driving the message home by reminding them that if they didn't tell us themselves, we'd most likely hear an expanded, more dramatic version via the parent network.

"Touché," I said to David. "Here's what I know."

I filled them in on Munchkin's condition and how he'd dragged himself home, what Detective Smith had told me, the details Stephen had given me, the contents of the letter he'd written, and finally what Stephen had asked me to do. I emphasized how important it was to keep the information within the family.

"Do either of you know this boy?" I asked. "Rafi Maldonado? His sisters? Or any other kids who work at the restaurant? Did you know Mr. Xiang?" Orchard View High School's district boundaries included parts of Mountain View, and it had an open campus. The older kids often went out for lunch, especially on Fridays. Rafi was older than David, but there was a chance they knew each other. Brian was more likely to know one of the sisters, though I still wasn't sure how old they were.

Brian shook his head. David stood up, moved to the counter, and lifted himself to sit on top of it. "I might know him," he said. "He may have been in my concert band class at the start of the year. I think he dropped the class, but he still plays bass with us."

It seemed like an odd arrangement. I frowned.

"It's not that unusual. The teachers do that with some kids—especially the older band kids they've known since they were freshmen. They're the only teachers who see kids all year, every year, straight through school, right? So they know us better than anyone. Better than the counselors who see us for, like, ten minutes once a year and don't even recognize us to say hi to in the quad. There are kids that the performing arts teachers keep an eye on and kinda look after. If Rafi is the guy I'm thinking of, he's one of those kids."

I thought for a moment. That was good news. Maybe one of the music teachers could put me in contact with Rafi, and we could meet in the band room if that seemed like a safe place to him.

David spoke as though he'd read my thoughts. "You know, if you have trouble getting in touch with Rafi, I'll bet Kathryn could help—Kathryn Sands, the band teacher." Kids calling their teachers by their first name had at first seemed odd to me. It might have been a laid-back coastal California thing, or a measure of the fact that Kathryn thought of her students as musicians, colleagues, and people. Regardless, it worked for Kathryn and in no way diminished the respect the kids had for her.

"You're right," I said.

David beamed, jumped down from the counter, and grabbed a fistful of cookies. "I've got a ton of reading to do for history," he said. "Will you let us know if you find out more? Or if there's anything we can look into at school?" He rummaged in his backpack and pulled out the crumpled papers he needed signed, tossed them on the table, and dashed up the back stairs, followed by Belle, who knew that David was good for sneaking her at least one cookie from his stash.

Brian looked at the table and frowned. Uh-oh. He was my sensitive kid. The most likely to feel things deeply and least likely to talk about them.

"Questions?" I asked. "Ideas?"

Brian shook his head. "It sounds like those girls are pretty little. And Rafi is even older than David. I won't find out anything at school. But . . . What do I say if anyone asks about Stephen?"

Whew. That was a good question. "I'm not sure. Maybe something like 'I heard about that, but I don't know the details. Stephen is a good guy.' "

Brian wasn't happy with my suggestion. "Lame, Mom. But never mind, I'll think of something." He stood and took his glass to the sink. He knelt next to Munchkin and massaged the dog's floppy ears. "Can he go upstairs with me?"

"Taking care of Munchkin is one of the most important things we can do right now," I said. "See if he needs to go out, and then I think a long snooze in your room while you keep him company and do your homework might be exactly what he needs. But take him up the front stairs—he may still be a little clumsy with the sedation and I don't want him to bang up those wounds too much." The kitchen stairs to the second floor were utilitarian, narrow, and steep. If I hadn't previously seen Munchkin manage them, I'd have questioned whether he would fit in the stairwell at all.

I was starting to think about dinner when Brian came back through the kitchen after taking Munchkin outside.

"Mom, did that man at the intersection know Munchkin? It sounded like he was trying to say Munchkin's name."

"I'm not sure, hon," I said. "I think so. But how would he have known him? On the other hand, Munchkin seemed to know him, too."

"He's probably at that corner every day. You could ask him."

Brian disappeared quickly through the dining room with Munchkin. He was absolutely right. Just as David had been earlier. But before I followed up on their ideas, I needed to make calls to the people Stephen had asked me to phone, and continue to bounce ideas off the boys and Max, when he got home.

I placed my palms on the table and stood. "Right," I said to no one in particular. "With a team like this, we'll certainly get Stephen out. Maybe even before I'm forced to tell Jason where he is."

But I was Jason's friend as much as I was Stephen's and I feared Jason would learn too much from the sound of my voice if I phoned him. I didn't want him to worry. I compromised by texting him. As Jason had explained to me, a text was more likely to get through the overloaded disaster-area communications system anyway.

I typed:

Found Stephen and Munchkin. Everyone healthy, well, and accounted for. Will start on project with Stephen tomorrow.

I knew that Jason would assume that the project I was referring to was the one we all had expected to start yesterday—sorting their belongings and organizing their home offices, storage, and new front room. I hated to mislead him, but the text would have to do for now.

By 6:30 p.m., the boys were finished with their homework and chores and were immersed in a video game. Max had called to say he was working late on the prerelease testing of a new product and wouldn't make it home in time for dinner. I wasn't surprised. It was all part of the predictably unpredictable life of being married to an engineer working to get a product out the door.

I called the boys away from their video game and Brian clattered down the stairs first, holding his laptop. "Mom, Rafi's on social media, but he doesn't post often. I'm guessing he doesn't have a computer at home. He probably uses ones in the library during a free period. There's nothing here that shows where he hangs out."

"If what Stephen told me is accurate, between working, school, and helping his family, Rafi doesn't have much time to hang out anywhere," I said. "Does he like any sports or music?"

Knowing his interests might help to get to know him—if I could find him.

"I can't tell," Brian said, clicking madly on his keyboard. "There's not much here to work with."

David, Belle, and Munchkin clomped down the back staircase with all the subtlety of a winning rugby team. A white streamer trailed from Munchkin's mouth. I reached down to pull it off.

"Toilet paper?"

"You don't want to see the bathroom upstairs," David said. "Maybe you can help me clean it up after dinner?"

"What on earth? Did he eat a whole roll?" I looked at Munchkin, unwilling to think about how to cope with the digestive system of a massive dog who had eaten toilet paper.

He looked horribly guilty and embarrassed, whimpered, sank to his haunches, and crawled under the table.

"Try a whole package," said David. "I don't think he ate it all, though. Shredded it and spread it all over the bathroom and the upstairs hall. We'll probably want to get to it before it turns into, like, papier–mâché. That dog can sure drool. Like he's performing as the erupting volcano in a school play."

I didn't know whether to laugh or cry. I decided to laugh. "Never mind. It sounds like a large garbage bag will do the trick. Poor Munchkin. He probably needs more exercise than he's been getting."

"What he needs is Stephen," Brian said as he filled a bowl with chili from the simmering pot on the stove and brought it to the table. Chili was our go-to family meal for busy times. "Did you get him out of jail yet?"

"No," I said, filling my own bowl and sprinkling it with cheese. "I've got the lawyer's number right here, though, and I'll call him in the morning. Rafi's grandmother, too, if I can figure out where she lives."

"What about that homeless guy on the way home?" David said. "He seemed like he knew Munchkin. Maybe he knows something about how Munchkin got hurt. Can you find him again?"

"Your brother said the same thing. I'll give that a try. Maybe one of the store owners down near the restaurant knows where to find him. A bunch of thugs don't attack a restaurant out of the blue. There must have been something brewing for a while. Maybe the stores have been hassled or held up, and this attack on Mr. Xiang is the first sign that it's intensifying."

My kids knew all about escalating violence, having experienced it firsthand, too close to home, when we moved to Orchard View.

"Wouldn't the police have already thought of that?" David reached across the table to grab a piece of sourdough bread from the basket next to my placemat. I passed him the bread and gave him my "mom" look. He looked guilty and grabbed a second slice while chewing the first.

"Sorry! Please. Thank you. Don't grab. And don't talk with your mouth full," he recited.

"Right, and . . . ?" I asked. The boys chimed in with "There's a fine line between a smart kid and a smart aleck. Make sure you're on the right side of the line."

I smiled. Message obviously received. Sometimes hunger and expediency overrode their manners, but they were definitely good kids.

"If you two take the dogs out on their leashes so they don't get too rambunctious, I'll tackle the dishes and Munchkin's art project upstairs."

"Deal!" said David. "You haven't seen the bathroom yet though . . ."

We cleared the table and I asked David to let me know if he saw anything about the murder at the restaurant on social media or on the web site of the local weekly paper.

"But be careful you don't reveal any information in the process," I said. "I don't necessarily agree with Stephen's need to keep this all quiet, but that's what he's asked me to do." I shook my head. "He must have a good reason."

"I already checked all the sites I could think of. There was nothing, which is weird. Stephen may be the only guy who knows that Rafi was there. When a rumor involves someone from school, the Internet blows up. There isn't even any discussion of Mr. Xiang's death or murder. Not on social media, the restaurant's web page, the police blotter, or any of the online newspapers. Has the restaurant been closed? It would have to be, wouldn't it? Do the police think the thugs were high school kids, or older?"

"Whoa!" I said. "Those are all good questions, but I don't have any of the answers. Not yet, anyway." While the boys took the dogs outside, I double-checked the restaurant's web site and the police blotter. As David had said, there was no mention of the murder. Was that usual, two days after a violent death in a town with a normally low crime rate and a citizenry that thrived on the Internet? I didn't think so.

Orchard View prided itself on maintaining a "rural atmosphere," which meant, among other things, no streetlights and no sidewalks. The boys took flashlights and bags to help them pick up after the dogs and warn off any skunks or raccoons scrounging for food.

I signed the kids' papers, fed the cats, did the dishes, and cleaned up the bathroom, which looked like a blizzard had hit it but wasn't that difficult to restore to normal. I put a new package of toilet paper out of Munchkin's reach on top of the medicine cabinet and hoped he wouldn't turn to shredding our towels in frustration. When the boys came upstairs and reported that Munchkin had suffered no digestive repercussions from his papier–mâché mess, I suggested they pick up any dirty clothes, shoes, and anything else they'd deposited on the floors of their rooms—in case Munchkin's plan was to branch out to other materials.

Holmes and Watson, our ginger-colored cats, followed me upstairs and "helped" me sort the laundry by attacking socks, subduing them, and dragging them under the bed.

Within an hour or so, I was tucked up in bed with my yellow-lined legal pad, making lists of the people I needed to call and the things I needed to do tomorrow. Contact the lawyer, Rafi's grandmother, and the proprietors of the stores near the Golden Dragon. I checked the web site of the local paper again but had no luck finding anything. The paper came out on Wednesdays and had already been printed and distributed by the time Mr. Xiang was killed in the early hours of Thursday night. My guess was that the few reporters and stringers the small paper still employed would be collecting details up until the last minute for next week's edition, hoping to print a more in-depth story with a local twist to differentiate themselves from the daily papers and nightly news. The aunt of a student at Brian's school worked at the paper, and I made a note to phone her. Then I crossed off her name and finally wrote it again with a question mark. While the reporter might be a good source of information, she'd want to know why I was asking. I wouldn't call her unless I absolutely had to, for fear I'd leak some part of Stephen or Rafi's involvement by mistake. Neither one of them needed to raise their profile with the police or the rumor mill by having their names appear in the paper.

I checked the *San Francisco Chronicle* and the *San Jose Mercury News*, but they'd posted nothing as yet. I made a note to check online again in the morning, but decided to avoid the television and radio news. I didn't have time to listen to an entire newscast of superficial information just to get a sound bite or two on a story they probably wouldn't cover anyway. Events occurring in the towns between San Francisco and San Jose were sparsely covered on the flashy nightly news programs, except in the case of very visual stories like a major wildfire, earthquake, or flooding, or anything that might affect the tech companies and their stock prices.

I sighed while I reviewed my calendar. If I was going to help Stephen, I needed to clear my schedule. It was a little painful to consider doing so, because I'd been working hard to build my client list since our move to the area last fall.

I was in the middle of a kitchen reorganization with one client, who hoped I'd be finished by the time she returned from a business trip in Germany. I e-mailed her about the unavoidable delay, offering her a ten percent discount. She quickly e-mailed back, explaining that she was awake early to go for a run before work. Her project had been extended by a month. She asked if I would mind convincing the post office to extend the hold on her mail and check to see if her neighbor was still watering her garden. Both chores would be easy for me, so I readily agreed. She thanked me for the extra work and suggested we forget the discount and call it even. I wished all my clients were that easygoing.

I called a few other customers, delaying an appointment to provide an estimate on a downsizing project, two for closet clean-outs, and a garage storage consultation. In general, the clients had seemed relieved. The reason they'd called for help in the first place was that they had an aversion to tackling the projects. By hiring me, they were scheduling time and hiring accountability and a second opinion. Having their personal organizer encourage them to procrastinate on a dreaded chore was good news.

But there was one client I knew I couldn't put off—Mrs. Bostwick. She was an exceptionally organized elderly woman with no family. I'd helped her clear out the sprawling city apartments of two of her siblings following their deaths. We'd dealt with everything from valuable antiques and artwork to treasured memorabilia. We'd grown close. But she'd had a stroke and now seldom left the house. She watched hours of home improvement television and called me every month or so to discuss an update to her systems.

This month's project was swapping out her yellowed and crumbling manila folders for brightly colored new ones. We'd planned to replace the old typewritten labels with new ones in a large, easy-to-read font. Her once-tidy hanging folders were coming unglued, so we were exchanging those for new ones with large print tabs.

She'd already provided a spreadsheet with all the file names.

We'd gone over it to determine if there were files she could combine or discard altogether. If she'd been a younger woman, I'd have suggested converting to online bill payment systems, but she was comfortable and adept at keeping her finances up to date using an old-school checkbook and register. I didn't want to mess with her success or force her to learn a new system that might make her anxious about safety and security.

All I needed to do was make the new labels, set up the folders, and keep an appointment in a little over a week to exchange the old files for the new. I figured I could easily fuss with those tasks in between bouts of working on Stephen's project, which I planned to have finished long before the appointment with Mrs. Bostwick.

But I had no idea at that point what helping Stephen would entail.

Chapter 6

Many organizers suggest that organized storage means
finding a designated home for every item you own. If
only it were that easy! I suggest starting with one
drawer. Remove everything that doesn't belong. Once
you remove invasive items, you'll have space to clean
and tidy what's left, decide where everything belongs,
and discover which items you can discard.

From the Notebook of Maggie McDonald,
Simplicity Itself Organizing Services

Saturday, February 18, Morning

When Max's team was releasing a new product, no matter how
many months of painstaking design and planning had been
done, disasters cropped up requiring last-minute testing and emergency bug fixing. Twelve-hour days, midnight calls from European
and Asian testing teams, and weekend marathons were the norm for
as long as it took to verify that the product was ready to go and
wouldn't pose problems for customers.

So I wasn't surprised when he rolled in at 1:00 a.m., gave me a
quick peck on the cheek, and fell promptly asleep.

In the morning, I found flowers on the kitchen table and a note
from Max expressing his undying love and asking me to remind him
of any appointments or family events he might otherwise forget
while keeping his current crazy schedule. No problem. I had his back

when he was busy, just as he had mine. But the flowers were a nice gesture and brightened up the kitchen on a gloomy February morning. After breakfast, I dropped the boys off at their Saturday activities. Soccer practice for Brian with an afternoon at a friend's house. David's plans were a little more free-form—Ultimate Frisbee followed by lunch with the other trumpet players from his band class.

I'd hoped to catch Max at home before he returned to work, but I found a note on the table that suggested I'd just missed him. I phoned his office and left a message, then poured myself a cup of coffee. I took it outside, along with the Saturday editions of all the newspapers I could find in the news racks near the soccer field. I sat in one of the rockers on our back porch, scanning one paper after another for news or an obituary for Mr. Xiang. Then I paged through them looking for something that might indicate that a pattern of violence or harassment had developed in the downtown business district. All I could find was a brief notice from a funeral home on the obituary page of the San Jose paper:

> *Jon Yuen Xiang, 75, born April 18, 1940, died February 16, 2016. Resident of Mountain View. Owner and manager of the Golden Dragon Chinese Restaurant since 1979. No services will be held. In lieu of flowers, please donate to your favorite charity.*

The notice seemed small and sad compared to the flowery mini-biographies of other elderly residents, most of which were written by grieving family members. They were capsules of California history, captured in the lives of individuals. I wondered whether the brevity of the announcement was due to the police keeping a lid on the details of the murder or a personal preference on the part of Mr. Xiang. I hoped it would be followed by a lengthier article or obituary later.

I dawdled over the rest of the paper, putting off interviewing some of the homeless people and shop owners near the Golden Dragon. I wasn't looking forward to introducing myself to the street people. Most of them weren't dangerous, I knew, but many lacked basic hygiene for a variety of reasons. Some had mental health issues that put them barely in touch with reality. And all of them tugged at my heart. I wished homelessness and treating incapacitating mental illnesses were problems that we handled better than we did.

A gust of wind set the rocker next to mine moving gently, as though Max sat beside me, unseen. I shivered. The homeless who couldn't find shelter were going to be in for a cold and uncomfortable night.

I couldn't do anything about the weather, and I needed to attend to things where I could make a difference. As quickly as I could. I phoned Forrest Doucett. If he was working over the weekend, he wasn't answering his phone, so I left a detailed message, asking for him or any of his colleagues who were working on Rafi's case to phone me back.

I hadn't heard from Max, so I texted him to avoid engaging in an ongoing game of phone tag:

Miss you. Lots of news here. I'll fill you in when you get home. Running errands most of the day. Text me if you need me to pick up anything. oxox

I phoned Paolo. "Hey, have you heard any news about Stephen?" I asked when he answered the phone. Paolo had little time or patience for small talk.

"It's not good. They've moved him to the county jail, though they've given him his own cell to keep him safe."

"What do you mean? Is he in danger?" I'd been worried about Stephen's mental well-being, but I hadn't given a thought to his physical safety. He was a retired marine who'd worked in special ops, and I'd taken for granted that he could look after himself.

Paolo paused before answering. I couldn't tell whether it was because of his normal reticence or if he was carefully choosing his words to avoid telling me something.

"Sometimes cops get targeted when they're in jail," he said.

"But Stephen isn't a cop. He didn't want me to tell anyone in the police department about his connection to Jason, and I didn't. So how would anyone in the jail know who Stephen is?"

"Oh, Maggie," Paolo said, as if he were addressing someone hopelessly naive. "Prisoners have very little to do in jail except gossip and they've got quite a network. Jason is responsible for putting men in jail. Stephen's probably worked with the few who are veterans."

He sighed. "They're both good-looking men who are often photographed at those police charity events. All it would take for word to get out is for one of those incarcerated men to have a suspicion that Stephen was connected to law enforcement. For that matter, most crooks claim they can spot a cop a mile away. Stephen's military bearing and his stint in the military police could have put a target on his back even if no one made the connection to Jason."

"But the guards will keep an eye on him, right? I should go down and see him. Do they have visiting hours on the weekend? Do I need any special paperwork?"

Again, Paolo was quiet.

"Paolo?"

"Yes, they have visiting hours. Normally, you'd need special paperwork but it can wait until next week, now, I think."

"Because?"

This time, in the silence, I heard a catch in Paolo's voice. "He's been injured and is in the hospital."

"What hospital? How badly is he hurt? What happened?"

"The hospital ward at the jail. He was targeted, I assume. His story is that he had an accident in the common area, slipped, and hit his head and arm on a table. He needed stitches, broke his arm, and has a number of nasty bruises. He's being observed for brain injuries."

"How do you know all this? Couldn't the bruises have been from the beating he took at the Golden Dragon?"

"I've got a buddy who works in the jail pharmacy. He knows Stephen and the situation. He'll keep quiet."

This time, there was silence on my end of the phone as I sifted through a storm of questions that came to mind too quickly for me to spit them out. "It doesn't matter what happened or why. We need to get him out of there as quickly as possible."

Paolo agreed. "Look, I don't have any more information on the case than I did yesterday, but I have the administrative phone number and a list of procedures for making contact with prisoners. You'll need to make arrangements with the chief warden if you want to visit Stephen, but you may want to wait. Normal practice is to restrict visitors to hospitalized inmates for at least a week. If he gets a visitor when he's not supposed to, it will arouse speculation."

"Do you know what they've charged him with? Why they're holding him there?"

"I don't know much more than I did yesterday, except that the district attorney is serious about putting pressure on Stephen to talk."

"Okay. I've got a list of things to take care of today for him. I'll let you know if I learn anything."

"He's safe enough for now in the medical facility, but . . ."

"I know. Thanks, Paolo. I'll talk to you later."

What neither of us said, but both of us knew, was that Stephen in jail was like a caged wild bird. He might survive, but he might never be the same after this experience.

At least I could take good care of Munchkin. I called him and Belle, leashed them both, and grabbed my raincoat. I put them in the back of my car, giving Munchkin a little boost when he had trouble jumping up. I needed information and Munchkin needed a walk. He was restless, injured, and unhappy. A walk might not help, but it couldn't hurt.

I drove to downtown Mountain View and was thrilled to find a rare vacant parking space in front of the corner Pet Wash. Both dogs were still remarkably clean and I didn't want to irritate Munchkin's healing wounds, but I stepped inside the store anyway. Wanda Daniel had been part of the downtown landscape for decades and knew everyone.

"Hey, Wanda," I called out over the noise created by a barking basset hound, running water, a clothes dryer thumping with heavy towels, and the chainsaw-like sound of a high-powered hair dryer. The room was lined with three tubs on each side, normal human bathroom tubs set at counter level to make dog washing less hard on their owners' backs. Ramps and small flights of stairs led up to the tubs, each of which was equipped with a hair dryer, a nonslip mat, and eyebolts for attaching leashes. Wanda supplied each human customer with a plastic apron, towels, and shampoo and conditioner in a variety of scents.

Wanda didn't hear me, but I waited while she finished drying a Bernese mountain dog who insisted on licking Wanda's ear. She turned off the dryer, fluffed out the dog's fur, and added a spritz of perfume. "No more rolling in dead birds, Buster," she said. "Although I do appreciate your repeat business." Buster licked her ear again.

Wanda looked up and startled when she saw me with the two dogs in tow. "Hi, Maggie. Wow, two? I don't have any tubs side-by-side right now but . . ."

"Don't worry, Wanda, these two are fine. Do you have a minute? I've got a couple of questions for you, and I wanted to give you some of my cards."

"Sure. Buster's people dropped him off so they could run errands while he gets his beauty treatment. I want him to air out for a minute and sniff him again. He found a dead bird at the beach early this morning and had a good long roll before anyone could get him back on his leash. It's a particularly persistent smell."

My nose wrinkled involuntarily. Munchkin and Belle tugged on their leashes, eager to make Buster's acquaintance. I was pleased to see Munchkin wagging his tail, but no matter how perky the smell made him, it would be a long time before I resorted to a field trip to roll in dead things at the beach. "Get a good sniff, Munch," I told him. "That's as close as I hope you're getting to anything dead for a good long time."

Wanda laughed, hung up her apron, and offered cookies to the dogs. I handed her a few of my business cards.

"Thanks, Maggie. I've been interested in going paperless with my files and stuff, but I don't have the money to pay you or anyone else to make the switch for me. And I can't carve out the time to do it myself. I hear customers talking about organizing projects all the time, though, and I'd be happy to give them your card."

"I can give you an estimate if you'd like. I offer a discount for friends."

Wanda chuckled. "My books are a mess. There's never enough time. I tell myself I need to sit down and attack them but then I start thinking how great it would be to have a glass of wine, curl up on the couch, and watch . . . almost anything on TV."

"I get that. You know, if you're concerned about the cost, we could think about setting up a class. If enough storeowners in the area are interested, I could do a group lesson with weekly follow-ups to keep the cost down."

"I'd go for that. As long as someone else organizes it and I get to bring my dog." Wanda changed the subject and I didn't press her further. This wasn't a marketing visit and delivering a hard sales pitch wasn't my style. "You said you had some questions. Did someone tangle with a skunk? Munchkin sure messed with something, didn't he?" She knelt down next to Munchkin and made sympathetic noises and said something about Stephen that made it sound as if she knew both of them.

"It's a little delicate," I began. "Do you know Stephen Laird?"

"Of course." She patted Munchkin and fended off a jealous Belle before patting her too. "We're part of one of their regular walking routes. I'm generally closed for business before they head out on their treks around the neighborhood, but they've stopped a few times to chat or help if I'm here working late."

"And did you hear about the trouble at the Golden Dragon?"

"Poor Mr. Xiang. He was such a sweet man. He wasn't too fond of dogs, especially the bigger ones, but he always said hello and waved and gave me money plants every Chinese New Year." She pointed to a row of healthy pots of bamboo-like pachira on the windowsill. "I don't know how he knew, but it seemed like every time I was having a bad day, he'd send one of the waiters down with a container of tangerine chicken, which is my favorite. It included a napkin with the characters for peace, strength, and happiness."

I was impressed. "You read Mandarin?"

"No, but that's what the waiters always said as they pointed to the characters." She smiled and spoke to the dogs while rubbing their ears. "For all I know he could have written 'scram, you witch,' but Mr. Xiang wasn't like that. I still can't believe that he's gone, or that someone decided to kill him."

"I saw the death notice in the paper," I said. "It was . . . brief. I was surprised that there wouldn't be a service. Does he have no friends, family, or business colleagues who'd like to say good-bye or pay their respects?"

Wanda hesitated, but finally said, "As far as I know, he has no family. But surely his long-term customers and employees would want to do something to honor his memory. I'll have to think who to ask, but I'll try to find out. It may be that his death was so unexpected and tragic that no one has had time to organize anything. You're right, though. He's been an active part of the community for almost forty years. Maybe one of the business associations he belonged to would like to do something."

"If you find out, will you let me know? My number's on the card."

Wanda agreed and walked back toward Buster. Before she could turn the noisy dryer back on, I followed her, trying to decide how much to tell her about Stephen's predicament and my plan to help him.

I knew Wanda pretty well. Every dog owner in Orchard View and Mountain View did. Washing Belle here, or having Wanda wash her for me while I did errands, was too great a luxury to pass up. Her rates were reasonable and there was seldom a wait for a tub. She was friendly and I'd never heard her pass along any gossip that wasn't completely innocuous. If I could tell anyone about Stephen, I could confide in Wanda. But I'd told Stephen I wouldn't tell a soul and I'd already talked to the boys. So I'd have to try to get information from Wanda without giving too much away. Interviewing people was much more complicated than either Jessica Fletcher or Miss Marple made it look.

I took a deep breath and pressed on. "I'm trying to find a witness who could have seen or heard what went on at the restaurant that night," I told her. "Or anyone who might know what sparked the violence. The police tell me that no one has come forward, but surely, a gunshot . . ."

I let my voice trail off, hoping that Wanda would fill in the rest and not be too curious about why I was asking. Her natural desire to be kind and helpful must have won out over her interest in my reasons for inquiring.

"I went home pretty early that night," she said. "Trying to fight off a cold. I stayed until maybe an hour after closing. Some of the other shop owners might know more, though. We've all been working later hours since the recession. Laying off help and doing the work ourselves. And then there are the homeless people. They might have seen something. They won't talk to the police but they might talk to you."

I hesitated for what must have seemed like a second too long. "Don't worry," she said. "All of the regulars are harmless. The Mountain View Police are pretty good about finding a reason to pick up anyone who is dangerous to themselves or others. But if you don't want to talk to them, I wouldn't blame you. They frighten me sometimes. I scare easily at night. I was attacked once, years ago. By someone who was after my moneybox. I've never felt safe in the dark since. I think Stephen Laird must have sensed that, because he has an uncanny way of stopping by when I work late."

I wasn't surprised. Anyone who knew Stephen was aware that he had a reputation for appearing out of nowhere when help was needed, much like a caped crusader. Max called him the Ninja Marine. But had Stephen been spending time here because he knew Wanda was fearful, or was he keeping an eye on a more serious problem? Had he sensed that trouble was brewing even before it boiled over in the violence at the Golden Dragon?

"I'm a little nervous about talking to them," I admitted. "But I'm sure I'll be safe with these two canines by my side. I'll wait though, until I've talked to the other shop owners. I'm sure someone must have seen something."

Wanda turned to reach under the counter behind her and pulled out a fifteen percent off card. "I'm sorry I couldn't help. But next time you come in, you can give Belle the works. A spa day. She'll love it."

"Thanks so much," I said, taking the card. "Have you been especially nervous at night lately? Have there been break-ins? Vandalism? Threats? Anything like that?"

Before she could answer, Buster barked and the rest of the dogs joined in. A young woman opened the shop door with a jingling of old-fashioned shop bells. I assumed she was Buster's owner, ready to take him home.

I thanked Wanda, excused myself quickly, and left with Munchkin and Belle. I'd wanted to ask her about Rafi and whether she'd seen him around the neighborhood. It would have to wait for another time. I reminded myself that he worked late and Wanda left early, so their paths were unlikely to have crossed. She had no hours posted on her front door or window, but I could check on my computer at home and find out if she was ever open in the evening. Regardless, I'd done all I could do at Pet Wash today.

"Who's next, guys?" I asked the dogs. Belle nudged at my pocket, hoping I had another treat hidden there, but Munchkin tugged us toward the flower shop. It made sense, I guessed, that he should be our tour guide. This was his territory and he knew it well. I'd brought him with me today to cheer him up and to keep him from eating all the paper products in the house, but he was doing double duty as a consulting detective and I appreciated his help.

A cold gust of wind tore my coat open and ruffled the dogs' fur, making them look larger and more aggressively protective than they actually were. I squinted and turned my head away from the dust the wind kicked up. I shivered as a cloud covered the sun.

I opened the door to the next shop and was greeted by the cozy smell of warm soil and the sweet perfume of hothouse flowers. It was like entering a rainforest and felt good after the gusty chill of the brewing storm. I wiped my eyes, which had begun to tear in response to the windblown dust out in the street.

Munchkin woofed softly and a short round man with a bald head and bright red apron bustled out from behind a counter. He only had eyes for Munchkin and knelt to greet him, touching his nose to Munchkin's with great deference.

"How are you, old boy?" he said with a hint of a British accent. "I've missed you. You haven't come by to see me in days and I've been worried. And what is this? Who has been hurting you? We can't have that. No. Certainly not. You give me their names and I'll see to things. They will not be welcome here, I can tell you that."

Belle scooted past me and nudged the man's elbow with her head, insisting that he also pay attention to her. Her persistent head-butting nearly knocked him sideways. He put out a hand to keep himself upright, looked up at me, and drew back in surprise.

"Oh, excuse me," he said. "Please, excuse me." He stood up with more ease than I would have expected, given the excess weight he carried. "I saw Munchkin and was expecting Mr. Stephen Laird to be at the end of the leash. How silly of me." He brushed his hands off on his apron and extended one to me.

"Maggie McDonald," I said as I shook it. "And you've met Munchkin's friend Belle."

He bowed slightly to Belle. "Indeed. I'm so pleased to make your acquaintance, Miss Belle." She responded by wagging her tail with enough enthusiasm to knock over two orchids and a ceramic gnome.

"Ed Bloom," he said, with a grin that told me he understood that the idea of someone with his last name running a flower shop was apt to spark a joke or two. "And yes, it's my real name. I used to be a software engineer, until I realized I'm not happy unless I've got my hands in some good rich loamy soil. I've been doing this now for five years and I love it. I just opened a second store in Orchard View with my brother."

"I've seen your sign but have never been inside your shop," I said. "It's lovely."

"Munchkin and Laird are frequent visitors. Stephen stops in for a cup of Yorkshire Gold tea and a visit on chilly evenings, and Munchkin generally accepts a cookie and a bowl of water. Straight up, no ice. Can I interest you and Belle in some refreshment?"

Ordinarily, I might have been a bit wary of Ed's invitation, but he was a friend of Stephen's and enthusiastically endorsed by Munchkin. Even Belle looked over her shoulder with a pleading look, trying to convince me she might starve if she couldn't have the cookie Ed was offering.

"Please," I answered. "May I help?"

Ed bustled toward the back of the shop. "No, no. Make yourself comfortable. It's no trouble at all. No trouble."

The dogs and I followed him through an arched doorway behind the register and into a narrow room lined with potting benches. Above each bench were rows of shelves stocked with every size and shape of flowerpot, from utilitarian to whimsical and beyond. Planters shaped like gnomes, small wheelbarrows, water wheels, and what I thought might be Flash Gordon's spaceship were stacked clear to the ceiling, and I had no trouble imagining them all falling to their deaths in the next earthquake. I ducked my head a little and followed Ed into a small side room. If I hadn't known better, I'd have thought I'd landed in a Hobbit hole. A small space heater took off the chill and was flanked by two chairs upholstered in worn autumn-colored chintz. Behind one chair was a credenza set up with a toaster, electric teakettle, and a hot plate. On the floor were a dog dish and a mini-refrigerator.

I looked around, half expecting to see a camp bed hidden behind a screen. The room felt too lived in to be merely a breakroom.

Munchkin went right to the water bowl but allowed Belle to drink alongside him when she joined him. Ed didn't seem to notice or mind that the dogs were spilling an expanding puddle of water on the floor. He turned on the kettle and pulled mugs toward it. "Will Yorkshire Gold suit you?" he asked, plopping tea bags into a flowered teapot without waiting for an answer. "It's the only kind I drink."

While the water heated, he gave each dog a small rawhide chew he'd selected from a cookie jar on the counter. He brought out a wrapped cylinder of English biscuits to share with me: chocolate-covered whole-wheat cookies.

When the tea was ready, Ed settled into the chair next to me with a happy sigh. "Are you warm enough?" he asked, turning the heater dial. "My HVAC system is on the blink again and the landlord doesn't seem to have a clue how to fix it reliably." His feet were saved from dangling in front of him by a short and well-worn wooden footstool. "It always feels so good to sit down. I never understood how much time shop owners spend on their feet." He lifted his legs and held them out in front of him, showing off a pair of bright red and well-padded running shoes. "Good shoes are my best friends."

I'd taken a big sip of hot tea and couldn't respond right away. Ed covered the awkward break in the conversation effortlessly. "So, Munchkin isn't saying a word, but do tell me why you are holding the end of his leash today and why he is out in the daylight and absent the company of his usual companion."

I introduced myself again, explained that Belle and I were friends of Stephen's, and gave him my card. He took it in both hands, held it out from his chest, and looked at it through the bottom of his smeared lenses, as though he were overdue for an updated prescription.

"Ah, an organizer. I could use your help I expect." He lifted his chin. I turned and saw an old-fashioned rolltop desk with some two dozen pigeonholes overflowing with paper. "The top still rolls, I think. Though I haven't been able to muscle it past any of those papers and books in years."

I nodded. "I'd be delighted to help you sort all that out, if you're ready, and if you think it would help. I've had enough experience to know that a messy-looking system isn't necessarily inefficient. If a system is working for you, it doesn't matter what it looks like."

"Just so." He took a sip of tea and carefully extracted a cookie from the package. "Though if you'd stopped in here last week, you'd have an entirely different opinion of my shop-keeping habits, I'm afraid. Someone bashed in the alleyway door, forced open the cash register, and knocked down my display shelves. It took most of the week to get a new register, throw out the broken items, and reorder stock. Luckily, they didn't touch my refrigerated cabinets and I didn't lose any flowers."

"That's terrible. Do they know who did it? I'm so glad you weren't hurt."

"The police are investigating, but I'm sure it has something to do with all those homeless people. I wish the police would round them all up. They're dirty, smelly, dangerous, and half of them are drug addicts. The other half are barking mad. They don't need help; they need to dry out and get jobs. The boozers and the druggies would kill to get the money for their next high. They're more pests than people."

I leaned back and took a sip of tea, stalling for time. I wasn't sure how to respond, especially since Wanda had given me a completely different assessment of the potential threat posed by the homeless, even though she'd said they made her nervous. Mr. Bloom, on the other hand, seemed angry instead of frightened and considered them a much more serious problem.

Before I could comment, he offered me another cookie, which took all my strength to refuse. Belle looked at me as if I were crazy.

"Never mind," Mr. Bloom said. "The mess has been cleaned up. Out of sight, out of mind. Please, tell me why you are here. And tell me what is wrong with my old friend Munchkin. He appears so melancholy this morning."

"He *is* sad." I spoke slowly, weighing how straightforward I should be with someone who was a stranger to me but obviously a friend of both Munchkin and Stephen. Once again I decided to err on the side of discretion. "Munchkin and Stephen got themselves into a bit of a mess," I said. "Munchkin is recovering with my family for a few days."

"And Laird? Is he hurt?"

"He and Munchkin are both going to be fine," I said, dodging the question.

Mr. Bloom winked at me over his mug of tea. "So it's like that, is it?" he said, holding out a placating hand as I started to explain. "No, no, it's fine. I trust you because you are a friend of two creatures who are dear to me. But I can see that you are struggling with a confidence, and I will not ask you to reveal any secrets. Tell me exactly how I can help you and I will endeavor to do so to the best of my ability."

I shook off the feeling that I'd somehow landed in the sitting room of Sherlock Holmes's brother, Mycroft, and began asking Ed the same questions I'd asked of Wanda at the Pet Wash, explaining that I was trying to learn more about the murder at the Golden Dragon.

"Ah, yes," Ed said. "Last Wednesday night. Or early Thursday morning. The police have already been to see me, asking similar questions. I live above the store here, but I sleep soundly after a day on my feet and heard nothing. But then, I didn't hear anything even when my own shop was attacked. There's always a certain amount of noise out among the dustbins in the alley. Raccoons and skunks, homeless people hunting for recyclables—after a few restless evenings I tuned it all out. Except for Mr. Xiang taking out his garbage. It was always the last thing he did every night, long after the alley was otherwise quiet. I'd hear a loud clanging thud from his dumpster and know it was time to put my book away and go to bed."

He tapped the side of his mug with a gold ring and moved his jaw from side to side. I could tell he was thinking about how much to tell me, so I decided to give him a little more information and see if it might encourage him to divulge more.

"What time did that typically happen? Do you remember whether you heard it Wednesday night?" I asked. "I talked to Wanda Daniel next door. Both she and Stephen thought it likely that one of the neighborhood homeless people might have witnessed what happened at the restaurant but is unwilling to come forward or talk to the police."

"I'm not surprised. Like I said, they're trouble. I sometimes go soft and offer them hot drinks on cold days, but seriously, there are shelters and that's where they should be. But they don't want help. Last winter I left out a heavy coat that no longer covers my girth. No one took it, even though one man was shivering in his ragged blanket. Sad." Mr. Bloom shook his head and made a *tsk*ing sound, but he didn't sound sad at all.

"I was surprised to learn from Wanda that there are homeless people that she considers to almost be residents of the alley out back. I seldom see anyone during the day."

"Probably there are a dozen or more. Just as they hide from the townspeople and the police during the day, they travel in the shadows at night. Many of them sleep in the park, but will only go there after full dark when they can't be seen."

"Do you know of anyone who might have seen or heard anything the night of the trouble at the Golden Dragon? Anyone who might be willing to talk to me? I'm surprised by the lack of information in the news . . ."

Ed frowned and leaned over the armrest of his chair to grab a newspaper from the basket at his side. "I'm sure I saw an obituary for him in one of the San Francisco papers."

"The painfully short death notice? I saw that one."

"No, no, this one had more. Have another cookie while I look." He offered me another chocolate biscuit, which I accepted. Belle wagged her tail, hoping I'd share it with her. "Chocolate is bad for dogs, Belle. You know that," I told her. I broke off a small piece of the cookie, popped it in my mouth, and allowed myself a moment to thoroughly enjoy it while Ed scanned the pages and kept talking.

"You're right. It's difficult to keep a secret around here under normal circumstances, but though they have less than most, the homeless have more to lose. They survive by keeping secrets." He hesitated before continuing.

"I don't know if this information is connected to poor Mr. Xiang's death," he added slowly, "but it might give you some background into what is happening in our busy little alley at night. We have a new health inspector in town. He has been strict with the restaurant owners about offering leftovers to the homeless and has warned us all about attracting rats by leaving food out at night. And when he says *rats* he clearly means the homeless people. He's been growing frustrated because someone continues to leave food out, but he hasn't been able to catch that person in the act."

I wasn't comfortable with Ed's anger toward the homeless and wondered what had sparked it. He had an odd look on his face and I wondered whether he knew, as I did, that it was Rafi and Mr. Xiang who'd been feeding desperate people leftover food. I couldn't tell for sure, but his stories were helping me understand the situation and the range of feelings the homeless provoked among the shop owners. The information might not help me get Stephen out of jail, but it could aid me in developing a strategy for approaching a homeless person. Despite Ed's feelings, I was with Wanda and far less afraid of them than I'd been when the man at the intersection had pounded on my window.

"Do people bother them? Do the police hassle them?"

"The police will bring them food from time to time and offer rides to the shelter when the weather is bad. They try to match them up with social services, veterans affairs, and job banks that could help.

But in the end, the aid that the police can offer doesn't necessarily match up with what the homeless people need or want. I think a get-tough approach would be more effective."

"If I decide I need to talk to one of them, what's the best way for me to go about it? What time would you recommend?"

Ed shifted in his chair. "Here it is." He cleared his throat, adjusted his glasses, and read aloud. "Jon Yuen Xiang, 75, born April 18, 1940, died February 16, 2016. Resident of Mountain View. Owner and manager of the Golden Dragon Chinese Restaurant since 1979.

"Jon was born in a small farming village in Taiwan. He was the third son and one of eleven children. An uncle, also the third son from a large family, provided money for him to attend medical school in Taiwan. When his parents died in a car accident in 1974 he emigrated to the United States and settled near his uncle in Mountain View, California. Though it was his parents' wish that he become a doctor, Jon gave up medicine and studied business at Santa Clara University, receiving a master's degree in 1976. Shortly thereafter, he graduated from the Silicon Valley Culinary Academy. He was engaged to be married, but his fiancée disappeared before they could be wed.

"He and his uncle created a partnership to buy a vacant bank building on Castro Street in Mountain View. After a complete renovation, they opened the Golden Dragon in 1979. Customers, suppliers, and employees describe Mr. Xiang as a savvy businessman who was warm and welcoming to his customers and treated his employees like family. He often employed high school students and awarded them scholarships to colleges and universities across the United States. 'It was his way of paying back his uncle's investment in his own education,' said Dr. Susan Huang, a gynecologist at Stanford University Hospital, who once worked for Mr. Xiang.

"His uncle died shortly after the Golden Dragon opened, and Mr. Xiang had no other family in the United States. A memorial service is being planned for a later date."

Mr. Bloom lowered the paper and folded it carefully, placing it back in the basket at the side of his chair. "That's interesting. There's no mention of how he died. And no story about the murder."

"Someone in San Francisco must have submitted the obituary," I said. "But who? Maybe one of those students he helped? I wonder if the police are keeping the details of the attack quiet. A murder in a cold-storage locker? I don't mean to be disrespectful, but that's pretty lurid stuff. You'd think the papers and the nightly news would splash it all over."

Mr. Bloom shrugged. "Sometimes I think the city papers don't know that the Peninsula even exists. They may have a vague idea of where Silicon Valley and San Jose are, but news coverage? It's nearly nonexistent for anything outside the city and county of San Francisco."

"Maybe the local paper will cover it next week. Everyone I've talked to says he was a wonderful man."

Mr. Bloom coughed. "Hmm. Maybe. He had a dark side . . ." He stood and took my teacup and his and placed them in a sink next to the credenza.

I started to ask what he meant by a dark side, but Mr. Bloom interrupted. "You should let the police take care of this. The homeless people may be troubled, hungry, and dirty, but they are not stupid, and they do what they must to survive. If they know something—and I'm not saying that they do—they are keeping quiet for a reason." He shifted again, as if his chair were suddenly uncomfortable. "Or maybe they feel entitled to take what they want from hardworking people. I don't know."

I leaned forward. "Do you know something about what they could have wanted from the restaurant? I know someone was there that night—someone who made an anonymous phone call after Mr. Xiang was killed." I nodded to Munchkin. "It may have saved his life. Is making a 911 call like that something you think one of the homeless people might do?"

Ed raised his eyebrows and leaned back in his chair. He sniffed the air, almost like Munchkin or Belle would do. "Maybe." He thought for a moment more. "Possibly. The street people can't all be irresponsible heroin-addicted vandals. They didn't *all* trash my shop. But tonight is not the night to contact anyone. Rain is coming. The homeless who are uncomfortable in shelters will be riding the buses all night or burrowed under thick cover somewhere. You will not find them and you will not want to be out and about yourself."

That made sense, but I shivered and scooted back in my chair to put some distance between us. I feared he was warning me of something more sinister than bad weather.

"They ride the buses?"

"Yes. Up and down El Camino. Stop after stop, all night long. It's warm and dry and relatively safe with the bus driver there to watch over them and call if there's trouble. Like me, I guess, they get used to the noise and learn to tune it out. Some of them are so doped up it wouldn't bother them if the bus crashed."

A sudden gust of wind blew the papers on Ed's desk and both dogs looked up. "Is there anything else you can tell me? Rumors you've heard of trouble?"

He tapped his fingertips together and stared at the ceiling. "There is one thing . . ."

I leaned forward, straining to hear as he lowered his voice to a whisper. "There's the health inspector. I've heard he's no good, but nothing specific. He's been around here more than I'd expect though, way more than his predecessors and some of the restaurant owners seem afraid of him."

"Any idea why?"

"No clue. Maybe he's ultra-strict about his inspections. Or is asking for money before he'll hand over a certificate of compliance with the health and safety laws."

"What about the neighborhood? You live here and work here, so you see all sides. Is it safe?"

Ed shrugged. "Safe enough for me, I guess. It's probably not a great idea to be wandering around alone after the stores and restaurants close." He peered at me over the top of his glasses like a beloved professor verifying that his class had absorbed the key point of his lecture. "A lot of people would like to see all these old shops pulled down and replaced by modern, green, energy-efficient buildings with high-density housing above the storefronts, solar panels on the roofs, and underground parking. That can't happen unless those of us with long-term leases throw in the towel. There's a lot of money in real estate around here, of course. It might be in someone's interest to encourage us all to leave. If that's the case, the violence is likely to get worse before it gets better."

"You think Mr. Xiang could have been killed over a *rental* agreement?"

Ed shrugged. I thought he was going to say more, but his demeanor changed when a customer called out from the front of the store.

"I'm sorry," he said. "You'll excuse me?"

"Of course," I said, in a more formal tone than I'd intended, but one that matched Ed's old-fashioned manners. "I'll take the dogs out through the back," I said, "and let you get to your customer."

Ed nodded and grasped my hand. "Thank you for coming. Give my best to Stephen. If you are going to continue looking into this, take Munchkin with you. He will protect you but the street people also know him and trust Stephen. The mastiff will unlock doors for you."

I thanked him solemnly and gathered up the leashes. He turned back and said, "Go to Cuesta Park at night—whenever the YMCA shuts its doors. They offer showers before closing. A discreet service, you understand? No one is supposed to know who is homeless and who is a member. Look for a woman with long gray braids. She walks at night like Stephen does, and she will want to help him. She may have seen something. I think her name is Annie."

He disappeared into the front of the store and I left through the back, into a deserted alley that smelled of dumpsters and the coming rain. I shook my head. On one hand, Mr. Bloom was angry with the homeless people. He blamed them for the damage to his shop. He also seemed frustrated with the police who weren't, in his opinion, doing their utmost to resolve the problems. But on the other hand, he seemed so gentle and protective of those who used the services provided by the YMCA, and he'd provided me with a number of leads. I made a mental note to check the local paper online for stories about the break-in at Mr. Bloom's shop. I'd ask Paolo whether he had access to police reports in Mountain View. I wasn't sure how far the cooperation agreement between Orchard View and Mountain View extended, but if anyone could gain access to the records, it was Paolo. He was the computer whisperer and knew better than anyone, even Max, how to find back doors and workarounds that would coax even an otherwise secure file to give up its secrets.

Raindrops spattered on the pavement, ending my rapid assessment of everything Ed Bloom had told me. The dogs and I raced back to the car, but we were drenched and cold within minutes. I was tempted to try another shop, but the wind howled through the alley and the clouds made it seem much later than it actually was. No store owner would want us dripping on their displays. Nor would they welcome dogs who might shake their coats dry without a thought to the expensive inventory they could damage.

It was time to give up for the day. The boys might have to change their plans given the unexpectedly hard downpour, and I'd heard nothing from Max or Paolo. If the rain let up, I could go out later on. Or tomorrow.

A squirrel ran down the fence next to us and leaped onto one of the dumpsters with a loud bang. Munchkin and I both jumped and then glanced at each other and looked away, embarrassed. In a world where someone like Stephen could be in jail and we were cold, wet, and tired, it was easy to imagine that danger could lurk anywhere.

Chapter 7

When you've separated everything that doesn't belong
from the things that do, it's time for the next step. Gather
all your containers of culled items and sort them. As
always, "toss," "recycle," and "donate" are your first
three piles. You'll also find items that obviously belong
in another room. Separate those belongings and deliver
them to the rooms where they belong. If you know
where the items go, great. Put them away. If not, confine
the pile to a box or bag you can get to later.

From the Notebook of Maggie McDonald,
Simplicity Itself Organizing Services

Saturday, February 18, Afternoon

On my way home, David and Brian each called to say they were
spending the rest of the afternoon and evening at the homes of
their respective friends. The rain turned to hail and my teeth chat-
tered. The dogs were curled up on the backseat, snuggled close together for warmth. I'd turned the heat and the defroster on high, but
both were having trouble keeping up. I wiped the inside of the wind-
shield with my sleeve so I could see the street and rolled my window
down so I could check for cross traffic on the windy and winding
roads leading home.

Our driveway had turned to a slick muddy track, and I skidded
twice between splashing great spouts of water from the potholes. I
grabbed the dogs' leashes and ran with them onto the back porch. All

three of us were equally bedraggled, and I wasn't sure that toweling off the dogs would do any good, but I unlocked the back door, grabbed our raggedy old dog towels from the shelf above the freezer, and gave each dog a good rub down, working gently around Munchkin's wounds. I knew they'd shake themselves off the minute they got inside, but at least I'd contained some of the mess.

Inside, I turned on a small space heater to warm up the kitchen, closed the door on the dogs to keep them from drying themselves on the living room sofas, and dashed upstairs to indulge in a long hot shower.

Shivering, and with my post-shower skin tingling, I dressed in my warmest socks, two sweaters, and a pair of flannel-lined jeans I typically saved for ski trips. Downstairs, I fed the dogs and fired up the coffeemaker. I hadn't seen the cats since we'd come home, but I didn't think it would take them long to figure out that the heat was on full blast in the kitchen, so I topped up their dishes with kibble and fresh water.

Max and Paolo walked in together just as the coffee finished brewing.

"Paolo, what a surprise! What brings you here?" I held up the pot and they both responded eagerly, stomping their feet and shaking their hands to get as much water as possible off their jackets.

Paolo was appropriately outfitted for a California rainstorm in waterproof storm pants and a lightweight breathable rain jacket with high-performance moisture-wicking layers underneath. My poor husband looked like a drowned rat in a sopping wet sweatshirt. He peeled it off and threw it in a laundry basket filled with my own wet things. I grabbed a hoodie from the line of pegs near the door and gave him a quick kiss as I handed it over. His face was freezing against mine.

They each gripped their coffee mugs as if I'd tossed them a lifeline.

"Let's head into the living room and light the fire," Max said. "I'm chilled to the bone."

"I checked the temperature earlier. It was about thirty-five degrees," I said.

"I'd better get warmed up quickly then," Paolo said. "If the rain weren't enough, temps like that will bring some ice tonight, which means overtime for me."

"I've got some leftover chili if you want an early dinner," I added. Paolo shook his head. "I'm good for now, thanks."

I still wasn't sure what had brought Paolo to see us today, but I knew he'd tell us in his own time. Max lit the fire and we each found a spot on our two enormous denim couches. The cats appeared out of nowhere and demanded lap space. Belle sat on my feet and Munchkin curled under the coffee table with a sigh. We all waited until Munchkin was settled to put our mugs down. He was more coordinated than his bulk would suggest, but I was never convinced that he could maneuver under the coffee table without wearing it on his back like a turtle wears his shell.

I asked Max about work, and he shook his head. "I won't have to go back until the morning, but this roll-out has been a beast. It's the last thing I want to talk about."

I knew enough about Max's work to understand that one phone call from engineers in India or Germany or Santa Clara about an unexpected bug could change his plans in a hurry. "Well, I'm glad you're home for now. The boys will be back later. They're both at friends' houses for dinner."

Paolo looked at me over the top of his coffee mug. "I need to bring you up to date on the Stephen situation. But first, I've decided I *am* hungry. Any chance of a sandwich? A cookie?"

I laughed. "I'll get Max caught up on Stephen while you go scrounge. There's leftover chili or stuff to make sandwiches and you know where the cookies are. Will you bring a plate of them in with you when you come back?"

Paolo nodded, as comfortable in our home as any of our family members. Belle followed him. Munchkin shifted and sighed in what I hoped was comfort.

Max kissed me again, more thoroughly this time, and sighed in a manner that duplicated Munchkin's so closely that I laughed.

"So, the old boy looks a bit banged up. What's he doing here with us and how is the Ninja Marine? For that matter, where's Jason? If Munchkin is with us, they must both be otherwise occupied."

"I'm not sure where to begin." I filled him in on Jason's emergency corps trip to Texas and how difficult it was to get in touch.

"But why would you need to talk to him?" Max asked. "I'm sure he's doing fine and that every law enforcement group they're working with is now planning to revamp their procedures to match Jason's. He's a wizard when it comes to team building and organization."

"I agree, but that brings us to the bigger problem." I outlined Stephen's predicament and my list of tasks.

"Not another murder investigation," Max said. "Can't you leave this to the police? This case sounds dangerous. Someone . . . or more than one someone . . . killed Mr. Xiang and could have easily murdered Stephen, Rafi, and Munchkin. Whoever they are, they aren't going to like you poking around trying to get the police to expand the list of suspects. And questioning the homeless people? Don't get me wrong, I feel for them but, Maggie, so many of them are, for lack of a more precise phrase, downright loony. And some of them are dangerous, particularly if you run around asking questions that make them feel afraid or threatened." He shook his head and put a hand on my leg. "This is a terrible, terrible idea. I don't like it. Not at all." He and Munchkin and Belle all sighed.

Paolo returned with a sandwich piled high with cheese and sprouts, pickles, tomato, and anything else you might consider putting on a sandwich. A plate of cookies was balanced on top.

I looked to Paolo for help, but he took a big bite of his sandwich and said in a barely intelligible voice, "My mouth is full. Go ahead."

"I haven't talked to any of the homeless people yet," I said. "I haven't even seen any of them, actually. I spent the morning talking to shop owners in the Mountain View neighborhood near the Golden Dragon. None of them knew anything, but the flower shop owner suggested I look for a woman named Annie with long gray braids. She hangs out around Cuesta Park after the YMCA closes for the night."

"That's a great suggestion," said Paolo. "The Y has fresh coffee and showers for people in the morning before the gym opens at 6:00 a.m., and sometimes offers more substantial food if they've had donations. After that, the homeless people disperse. Some for jobs—a surprising number are well employed but can't afford housing. Others head out toward various panhandling locations, to ride the buses, or for programs at the Mountain View Day Laborer Center or the veterans hospital in Palo Alto."

"Jobs?" said Max.

"Absolutely," answered Paolo. "You know the state of the economy around here. How many people, especially those with mental health issues, can afford market rates for rent let alone a security deposit and initial payments?"

Max took a big sip of his coffee. His face reflected a complex combination of fury, surprise, and problem solving. Unless I was completely wrong about my husband, he soon would be making a visit to his company's human resources department, insisting that they offer roommate-matching services to all employees and try to learn whether any of them were homeless. If anyone on his team was living in a car or sleeping on the streets, I could bet they'd have a roof over their head within a few days. The problem of the homeless might be difficult to solve on a global, national, or even a local scale, but Max would make sure that everyone on his team was cared for and had the help they needed.

I feared we'd all lost focus on our primary goal. "We have to get Stephen out of jail," I said. "The fact that he's in the infirmary or the hospital wing or whatever you call it proves that he's not safe. I have no idea how long he can stay cooped up and remain sane. He's got no Munchkin, no Jason, no endless nightly walks, no veterans or dogs to help with their own PTSD issues. He's been completely stripped of every single one of his coping mechanisms and is afraid to talk to anyone for fear of spilling the beans and getting Rafi deported."

"Have you connected with the lawyer?" Paolo asked. "What has he said about the odds of finalizing Rafi's citizenship papers? Is it even possible? Has the lawyer even met this Rafi kid? Have you? Is he worth all of Stephen's sacrifices?"

Paolo was picking up my AK-47 style of firing questions. I shook my head and pushed my hair back, holding it in a ponytail and tugging on it gently, as if that would help me think better. "I've left a message with Forrest Doucett but I don't even know if he's the right person to call. Stephen gave me his name, but he's a criminal lawyer and doesn't deal with child welfare issues or immigration concerns. I'm sure he farmed it out to someone else, maybe this Nell Bevans person who is also on the list Stephen gave me."

I leaned back, dejected. From where I sat, all warm and cozy with my animals, friend, and Max for comfort, it looked like we'd never be able to get Stephen home and safe. At least not before he went stark-raving mad.

Max rose from the sofa and grabbed a cookie. "I'm going to call

Forrest right now. I've got his home number and a couple of other work numbers for him. Unless he's somewhere without cell coverage, I should be able to catch him. Whether he can help is a whole other matter, but at least if I can talk to him, we'll know where we are. He may be able to tell us more about why Stephen thinks Rafi is worth going to jail for." He moved into the adjacent dining room, which had become our family office in lieu of the work areas we were still planning to set up in our rebuilt barn. We were a perfectly normal family with two busy young teens, which meant that ninety percent of the things that Max and I wanted to do for ourselves never got done. And that was okay with us. But right now, Stephen's problem was a priority. Family first, with friends a close second.

I turned to Paolo.

"Do you know a thin older man with missing teeth who panhandles at San Antonio and El Camino in the evening? Or this woman with the gray braids that Ed Bloom mentioned? Is Bloom his real name? Do you think it's worth continuing to talk to the store owners? I get the sense that there is something else going on down there. Maybe in the alley behind the stores. I don't think they're telling me everything they know about Stephen and Munchkin and the Golden Dragon. Ed Bloom mentioned a dodgy health inspector and a property development scheme, and a possible pattern of vandalism that might be related to both."

Paolo looked bewildered by my barrage of questions. I sipped my coffee and dismembered an Oreo while I waited for him to process it all. Trying to clarify my concerns would make it worse for him. It was amazing that the two of us could be friends or work together. Our thought patterns were so different. But we both wanted the same thing and were willing to work for it.

"So, responding to your interrogation in order . . ." Paolo held up his hands and touched the pinky of his left hand with the pointer of his right. "Dental hygiene generally comes in lower than food and shelter on a homeless person's priority list, so your description of a thin man with missing teeth could apply to any number of people. But I'll ask around. I've seen the woman with the braids, but don't know her name. I can ask some of the patrol officers at the station. Once I've got a first and last name for her, I can check to see if she has a record or if we know more of her story."

He touched his left ring finger with his right pointer. "Ed Bloom is the florist's real name. He has a second store in Orchard View that his brother runs for him. We ran a background check on Ed when he volunteered for our after-school program for at-risk kids. We did another when he applied for a concealed weapon permit. He wanted a handgun after there were a series of break-ins downtown last summer."

I raised my eyebrows at that one. *A handgun?* I wondered if it matched the gunshot wound Mr. Xiang had sustained. But I'd asked Paolo enough questions for now and he continued to plow through them, one by one.

"As far as talking to the store owners goes, I do think it's worth it," Paolo said. "Stephen suggested it, which he must have done for good reason. He has military police training and I trust both his judgment and experience. So does Jason. Even if you don't get any more information, we want to be able to tell Stephen we're doing everything he asked of us, right?"

I nodded and Paolo continued. "It's interesting that you picked up some kind of an undercurrent of . . . what? Fear? Anxiety?"

"I'm not sure. It could be that they don't trust me and are protecting Stephen and Rafi. They certainly know Munchkin well. He's comfortable with them, so stopping in and talking to the store owners must be a regular part of Stephen's routine . . ." My voice trailed off. I had the feeling that if I could make my brain work a *little* harder or if I had a bit more information, I could connect the dots. But not yet.

Paolo stroked his hairless chin as if he were a wizard with a long beard. "Let me ask around at the station and see if anyone is working with the Mountain View Police on cases that involve those shops or the homeless people. There is so much crossover in our jurisdictions that it's entirely possible one or more teams are working similar cases in Orchard View."

"Can you ask those questions without revealing Stephen's problem?" I asked. "Stephen's got friends throughout the department, any one of whom might spill the story to Jason or even get Stephen out of jail before Rafi's immigration status is finalized."

"No, they all still think of me as the new kid, and I have a reputation for asking too many questions." He smiled as though he'd been caught tasting the cookie dough. "Usually, I try to shake that reputation, but I can make it work for me . . . and for Stephen. Jason's pretty much out of reach in Texas anyway. I heard another huge storm system barreled through there this morning."

"Those poor people . . ." I shook my head, took another Oreo, and passed the plate to Paolo. "I'll try to get to the rest of the shops tomorrow then. Seems like we've both got a plan."

Max returned from the dining room. "I got in touch with Forrest. He asked to be remembered to both of you. He'd heard from Stephen a couple of weeks ago about Rafi's case and passed the information along to an associate, Nell Bevans, who worked immigration cases for the Legal Aid Society while she was in law school. He says she's more experienced than her career level might suggest, and if anyone can help Rafi and his family, she can. Unfortunately, Nell is camping on some remote US Forest Service land near Yosemite for the long weekend and has no cell service." He handed me a slip of paper. "Here's her name and contact information though, in case you want to send her an e-mail. Forrest says she usually gets in early and returns calls quickly. He couldn't say enough great things about her."

I looked at the paper. If Forrest Doucett trusted her, I would too. If only Monday weren't a holiday.

Chapter 8

If you've been following along, you've made progress,
but you've still got stuff you don't know where to store.
Sort those items into piles of like items. Where would
you buy them? Where would you use them? I store
groceries in the kitchen, hardware and tools in the
garage or basement, and drugstore items in the
bathroom. Items used once a year can be stored with
other seasonally used boxes in a less-accessible area.

When you've figured out where items belong, you can
determine whether you need fewer things or more
drawers, cabinets, and shelving.

From the Notebook of Maggie McDonald,
Simplicity Itself Organizing Services

Sunday, February 19, Morning

Sunday morning we all slept in. By the time I got up, the rain had
ended and sunlight reflected off the dewy surface of every leaf,
twig, and blade of grass. I adjusted the mini-blinds in the kitchen
windows to cut the glare. On autopilot, I moved through my morning
routine.

I was the cats' chosen one this morning, the one targeted for an
early wake-up call and relentless nose patting. The rest of the house
was quiet save for Holmes's noisy crunching on his kibble. Watson, a
speedy eater, had turned her attention to stalking a plastic ring that

had escaped from a gallon jug of milk. She crouched with her tail lashing, carefully selecting the perfect moment to deliver the fatal pounce. I'd never felt so well protected from plastic milk jug rings, but I knew better than to laugh or even think about laughing or in any other way insulting the dignity of our beloved investigative pair.

I chewed the last of my toast, chased it with a swallow of coffee, and checked the time. It was past nine o'clock. All the stores, including the ones near the Golden Dragon, were running promotions for Presidents' Day. If I dressed quickly, I might get a chance to talk to some of the owners before they became too busy with an influx of customers.

I left a note for the boys and Max, leashed the dogs, and was on my way. I found a parking spot directly in front of the quilting store and quickly unloaded the dogs and untangled their leashes. Shop hopping with two large canines was not optimal, but per Mr. Bloom's advice, I needed Munchkin's endorsement if I hoped to encourage the business owners to trust me with their secrets. And Belle's pride would have been wounded beyond repair if I'd taken off with Munchkin and left her at home.

Max still wasn't comfortable with my investigation and feared that I'd uncover a seething pit of rattlesnakes where I least expected them. His analogy gave me the creeps, but I respected his opinion and his concerns about my safety, especially when he was under so much pressure at work and couldn't be with me.

And so we compromised. I'd take the dogs, both dogs, with me. If they hesitated or showed any discomfort, I'd back off, quickly. I'd make sure he and Paolo knew where I was. And I'd investigate on my own only during daylight. After dark, Max would be my designated sidekick. Realistically, I didn't know what Max might be able to do to protect me in an emergency. But he'd provide a second set of eyes, a second opinion about the investigation, and I enjoyed his company.

For now, I peered through the front windows of the quilt shop, which featured row after row of brightly colored cotton fabric arranged by color. Hanging from the ceiling were finished samples of various patchwork patterns, each one more gorgeous than the next. A woman I took to be the manager was cutting fabric pieces at a central counter, performing a demonstration of what looked like an intricate design. She saw me peeping in the window and I was relieved when she smiled and waved me in instead of calling the police and reporting me as a stalker.

I opened the door, smiled, introduced myself, and held up the leashes. "I'd like to ask you a few questions when you have a minute, but I'm quite sure these drooling monsters would add nothing to your demonstration."

"That's fine," said the manager. "I'm almost done here, and then we're going to take a break and I'll have time for a chat. If you like, you can go around back. My business partner is there with my own dog, and yours can get to know him as we talk."

It took me another moment or two to disentangle the dogs without tripping over either of them or the two quilt shop patrons who wanted to get past us and into the store. I apologized and performed the dance steps required to avoid a collision. Eventually, we made our way to the end of the street and around the corner to the alley. We had a couple of dicey moments when Belle thought it would be a good idea to help a small child finish his ice-cream cone, and again when Munchkin blanched at entering the alley full of dumpsters. Belle licked his ear in what I assumed was encouragement but might have been an effort to clean up a stray bit of drippy ice cream.

In any case, Munchkin recovered quickly so I didn't count his behavior as hesitating or exhibiting discomfort. Dumpsters were a known trigger for Munchkin's PTSD, as Stephen had explained to me when we were all first becoming friends. If there was anything else in the alley that worried him, he didn't let on and was soon wagging his tail and exchanging polite posterior sniffs with a salt-and-pepper-colored short-haired, pointy-eared dog of nicely blended heritage.

"His name is Mr. Tweed. I'm Patty," said a young woman wearing leggings and a shirt that could only be called "wearable art." If someone other than a gifted artist had tried to duplicate her tunic, it would almost certainly look as if it had been rescued from a junk heap. Instead, it was a stunning combination of at least twenty different fabrics in a wide array of textures and hues that had been pulled together in a way that looked comfortable, flattering, and gorgeous. I immediately wanted one like it, though its composition ensured that a duplicate couldn't possibly exist. I introduced myself and the dogs and told Patty how much I admired her outfit.

She glanced down as though she'd forgotten what she was wearing, then drew her head back as if startled. "My sister makes these using scraps from fabric she weaves. I love them because my sister makes them, but they're a bit bright for me." She squinted and went back to her project, which was set up on a sheet of plywood balanced on sawhorses.

"Do you mind if I continue working while we talk?" she asked. "Eileen—sorry, that's the manager—should be out in a moment."

She didn't wait for a response from me, which was fine, because I was fascinated by what she was doing.

"I'm making a quilt sandwich," she said. "Getting the top, batting, and backing smoothly put together prior to the actual quilting process." Patty smoothed a layer of fabric, then sprayed it lightly with aerosol glue. She wrinkled her nose.

"Why is it that whenever your hands are all gummy your nose itches? As soon as I'm finished here, I'm headed over to Ed Bloom's to take a shower and ditch these gummy clothes. This is my third quilt today and I'm ready to be done."

I made a mental note that all the shop owners seemed comfortable with Ed Bloom and were at ease running in and out of each other's stores and even Ed's apartment. I assumed Patty did not live above her shop or she wouldn't need to borrow Ed's shower.

Eileen came out and helped Patty finish up the quilt top. She then shooed off her younger coworker and invited me back into the store's work area, dogs and all.

"So, how can I help you?" she asked.

I handed her one of my cards and described some of my services. Eileen thought for a moment. "I've got my stock pretty well organized," she said. "We have to work hard and stay on top of it to keep those tiny sewing notions in stock and all the thread easily accessible. They get misplaced so easily by browsing customers. I close about half an hour earlier than any of the other shops to set it all straight."

"Sounds like a great system," I said. "Then, when you arrive in the morning, everything is as it should be."

She nodded slowly. Her expression gave me the glimmer of a feeling that she was keeping something from me. Something important.

"I use an old-fashioned accounting system and do the books myself, but I'm comfortable with it. I don't want to mess with success."

She sounded confident, but wouldn't look at me, and I wondered whether she was particularly shy for a shopkeeper or if she was skirting the truth.

"No problem. I'm just introducing myself to everyone. I'm relatively new to the area. If you change your mind, my e-mail's there on the card. Do you mind if I ask you a few questions about something else?"

"Not at all. How can I help?"

I gave her a shortened summary of my investigation into what had happened at the Golden Dragon. I also asked if she recognized Munchkin and if she knew Stephen or Rafi.

Munchkin wagged his tail at the sound of his name.

"I thought I recognized Munchkin," said Patty. "I don't know Stephen and his dog well, although I know they are regulars around here after hours. As I said, the other shop owners tend to stay open much longer than I do. I'm here late on rare occasions. Patty closes for me most of the time.

"I'd heard about the murder, and I know that the comic book store has been broken into two or three times since the holidays, but I don't think there's anything I can tell you by way of being a witness or anything. I was long gone by the time anything happened in the Chinese restaurant. Probably sound asleep."

"What about the homeless people? Do you know a woman with big skirts and gray braids? Or a thin man with no teeth?"

Eileen bristled. "You can't be suggesting one of them hurt Mr. Xiang. They have problems of their own to worry about. If anything, they go out of their way to avoid other people and any sort of conflict. I get so tired of people blaming them for everything that goes wrong around here, as if there aren't all sorts of bad people in the world."

I tried to hide my surprise at her vehement reaction and wasn't sure which part of her statement to address first. I decided I'd get no more information from her unless I reassured her I was on her side.

"I'm sorry. You're right. I was trying to get a clearer picture of what might have happened and wondered if you knew any of the homeless people who could have been witnesses. None of them have given any information to the police, but if they saw something that worried them, I wondered if they'd mentioned anything to you. You all seem more comfortable with the street people than I would have imagined. Patty sets up her sawhorses and works alone in the alley, for example."

Eileen leaned back, relaxed, and sighed. "She's not alone. She has Mr. Tweed. And the other business people are in and out of their stores all day. Some of the long-term residents use the alley as a cut-through to avoid traffic. But you're right; we don't worry much about the home-less people. The possibility of violent people or greedy people worries me much more, which is another reason I like to leave early when I know that everyone else is still here."

"Have you had any recent problems? Mr. Bloom told me about a break-in at his shop. And Ms. Daniel told me she'd been attacked years ago."

She frowned and rubbed Mr. Tweed's ears. "Not for a long time," she said. "Maybe a year ago our front window was broken and some-one spray-painted the front door. But we restored it all quickly. And then we got Mr. Tweed here, our head of security. He looks after Patty and me while we're at the store. I guess people assume he's here all the time, but he comes home with me at night." She ruffled Mr. Tweed's ears and he looked up at her in adoration. "Dogs don't like to be on their own, do they, Mr. Tweed?"

She turned her attention from Mr. Tweed back to me. "We help the homeless people when we can. Patty and I are both single moms. We know what it's like to be poor and hungry. And what it's like to have someone offer to help when you have nowhere to turn. I think they call it 'paying it forward' now, or 'giving back.' But it's just being kind to someone who desperately needs it. Everyone wants to quilt the cute little blankets for the babies in the hospital. The fabrics are sweet and the babies are adorable. The homeless aren't cute, so it's harder for them to get help."

"Like sea otters," I said. And then I looked up, alarmed at what must have seemed like a total diversion to the conversation.

Eileen laughed. "I know what you mean. Animals that look like floating teddy bears get lots of money and attention. But if you're an endangered mud worm or a bad-tempered shark, well, not so much."

We chuckled together and I felt I'd made a friend. She must have thought so, too, because she leaned forward with her elbows on her knees. "There's another reason we help the homeless, Patty and me. My son was homeless. Came back from the war a drug addict. He's clean now, but we know better than to take it for granted. Any minute.

Any tiny thing"—she snapped her fingers—"and he could be back on the streets. If there are other mothers somewhere, wringing their hands in worry over any of our regulars here, I'd like to do what I can to make sure their children have a chance to get clean and go home." She shrugged. "I'm not sure how much it helps them, but I do what I can."

With that she stood, brushed off her jeans, and rolled up her sandwich wrappings. "I need to get back to the front of the shop," she said, holding out her hand. "I'm delighted you stopped by. I'll e-mail that link to you, and I'll let you know if I hear anything about poor Mr. Xiang."

And that was all I could ask of her. I shook her hand. "I look forward to seeing you again."

Outside in the alleyway, Patty had nearly finished cleaning up her tools and putting them away. Her arms were full, so I held the door open for her. "Thanks for walking me through your quilting preparations," I said.

"No problem. We run classes all the time from beginner to expert. You should take one."

I shook my head, thinking of my already limited spare time, but I answered with the exact opposite of what I'd been thinking. "I'll do that, thanks."

I followed Patty back into the shop, where she unloaded her supplies into cubbyholes designed and labelled for that purpose. No wonder Eileen hadn't had much interest in hiring an organizer. Her storage area was as regimented and tidy as that of any professional I'd ever met.

As I handed Patty the tools I'd brought in, I thought of another question. "Do you know a boy named Rafi Maldonado? A teenager who worked nights at the Golden Dragon?"

Patty turned away quickly and straightened scissors and other items hanging on a pegboard over the cubbies. "We don't get too many guys in here," she said, which didn't quite answer the question. "I thought Mr. Xiang hired mostly relatives in the restaurant."

"Do you know of any reason why Mr. Xiang might have gotten involved with bad guys who would beat him up and shoot him? Were there rumors of any illegal activities going on there or in any of the other businesses?"

Patty stiffened and her hands froze in the process of straightening a stack of plastic quilt templates. She turned around, red faced, with her hands on her hips. "Of course not. What do you think this is?" She waved her hands to take in the whole shop and maybe even the whole neighborhood. "We're shopkeepers—small operators trying to keep afloat. There's barely enough money in these businesses to keep the owners and their families alive. If crooks want to steal something valuable, they'd be much better off breaking into some of those big mansions in the hills."

She grabbed a stack of rulers and waved them in the air. "Unless they have some sort of measuring or sewing fetish." She laughed awkwardly and I did the same. Then I thanked her and left through the alley, closing the shop door behind me.

Sunshine filled the alley and a dumpster clanged as the metal expanded in the heat of the sun.

Munchkin and I startled at the sound but Belle pretended not to notice, just looking at me with a *What's next?* expression.

Before I could collect my thoughts and figure out exactly how badly I'd mangled my so-called investigation in the quilt shop, my phone rang. I juggled the dogs' leashes so I could pull it from my pocket.

"Hey, Paolo, do you have any news?"

"News? Yes. Good news? I don't think so. I wanted to give you the number of Stephen's court-appointed attorney."

"Court-appointed? Can they do that? He has plenty of money. And Forrest Doucett was going to try to reach him."

"Stephen still won't see anyone except you, or take any phone calls. I think the DA's office assigned him a lawyer when he was arraigned and charged. A trial date has been set."

"A trial date? Seriously? I guess I didn't realize how quickly these processes move . . ."

"Normally, there are lots of places for attorneys to slow things down until they can examine the evidence and prepare a case or even get the case thrown out. But since Stephen won't talk to anyone, nothing is happening normally. Theoretically, he could be at trial in six weeks and convicted shortly after that if he's not going to aid in his own defense. The forensic evidence makes it look an awful lot like he killed Mr. Xiang. The DA's office is in a bind, which isn't endearing Stephen to the powers that be."

"I get that, but I guess I never thought it would go to trial."

"We're still working to avoid that, have the charges dropped, and get Stephen out of jail. But now that he's been arraigned, events are moving forward on their own schedule. If the DA deviated from customary procedures, it could be argued that Stephen is getting special privileges because he's connected to the police and because he's white and reasonably well off. In the current political climate, I'm sure you can imagine what the headlines would say. And if you put those headlines side-by-side with the ones that say, Chinese-American restaurateur brutally slain . . ."

I wrinkled my nose and frowned.

"Well, you get the picture."

"I get it, but I don't have to like it."

"And that's why I'm giving you the lawyer's name and number. Do you want to write it down or should I text it to you?"

I rummaged in my bag for a pen and prepared to write the information on my palm. It seemed ridiculously old-school, so I changed my mind and asked Paolo to e-mail the information so I'd have a record of it. While I waited for the information to zip up to a cell tower and back down to my phone, I asked Paolo if he'd learned anything from his sleuthing in the police department records or if he'd found any officers who knew anything about the gray-haired woman or any of the shop owners.

"Is there any hint of a protection racket putting pressure on the shop owners?" I asked. "Maybe Mr. Xiang didn't pay and somebody sent the thugs to rough him up. Mr. Xiang was elderly. Maybe he was more fragile than they thought and a warning turned into a homicide."

Paolo took a moment to answer. "I'd buy that if they'd beaten him and left it at that. But the knife cuts and the gunshot wound were literally overkill if they were only trying to scare him. This isn't a screen play, Maggie. This is Orchard View. Or Mountain View, I guess in this case, but that's nearly the same thing."

"Would you check into the possibility of a protection scheme though? For me? We need something to break open this case. Some clue that will lead to the rest of the information we need to prove that Stephen is innocent."

"You still sound like you walked out of a late 1940s film noir, but I understand, and I'll work on it. It's more difficult on the weekends. Not so many people are here."

"Maybe you can get the more informal atmosphere to work for

you," I suggested. "Ask questions of people who might be more willing to speculate."

"I'll try. But what's your next step?"

"Coffee first, I think. Then I'll stop by the comic book store. One of the other shop owners said it had been broken into more than once. And then maybe the Golden Dragon."

"Be careful, Maggie. Max will skewer me if anything happens to you."

"And Stephen will do the same to me if I lead Munchkin into any danger. I'll be fine."

I was about to hang up, but didn't. "Paolo?"

"Yeah." His voice was distracted, as though he'd already moved on to his next task or problem.

"Find something. Today. Please?"

There was silence on the other end of the phone. Then I heard Paolo clear his throat.

"You too, Maggie."

It was only after Paolo disconnected the call that I remembered what Detective Smith had said: that the DA wanted to try Stephen for murder. California was still a death penalty state and murder committed in combination with a robbery was a capital offense. Stephen's noble gesture to protect Rafi could not only risk his mental health but put him on trial for his life. I gulped. The stakes were high and getting higher.

Chapter 9

Your goal is to minimize confusion about where items belong. I recommend my clients keep one easily accessible small open container. We label it "Odd things that might be important." After a year, they sort through the box and either re-home the items within or throw them out.

From the Notebook of Maggie McDonald,
Simplicity Itself Organizing Services

Sunday, February 19, Late morning

I phoned the public defender and tried to leave a message but his voice mailbox was full. When I checked my own phone, I discovered that Max had left a voice mail to say that he and the boys had filled in some of the worst potholes in the driveway, called and made arrangements to get a quote on having it paved next week, and were off for a hike in the hills behind the house. A muddy hike.

I was tempted to call Jason, but I knew that if I did I'd spill Stephen's secret. To be honest with myself, that was the reason I wanted to call him. Keeping secrets was difficult work and it wasn't my strong suit. In fact, my career depended upon uncovering my clients' secrets so that we could find ways to work around them and construct an organizational plan to help.

Belle whined quietly and tugged on my leash. I looked at her, smiled, and she wagged her tail.

"Coffee shop?" I asked. She wagged harder until her entire body was awiggle and she bounced a bit on her front legs. My favorite among Mountain View's many independent coffee shops offered an order window for dog owners that included biscuits and a bowl of water with every order. Outdoor seating abounded.

But once I'd ordered coffee and a cookie, and settled the dogs with their complementary biscuits, the manager refused to talk with me. She was wiping down tables outside and gathering up stray plates and mugs. I handed her my card and asked if I could talk to her for just a few moments. She took the card, but shook her head. "It's so busy today. Come back next week?"

"I just have some quick questions about Mr. Xiang and the Golden Dragon," I said. "It will only take a moment. Please?" The owner took a half-step back and widened her eyes in what looked like alarm. She shook her head. "I'm sorry. I can't talk now." She walked away as I was telling her I'd stop in again.

I wasn't sure what had spooked her. Was she, like some of the other merchants, nervous or hiding something about Mr. Xiang's death and recent events? Did she think I was a newspaper reporter prying for a lurid story? Or had she, like the other business owners, cut her staff to lower her overhead and had she, as a result of those cutbacks, become too busy to talk to customers? I had no way of knowing for sure, but her refusal to talk to me increased my anxiety about the state of my investigation. I left without finishing my coffee.

"On to the next interview," I told Belle and Munchkin and we strode down the street to the comic book store. It was closed, with a hand-lettered sign that said, SORRY, DUDES. HITTING SOME GNARLY WAVES. I laughed out loud. I happened to have met the owner previously, as I'd designed a storage and inventory system for him. He was nearing fifty with a conservative short haircut. He wore cotton sweaters, button-down shirts, jeans or khakis, and tennis shoes or loafers. Reading the sign, I'd have assumed he wore board shorts, flip-flops, sunglasses, and had long sun-streaked hair that fell across a tanned face.

"We'll stop in here next week when we talk to the coffee shop owner," I told the dogs, though I hoped that by then all our problems would be solved. Munchkin woofed. It was the first positive communication that I'd heard from him in the past few days and I took it as a sign that his usually sunny disposition might reappear. Or maybe

I'd misunderstood, and his woof was intended to prod me into kicking my investigation into a higher gear. I looked at Belle to see what she thought. She scratched her ear with a hind leg.

"Okay, then, Munchkin, I'm in your paws. What do you think we should do next?" Munchkin engaged in a full-body shake, looking for all the world like a sprinter getting loose before a heat in the hundred-yard dash. Without looking back to see if we were keeping up, he headed deliberately down the street and around the corner to the last place I thought he'd ever lead me: the dumpster-filled alleyway behind the Golden Dragon.

Munchkin's pace slowed as we entered the alley, and he looked at me over his shoulder several times for reassurance. A bit of yellow crime-scene tape still adhered to the framework of the restaurant's back door. White candles and flowers had been placed on the loading dock.

"I guess this is the crime scene." Munchkin tugged me up the steps of the loading dock and then slowly down again, giving me plenty of time to examine what looked like the faint outlines of bloody shoe prints that someone had tried hard to wash away.

Indistinct brown finger smudges marked the board fence that separated the alley from the properties beyond. I doubted I would have been able to spot them let alone identified them if I hadn't already had some idea of what I was looking for, but I was sure they were evidence someone had unsuccessfully attempted to clean up.

I assumed that the entire scene had already been well-photographed and blood samples had been collected, but I pulled out my phone and took pictures anyway. The images might not help get Stephen out of jail, but taking them it made me feel like I was doing something, anything, to rescue Stephen.

The dogs sniffed around the dumpsters and at the base of the fence. Munchkin took particular interest in one of the drains. I didn't want to think about the animals that might choose to make their homes down there, or why it might be of particular interest to Munchkin. I gave it a quick glance, just in case, but then I heard a squeak and rustle from deep in the dark of the drainpipe, and I jumped back, trying to find something else on which to focus my attention.

The back door of the restaurant opened quickly, slamming against the wall of the building with an echoing bang. I stepped backward and covered my mouth with my hand, trying not to yelp in fear. My heart pounded. Belle barked and pressed herself against my leg. Munchkin strained at the leash and wagged his tail.

It was Munchkin's demeanor that helped me relax as a group of teens and young adults trooped down the concrete steps of the loading dock carrying buckets, mops, brooms, and other cleaning supplies. The moment it took them to realize I was there gave me a chance to slow my heart rate and compose myself.

First down the steps was a young woman with shining straight black hair pulled into a ponytail. She stopped suddenly when she saw me, and the other members of the group jostled each other until they all halted behind her. A tall, thin young man in an orange Princeton hoodie stepped forward protectively. "Can we help you? The restaurant is closed."

I hesitated a moment, scanning the group, all of whom appeared to know one another. Each wore a sweatshirt or jacket with collegiate insignias. Some I recognized as Stanford, UCLA, Santa Clara University, or UC Berkeley, others were unfamiliar to me.

"It's okay, Daniel. I recognize this guy." The young woman at the front of the group knelt in front of Munchkin and rubbed his ears while he slobbered on her gray Santa Clara University sweatshirt.

"I'm Maggie McDonald," I told them. "I'm a friend of Munchkin and his owner, Stephen Laird." Belle abandoned protecting me, butted her head against Daniel's hand, and sat on his foot. "Are you helping to clean up? Have the police finished their investigation?"

I was certain the group, whoever they were, had meant well, but I feared they might have eliminated evidence or endangered themselves by tromping around the restaurant. I knew from experience that the police generally required a hazmat-certified clean-up team to sign off on a crime scene before they allowed owners or members of the public back inside.

The young woman stood and held out her hand. "I'm Becca Hsu," she said. "This is Daniel Chiang and, well, everyone." She waved her hand in an arc to take in the whole group. "I guess you know what happened here."

I nodded. "I was very sorry to hear about Mr. Xiang. Were you friends of his? Did you work here?"

"I worked here all through high school," Becca said. "We all did. We heard about Mr. X and thought we all needed to get together and talk about it. To be sad together. But then we thought it would be better to accomplish something and contribute." Her voice broke and then trailed off. She knelt next to Munchkin and hugged him, seeking a comfort that Munchkin looked more than happy to provide.

Daniel continued. "He helped with our college applications and with tuition, books, and fees. He'd either give us money directly, help us apply for scholarships, or hire us to work catered events when we were home on school breaks." He looked over his shoulder at the door to the restaurant. "The police were finished, and Becca still had a key, so we went in to do a last clean, and then close and lock up. We cleaned up the kitchen, washed the dishes, and threw out all the spoiled food from the cold-storage locker." He shuddered. "It was eerie being in there where he died. His overcoat was still on the hook by the door. The one we all wore if we had to spend any length of time in there. It was too cold to work in the refrigerated room without it. The police had left the door propped open, and today it was warm. And that's just so wrong." He looked up with tears in his eyes. "I mean . . . well, Mr. Xiang being killed was worse, of course, but the warm room brought home how much everything has changed. I don't know what will happen to the restaurant now."

"Do you know when the restaurant will reopen?"

They all looked at one another before Becca answered. "It may be permanently closed. As far as anyone knows Mr. X had no family. We'd all talked about seeing if we could buy it and run it, but we don't have any money and we know nothing about running a restaurant."

They weren't much older than Brian and Daniel, and I felt compelled to reassure them. "I'm sure Mr. Xiang wouldn't want that for any of you. He helped you with your education and I'm sure he'd be pleased to see you going ahead with your plans. If there's no obvious heir to inherit, Mr. Xiang surely had a will. It's a confusing time, but it will all get sorted out."

"But what are you doing here, Mrs. McDonald? Why is Munchkin with you instead of Mr. Laird?"

"I'm taking care of Munchkin for a few days while Stephen is away. He and Belle here are having a play date."

The kids laughed and accepted my explanation, which told me they probably didn't know that Stephen had been arrested. Daniel confirmed that by asking, "Have you heard anything about the murder? Do they know who did it? I keep looking at the police blotter online, but there's nothing. Not in the papers, either. It's strange."

"The local paper will probably have something next week. But you all probably knew Mr. Xiang as well or better than anyone. Do you have any idea why anyone would want to kill him? Was anyone jealous of his success? Did anyone threaten him? Were there any routine visitors that he tried to hide from you? Anything that seemed strange or you didn't understand?"

A girl in the back sobbed and was comforted by a boy wearing a Berkeley hoodie. Becca shook her head. "It's just a restaurant. Nothing complicated. There were private family parties where we all served as waitstaff, but nothing secretive. And he welcomed us here whenever we had the time to work, so he couldn't have been hiding anything. Not from me, at least." She turned to look at the other kids, but they all seemed confused and shook their heads.

They all broadcasted misery with their dejected posture and I felt compelled to cheer them up. "I think it's great that you all found a way to honor Mr. Xiang. I don't know when any memorial services will be planned. I found an obituary in the *San Francisco Examiner*, but it just noted that a service would be announced later."

Becca and Daniel looked at each other, then at me, and back at each other. Becca nodded and Daniel explained. "We've been talking about getting all of the people together that Mr. X helped over the years. Maybe asking them to donate to a scholarship fund in his name. And holding a service or maybe a volunteer day to do something for the community. But we're not sure where to start." Daniel looked at me expectantly and hopefully.

"Hmm . . . Are you asking for my advice?"

Becca nodded.

"If I were going to do something like that, I think the first step would be to find out if Mr. Xiang had a lawyer, someone who is handling his estate. The funeral director would be able to put you in touch with him, and I believe the funeral home was responsible for the obituary in the *Examiner*." I dug in the pocket of my jacket for my card. "If that doesn't work, please give me a call and we'll figure out what to do next."

"Did you know Mr. X? Is that why you're here?" Becca asked, taking the card.

I dodged the question. "I'm saddened by his death. He seemed to do a lot of good in our community. And he was a friend of Stephen and Munchkin here." Munchkin wagged his tail at the sound of his name. Belle had fallen asleep on Daniel's foot.

Becca thanked me and the kids dispersed. I watched them go and then walked slowly back to my car. I realized that although I'd said that Stephen was a friend of Mr. Xiang's, I didn't really know if that was true. Rafi was a trusted friend, and he worked at the Golden Dragon, but Stephen had never mentioned how he felt about the restaurant owner. Could it be that Stephen and Munchkin patrolled this alley at night because something wasn't right here? I'd assumed they'd performed a protective role, but they could have just as easily been trying to prevent some kind of criminal behavior.

I didn't think it likely. I'd only heard people speak well of Mr. Xiang. But I needed to remain open to all the possibilities.

I was halfway home when my phone rang. "Hello?"

"Mrs. McDonald?"

"Yes, this is Maggie McDonald."

"This is Bruce Renwick, Mr. Laird's attorney. I wanted to let you know that he's asking for you. If you want to see him, you'll need to come by within the hour. He's being transferred out of the hospital and back into the general population."

"I'm in Mountain View, the traffic is terrible, and I have two dogs in the car. There's no way I can get there in an hour. Are you sure they can't stretch it to two?"

"Mrs. McDonald, this is the Santa Clara County Jail we're talking about here. You do understand that? Your friend is in jail and his life now runs on jail time. Jail time does not stretch, bend, contract, or otherwise accommodate itself to anyone."

"I'm sorry," I said, as if I actually had something to apologize for. "Can I see him in the jail after that, if I come straight down?"

"Once he's back in the general population, regular visiting rules will be in effect. You'll have to wait for paperwork to go through and then apply to see him. You might be able to make all that happen by next Saturday's visitation, but it will more likely be the week after that."

"Is there any way you can pass along a message for him? Do you know what he wants?"

I heard a heavy sigh from Mr. Renwick's end of the phone, and his next words were clearly forced out through clenched teeth. "That is what I have been doing, Mrs. McDonald, passing along the message that Mr. Laird would like to speak to you. And if you're inclined to accommodate that request, you need to be here within the next forty-five to fifty minutes."

There was nothing I could do. I checked the clock in the car three times, then checked it again against my watch. If I turned around right this minute, I'd never make it in time. Even if I did, I'd have to leave the dogs in a huge unshaded parking lot that would probably make the car unbearably hot.

"I'm sorry, Mr. Renwick. I could break every traffic speed limit between here and Santa Clara and I still wouldn't make it in time. I'm afraid I can't overcome the laws of physics. I will phone the jail and do everything I can to get in to see Stephen as quickly as possible."

Mr. Renwick sniffed. "I guess Mr. Laird should have selected another friend to contact."

I was furious, hungry, tired, and frustrated. I was also stopped at a red light. I slapped the steering wheel and my eyes stung. I was doing everything I could think of to help Stephen and his public defender's disdain was the last thing I needed. So I let him have it. But tried to remain unfailingly polite as I did so.

"*Mister* Renwick," I said, enunciating every syllable. "When I meet with Stephen, I will ask him when he spoke with you and what time it was when he asked you to relay the message. When I do that, what will Stephen tell me?"

"I have no idea, Mrs. McDonald."

"Do you remember when you met with him? You attorneys keep careful notes on your billable hours. Could you consult those records and tell me what time you spoke with Stephen today?"

"Ten o'clock."

"And that was six hours ago. Six hours in which you could have phoned me, giving me plenty of time to meet Stephen. Did you deliberately wait to relay the message to sabotage me or Stephen? Are you overworked, corrupt, or cruel?"

"Er . . ."

"Look, Mr. Renwick, I apologize. I don't know what the problem is, but I am doing everything I can to help Stephen and I hope that as his attorney, you are too. We're on the same side and I don't need your disdain. Do you understand me?"

"Erm . . ."

"Is there anything you want me to ask him when I do get a chance to see him? Is there anything you or anyone else might be able to do to speed up the process? Anyone we could talk to?"

"I can look into that and text or call you when I find out."

"Thank you. As I said, we're on the same side." I accidently ended the call by gripping the steering wheel too hard in the wrong place. I hoped that Mr. Renwick wouldn't think I'd hung up on him.

In any case, I was home shortly and let the dogs out. Belle ran circles around the yard before unearthing a muddy old tennis ball cleaved in half by the mower. She bounded up the back steps. Munchkin followed at a stately pace.

The kitchen was filled with the comforting smell of slow-cooker beef bourguignon—one of Max's favorite meals. Two loaves of crusty homemade bread rested on cooling racks on the counter. I sliced off the heel of one, slathered it with butter, and took a big bite.

"What are you doing? Dad told us we couldn't have any until dinner. We hiked the whole PG&E trail loop this morning and now he's got us doing laundry and vacuuming." While David's voice was one hundred percent aggrieved teenager, he had the happy, healthy look of a kid who'd spent most of the day outdoors with his dad.

"Are those clean clothes? Folded even?" I mumbled around the mouthful of bread and inclined my head toward the laundry basket David held in both hands. "A bazillion points for you. Kid of the week!"

Brian came down the back stairs, carrying a garbage bin in one hand and a paper grocery sack full of recyclables in the other. "What about me?"

I messed up his hair, kissed his head, and said, "I love you, too, Bud. A bazillion points all around. You're the kid of the week, too."

"Did you get Stephen out of jail yet?" David asked.

"Or figure out who hurt Munchkin?" added Brian.

I shook my head and sighed, thinking that I'd accomplished very little today despite all my efforts. "Unfortunately not . . ."

Before I could elaborate, Max came through the pantry from the dining room. He gave me a hug and snagged the rest of my slice of bread.

"No fair. Can we have a slice, since Mom took one?" David asked.

"When your chores are finished," Max said. The boys rolled their eyes. My phone rang. Startled, I dropped it on the floor in the process of trying to answer it. The ring tone cut off. My heart sank. The last thing I needed right now was a broken phone. I'd only recently become familiar with all its capabilities and did not have any inclination to upgrade to the latest version until I was forced to do so.

Max picked up the phone, looked at the screen, swiped a few times, and pushed some of the buttons. "It looks like it's working fine. Do you have a secret admirer in Texas? Area code 972. I think that's Houston. No, it's Dallas. Definitely Dallas."

I peered over Max's arm and looked at the call log. "It's probably Jason. He told me communications would be spotty. Did I tell you that his emergency team deployed to the flood zones after all those tornados?"

Max handed the phone back to me. "Call him back. Over dinner you can catch us up on your investigation." Munchkin woofed and wagged his tail.

Max knelt down and rubbed the dog's ears, laughing. "Good boy! Great tail wag. We've been worried about you, buddy. Let's see more of that." Munchkin complied. "I'm thinking he likes us talking about getting Stephen out of jail. Maybe we should be calling this *his* investigation."

I tried calling Jason directly, but the call didn't go through. I wasn't surprised. All of our earthquake preparedness exercises told us that between damaged phone lines and overloaded systems, contacting loved ones following a natural disaster could be difficult for days. The phone emitted a grating alarm before the mechanical voice began: "All circuits are busy. Please hang up and try your call again. We're sorry. All circuits are busy. Please—"

I sent Jason a text saying that I hoped the storms were ending. I added the news that everyone here in Orchard View was healthy and well. I wasn't completely confident that Stephen was safe in the general population at the county jail, since he'd already been injured once. But, for now, it was the best I could do.

Later, over dinner, we talked about Stephen and Jason. Max was still nervous about my plan to question homeless people, particularly since the shop owners had suggested approaching them at night when they seemed to be less skittish.

"I know most of them are harmless," Max said. "But what about the ones who are off their meds and might be hearing voices telling them you're dangerous? I don't mean to be disrespectful, but neither one of us knows enough about serious mental illnesses to spot red flags that might predict violence." I could hear the frustration in his voice. He stood to clear the table.

"I'm not excited about it, either," I said. "But I'd like to visit them in the park after they've had a chance to wash up at the YMCA and while there are still people coming and going in the parking lot. Ed Bloom suggested I look for Annie, a woman with long braids and colorful clothing who he says is friendly, talkative, and mostly stable in mind and body. He told me where she hangs out, so I'm hoping I can consult her quickly and then come straight home. I'll also have Munchkin with me. Apparently most of the regulars know him and Stephen. Anyone who doesn't know Munchkin is bound to be afraid of him, based on size alone. And you'll be with me too. I promised I wouldn't do any sleuthing at night without you."

Munchkin hung his head, uncomfortable with our concentrated attention, but then looked up at us from under the wrinkles that had collected on his brow. The boys laughed. "He looks like he ate all the cookies and half the cake but wants you to tell him it's okay because he's so darn lovable," Brian said.

"It's a look you should know," said David. Brian ignored his brother's barbed comment.

Max started the kettle and plunked tea bags into two mugs, one for him and one for me. "Do you boys want anything?"

"Is there dessert?" David asked.

Brian grabbed a tangerine from the fridge and tossed it to David. "Mom, I think besides this Annie person, you have to try to find the guy from the intersection. The one that recognized Munchkin. How hard can it be? Drive past the intersection again. What can he do, push you into traffic?"

Max blanched, but I laughed. "And that's supposed to make me feel better?"

"Well, he wouldn't do that, would he, with all those witnesses? And we already know he *wants* to talk to you and that he has something to say."

"You're right, Brian. I'll check on Tuesday."

But David urged me to go sooner. "Let's go tomorrow. Dad, you can come too, if you're worried. What are the odds that a homeless person has an electronic calendar that reminds him it's a national holiday?"

"Are you going to go to the park now?" Brian asked. "It's dark. They'd probably be there."

Max shook his head and opened his mouth to answer, but I interrupted. "Mr. Bloom suggested I bring sandwiches, clean socks, Band-Aids, and a few other useful items. I'll get those together tomorrow so we're ready to go."

What I didn't realize then was how far away our cozy Sunday evening dinner would seem by the time Monday night arrived.

Chapter 10

Label your storage drawers, boxes, and bins. Some
families need big labels (or pictures, for those who don't
yet read). For some, small reminder labels on the inside
of the drawer will do.

From the Notebook of Maggie McDonald,
Simplicity Itself Organizing Services

Presidents' Day, Monday, February 20, Morning

I woke up to a call from Jason that again was cut off before I could
answer it. I knew Jason wouldn't be able to reach Stephen, and I
wondered how many people besides me he was trying to reach to
find out why his husband was not returning his calls. I sighed.
Despite Stephen's pleas not to tell Jason anything, I couldn't hold out
much longer and I didn't think Jason could either. I was sure he was
growing frantic, and I vowed that I'd provide a full report the next
time he phoned. I wasn't up to explaining it all in a text message.

I went downstairs to start the coffee and went through the now
routine list of calls I was trying to make. Trying and failing. Paolo:
left message. Nell Bevans: left message. Bruce Renwick: left message.

It occurred to me that Rafi's family might be home, since today
was a school holiday, but Stephen hadn't given me an address for
Mrs. Maldonado. The days of everyone having a landline were over,
and I no longer kept a phone book, but I looked up Rafael Maldonado online, hoping the great and powerful Internet would reveal his

grandmother's phone number or street address. As usual, the Internet provided way too much information. There were hundreds of Maldonados living locally. I made a copy of the list and transferred it to a spreadsheet. Stephen had said that Rafi lived in his grandmother's house. I double-checked the location of some of the less familiar streets, then highlighted and deleted all the Maldonados who lived in areas I knew were predominantly populated by apartments and condos. I circled the ones in neighborhoods with single-family homes.

I spent half an hour on it before I was itching to do something more active. I phoned my friend Tess, but ended the call when I remembered that she was up near Lake Tahoe skiing with her family and wouldn't be back until late evening. A number of local families, or "everyone," according to Brian and David, were skiing over the long holiday weekend.

I decided to get a start pulling together the cookies, sandwiches, toiletry items, and socks that I'd hand out to some of the homeless people. I began making a list of the grocery items we needed too.

I glanced at the clock and the thermometer outside the kitchen window. It was cool, with a brisk breeze. Taking the dogs with me yesterday had been a big help in cheering up Munchkin. Though I didn't intend to do any sleuthing today, I rattled their leashes to invite them to join me. I left a note for Max and the kids to let them know where we were headed and took off.

A gust of icy wind blew the ears of the dogs and pulled my hoodie open as I walked to the car. That was February in the San Francisco Bay Area. It could be warm and sunny with a light breeze one day while the next would bring the high winds we called the Pineapple Express, with days of rain that flooded small streams and created mudslides before moving on. Other days, like today, it felt like someone had opened an enormous freezer door. Our air came straight from the Gulf of Alaska and taxed our wardrobes and heating systems to their limit.

Outside the supermarket, I parked and grabbed my reusable grocery bags. But Munchkin looked exceptionally anxious, even for him. Belle whined.

"What is it, guys? You don't usually mind waiting in the car." I looked at them closely, trying to figure out what they were struggling to communicate. I checked Munchkin's wounds, remembering that

I'd neglected this chore that the veterinarian had told me would be so important to Munchkin's recovery. His left flank was a bit warm. I used my other hand to compare the temperature of the undamaged skin on Munchkin's right side. Both dogs seemed uncharacteristically impatient with the process. "But I'm not going anywhere interesting," I insisted. They literally pushed back.

"Bathroom?" I asked. They both wagged their tails, so I shrugged and grabbed their leashes. They did a quick sniff around the parking lot, but then Munchkin pulled toward the street where a garbage can at the bus stop overflowed. "I'm sure it's full of great smells," I told him, "but you don't need that trash in your system." I smiled to myself, thinking that food scraps were literally "junk food" for dogs.

"You're certainly focused this morning," I told Munchkin as he continued to tug me toward the bus stop. "I'll do my good deed and pick up the trash, but then I need to finish the grocery shopping. It's part of the plan to bring Stephen home and I know you want to help."

As we grew closer, I saw a pile of old clothes and blankets on the bus stop bench and assumed someone was sleeping there. I didn't want the dogs to disturb him so I turned back toward the car. With an uncharacteristic burst of speed and bad behavior, Munchkin pulled the leash from my hand and ran toward the bench. He snuffled through the pile of clothes, nudging them aside, and licked the face of the sleeping man he uncovered. Belle and I approached cautiously, but it was soon clear that Munchkin had found an old friend. His tail wagged with an enthusiasm I hadn't seen in days.

As we drew closer, I called out, "I'm so sorry. I didn't mean to disturb you." The man laughed and said in a rumbling bass voice, "Well, this old guy certainly intended to wake me." Munchkin bounced like a puppy and wriggled with joy, licking the man's face again, jumping on the seat next to him, and leaning until the man fell off the far end of the bench. Laughing and patting Munchkin, rubbing his ears and his chest, the man began to fold up his gear.

"And where's your companion, Mr. Munchkin?" he asked. "Where is your friend Stephen?"

He looked up at me. "Hello, friend of Munchkin," he said. "I, too, am a member of that club. Harry Franklin." He held out his hand, which was clean and well kept.

I took his hand, shook it, and introduced myself and Belle.

"Would you like a seat?" he asked, waving toward the bench. Munchkin remembered his manners and jumped down, but continued to lean against Mr. Franklin's leg and gaze up at him adoringly.

I sat and noticed that the man didn't smell. His clothing and blankets were well worn, but clean and cared for. Mr. Franklin chortled . . . a sound I thought I might never get tired of hearing. "Not what you expected from a bum on a bench?" he asked.

I blushed, embarrassed that my inner thoughts had been so clearly and loudly projected.

"I didn't say that," I protested.

"Never mind. I'm not a bum. I live in veterans' housing near the hospital where Stephen and Munchkin work. Stephen's been gone for days, and I know he has a habit of walking around and keeping an eye on some of the nighttime crowd. I figured I could fill in. I don't usually see Munchkin and Stephen except when they're together. Has something happened? Is Stephen well?"

Before I could reply, before the question of what to tell him had materialized in my brain, the man frowned. "Oh dear. I can see from your expression that something is terribly, terribly wrong. Can you tell me about it?" He peered into my face, his own lined with concern.

We were both silent for a moment as he gave me time to work out what to say. Again, I decided to rely on Munchkin's endorsement. I told him about Stephen's predicament and my plan to talk to some of the street people who might have witnessed what happened on the night that Mr. Xiang had been killed.

"I should have known Stephen's absence and Mr. Xiang's death were connected in some way," Mr. Franklin said. He shook his head slowly and rubbed his face with his hands. "Stephen will not do well in a cage. You must get him out, and soon."

He was stating the obvious and I felt guilty that I'd still made such little progress toward releasing Stephen. The man leaned toward me and put his hand on my arm. I jerked away, partly involuntarily, but also in response to his unspoken rebuke.

"No, no," he said. "You misunderstand. I want to know if you will accept my help."

I nodded, wondering what he could do.

"I can introduce you to some people. We'll find Annie and Freddie, the guy who works the corner you were talking about. I know them both. You're right to plan on talking to them after dark. And the YMCA parking lot is a good place to meet them, too."

"I was going to bring socks and sandwiches, and maybe some cookies."

"Cookies never hurt. I'm an outsider, too, but they'll recognize me. If you bring your cookies and Munchkin, we'll find you someone to talk to, even if Annie and Freddie aren't there. In the meantime, there's someone else you should meet."

He gathered up his blankets and stretched while his joints creaked and cracked. "I sat down for a moment last night, around 3:00 a.m., and here I am hours later. Anyone could have attacked or robbed me in the night. That's the real danger. Folks on the street need to keep walking during the day, as they get rousted from one place after another. By the time they crash, they're exhausted. They're so soundly asleep they're easy prey for thieves and the like."

"Lately, I've learned more than I thought was possible about the homeless problem," I said.

"That's the tricky bit. It's not a *problem*, but *problems*. Every person's story is different, with a completely different solution, and a different agency or even several different agencies might be required to provide help. With families, it's even more difficult. A shelter that takes Dad won't take Mom and the kids, and vice versa. And none of the shelters will take animals, even though pets are often the only living connections these people can make. What can we do, except help where we can."

I shook my head. "I guess if anyone had the perfect answer, we wouldn't still have a homeless problem."

"And that's the most brilliant assessment I've heard in months," he said. "Only the wise can admit what they do not know."

I laughed. "I can see why you and Stephen are friends."

"He's one of the good ones."

As Harry Franklin led me behind the grocery store where I'd planned to do my shopping, I asked if he'd known Mr. Xiang. He shook his head. "Never met the man. Never ate in his restaurant, either, though people say his loss will leave a gaping hole in the fabric of Mountain View. He's lived here for decades and understood our history unlike the dot-com newcomers who mean well but want to turn us into something we're not."

As we approached the supermarket loading dock, I could see flies investigating stray leaves of cabbage and bits of dirty watermelon rind. Harry picked up the trash and placed it in a garbage can, making the world around him a little tidier. He approached the back door and rang the bell. In a few moments, a man in a tie, wearing heavy black steel-toed shoes and an apron covering a slight paunch came through the hanging plastic strips of the loading bay door already waving us off and shouting for us to leave.

"We can't have—" he began, before dropping his arm. "Oh hi, Harry," he said. "What do you need?"

Mr. Franklin turned to introduce me and I handed the man my card. Harry told me he was the manager, but didn't give me his name.

"Organizing?" he said as he read my card. "Like the union?"

"Like making life more efficient," I said.

"I've got corporate folks like that. They're always in here rearranging aisles and shelves to maximize sales."

"That's fine," I said. "You're all set then. I was wondering, though, if you'd heard about Mr. Xiang's murder, and whether your late-night employees thought they might be in danger too."

The manager looked a little nervous and glanced up and down the alley on either side of the loading dock. "No, no, not at all." He lowered his voice. "We save food for the homeless people in the neighborhood. Day-old bread, coffee, leftover deli items. In exchange, they kind of keep an eye on the place for us. Make anonymous calls to the police when something's not quite right. That sorta thing."

"Wow," I said, with a distinct lack of the wisdom Mr. Franklin had noted earlier.

"We get to know them. As well as anyone does, anyway. Some of our employees bring them warm clothes when the weather gets cold and will give anyone interested a ride to the shelter. Most won't get in a car, but some will when we get these blasts of Alaskan air or when the rain washes out the culverts where they sleep."

"Don't the police do that?" Ed Bloom had earlier implied that they did. It was interesting that among the people who lived and worked most closely with the homeless there was still a difference of opinion regarding the options open to them.

"They used to. The current night-patrol supervisor is new to our police department, but he's old-school. He treats the homeless like criminals." He paused for a moment. "You know, the person you want to talk to, probably, is this old woman who is the closest thing they have to a leader. An elder, you might call her. She wears fingerless gloves, several layers of big skirts, braids, and either a headscarf shawl kind of thing or a striped knit hat with one of those big bobbles on it. I sometimes see her feeding squirrels at the park. Sometimes she knits, badly, but she always seems to know things others don't, and she doesn't mind talking to people."

"Would that be Annie?" I asked.

He nodded. "Are you going over there tonight? If you are, I have some things you could take with you. Socks from opened packages, crushed bandage containers, recently expired pudding packets, that kind of thing."

"I was actually here to buy some of those items, along with my groceries," I said. "If you give me a minute to get the dogs in the car, I'll meet you at the front of the store."

He agreed, and Harry Franklin walked me back to the car. I got the dogs situated, and they both promptly curled up, their mission accomplished. Munchkin gave a satisfied sigh before resting his head on Belle's back and closing his eyes.

Mr. Franklin, who insisted I call him Harry, promised to meet me at the Y at dusk.

"Can I drop you somewhere?" I asked. "After I've done the shopping?"

"The bus stops right in front of the VA," he answered. "I'll be home before you've rung up your bananas." He took off with a limping, loping run that indicated to me that he might be in need of a hip replacement. Before I was halfway across the parking lot, he'd reached the bus stop and climbed aboard an articulated transit bus that arrived at the curb at the same time he had.

Chapter 11

For me, hiring a housekeeping service to clean my
floors, kitchen, and bathrooms twice a month means I
don't have to nag my family. I can overlook grubbiness
between cleanings.

If you can't afford a service or don't want to use one, try
to find another way to let go of the need for a perfect
home. I'm quite sure that even in the pristine fantasy
photo displays found in interior design magazines, the
everyday trappings of normal life are shoved to the side,
just out of the frame.

From the Notebook of Maggie McDonald,
Simplicity Itself Organizing Services

Presidents' Day, Monday, February 20, Morning

On the way home from the store, I decided to try again to talk to
the owner of the comic book store and maybe one of the other
shops. I knew there was some piece of the puzzle that I was missing.
Something that linked Rafi, Stephen, Mr. Xiang, the health inspector,
and the shopkeepers together. Something more than proximity that
would explain the pattern of damage to the shops, the attack on Mr.
Xiang, and why Patty and Eileen seemed so nervous when I questioned them.

It was still chilly and I found a shaded parking spot so I left the
dogs in the car with the windows partially open. The comic book store

was still closed. I hoped there was nothing wrong with the owner. It wasn't like him to be closed on a weekend when all the kids were out of school. The knitting shop next door was open and the chimes rang cheerfully when I stepped inside.

"Back here," a voice called out. "Feel free to look around. I'll be out in a moment."

Like the quilt shop, the knitting store was a delight to my eyes. Cubbies on the walls held every shade of wool, from deep reds to crystal sky blues, snowy whites, and a dozen shades of black. Bundles of yarn were divided into sections reserved for man-made fibers, blends, cotton, silk, and bamboo.

I tore myself away to speak to the owner in the back.

A gray-haired woman with a young but weary face looked up as I walked through the saloon-type doors to the back.

"Can I help you?"

"I should say the same to you," I said. "Do you have another mop?"

She pointed toward the corner and I introduced myself as I grabbed the mop and began swabbing at a foul-smelling, tea-colored puddle mixed with clumps of garbage. It covered the floor of the shop's back room.

"I'm Liz," she said. "At least I thought I was when I woke up this morning. Now I'm hoping I'm someone else. Maybe someone in the witness protection program who is really an heiress. I'm waiting for the US Marshalls to whisk me out of here any minute."

I laughed. The mess was dreadful and the smell made my eyes water, but Liz's sense of humor was infectious.

"What *is* all this?" I asked. "Did your sewer back up?" I looked at my feet, for the first time realizing the kind of muck I might be wading through. I was wearing my white sneakers, which, thankfully, could be bleached and thrown in the wash. Or thrown out.

Liz wore knee-high rubber boots. "Someone hooked up a hose to the tap out back and left it running in the dumpster overnight."

"Were they cleaning it?"

"Oh, I don't think so." Liz kept mopping without looking up as she explained. "They stopped up the drains in the alley. I think all this was exactly the result they were after. Luckily, I couldn't sleep last night, so I came in early this morning. The water didn't have a chance to get into the front room and soak the carpet or my stock."

She sniffed the air. "Though I'm afraid the smell alone may ruin everything and drive my customers away." She shrugged. "One thing at a time. I can only worry about one thing at a time."

We worked in silence until we had all of the puddle mopped up. We rinsed out the mops and suspended them from hooks attached to the outside wall of the shop.

Liz glared at the dumpster. "If there were any room in that thing, I'd just throw the mops away and get new ones." Sunlight glinted off an oily sheen on the water flooding the alley.

"How will you deal with *that*?" I asked. "Do you have a pump?"

"I called the landlord and the police earlier this morning. I'll let them figure it out. I came in early to get caught up and now I'm further behind than ever."

"I'm surprised I was your only customer."

Liz shook her head. "I had a big rush before the long weekend. The big-box stores get hordes of people in for their Presidents' Day sales, but all the knitters are up in Tahoe skiing with their families this weekend. They'll be back in here tomorrow asking for help straightening out the muddles they created attempting patterns that were just a little too difficult. I hope I can get the smell out of the store before then."

She brushed her hair out of her eyes and let out a sigh. "Please, pick out whatever you want. It's on me. It was so nice of you to help."

"Oh, I'm no knitter. I don't crochet either. I grew up with four older brothers and spent my time trying to keep up with them. They weren't much into the fabric arts, so I never learned."

"Then what brought you into my store?"

I told her about investigating the attack on Mr. Xiang at the Golden Dragon, explaining that a friend was a suspect and I was sure he was innocent.

She offered me a seat at a round table. "What have you learned from the other shop owners?"

I outlined the information I'd picked up from Wanda Daniel, Ed Bloom, Patty, and Eileen. I added that I'd tried to stop in at the comic book store, but the owner had been gone for at least twenty-four hours. "I'm surprised he'd want to miss the sales from such a busy weekend," I told her. "I hope nothing's wrong." For the first time, I wondered if he was responsible for Mr. Xiang's death and had left town to avoid being questioned by the police.

Liz laughed softly. "His clientele is as likely to be up skiing as mine is. He'll be back on Tuesday, I'm sure. He lives and dies for the surfing in at Pleasure Point in Santa Cruz, and I suspect he may have a girlfriend over there who works more conventional hours than a retail store owner does. He was talking a few weeks ago about hiring someone to close up the store at night so he could leave earlier."

"You all work very hard," I said.

She nodded. "It can be a strain, particularly on families. The store hours are long, and that's only the beginning. We track inventory, order stock, keep the books, and, as you saw, do the maintenance. We're like teachers, nurses, and police officers, I guess. Our work involves so much more than what's reflected in our take-home pay. If you calculate our hourly salary, we don't make anything even close to minimum wage."

"Then why do it?"

Liz blushed and looked like a small child caught doing something she knew she shouldn't. "Because we love it. I miss my customers when I'm away from the store, and I feel more at home here than I do in my apartment. You know that old expression 'a man's home is his castle'? To a shopkeeper, the store is *everything*."

Which made me think that any of the business owners might have been willing to step outside the law to protect their stores. But how far might they go over the line? Could one of them have been driven to murder? I tried to pose the question delicately.

"Something like flooding the dumpster, the alley, and your store . . ." I began slowly. "That's more than a prank then. It's an attempt to get at the heart of everything that's important to you."

"I'll say. But I wasn't the target here. It was Eileen. I'm sure of it. She's responsible."

I stared at her, uncertain whether she was joking. "Seriously? But why? She seemed so nice. She *quilts,* for Pete's sake."

"Yes, she quilts, but that doesn't make her any less guilty." Liz pulled her chair closer to the table, leaned forward, and whispered, "I don't mean she *did* this, but she's responsible all right. And I'll get her for it too."

"But—" I was starting to think I'd made a terrible mistake offering to help Liz.

"Oh, I don't mean revenge, but it's just more proof that she's making life miserable and dangerous for everyone around her. She doesn't care so much about me, but she won't want any harm to come to Patty or Mr. Tweed."

"But—"

Liz looked down at her hands, which gripped each other tightly. She sighed and began rolling a stray piece of yarn into a coil. "I probably shouldn't be telling you any of this, but I'm so tired of keeping secrets and covering for her, enabling her." She straightened out the coil and began winding it again. "I've been waiting too long for her to come to her senses, realize what a mess she is and what trouble she's causing. That may never happen."

She pushed back her chair, stood up, and threw the piece of yarn into a scrap bin, then looked wide-eyed around the store as though she was desperate for a project to occupy her hands. She picked up four small containers of stitch markers and dumped them on the table, separating them and organizing them by color and size.

"I've known Eileen forever," she said as she worked. "We're friends. Almost like family. But I can't keep her secrets anymore. It's eating away at me and damaging my business, like you saw this morning. It's not doing her any good either, I don't think. I love her, but I also need to look after myself and my own life."

She spread her hands on the table and looked at them. I had the sense that she was seeing something there other than just her hands. Something that wasn't visible to me, but that represented her history with Eileen.

The silence dragged, but I said nothing. Liz was struggling with a decision. Nothing I could say or do would sway her one way or another. Interrupting her thought process might remind her that I was here and she was about to unburden herself to a virtual stranger.

Liz let out a long breath and then said in a rush, "She gambles. High-stakes poker. And like many compulsive card players, she owes money to people who aren't very nice when you owe them money." She waved her hand in an arc. "All this was a warning meant for her."

I still stared at her in disbelief, unable to think of a word to say.

"Look, I'll show you."

She took me to the back of the store, where the wet floor had nearly dried. She opened the outside door and stepped out into the alley. I followed her and she closed the door again. Badly faded let-

ters arced across the top panel spelling out PORTER'S SEWING MA-
CHINES AND NOTIONS.

"This was a dry-goods store some thirty years ago. It was a fly-
fishing place and a saddlery in a more robust economy, but then I
took it on. The landlord won't repaint the back, and I saw no need to
do it. I just tell delivery people the address and to look for the sign
that says 'Porter's.' But those nitwit goons the loan sharks sent must
have seen 'Sewing' and assumed this was Eileen's shop. Did she tell
you they broke her front window and spray-painted her storefront
last year?"

"She didn't mention why it happened," I said. "Are you sure it
was the same people?"

"Of course it was the same people," Liz said impatiently. She
opened the door and invited me to enter the store before her. We re-
claimed our seats at the table, and she resumed the story.

"Everyone else around here leads an exceptionally boring life. It's
work, eat, and sleep, and sometimes we skip the eat and sleep part." She
leaned back in her chair and looked at the ceiling, then back at me. "It's
gotten so much worse so quickly for Eileen. In the past, she's always
been able to win enough to pay back what she owes. But Mr. Xiang
told me last month that she was in debt up to her neck and about to
lose the store. He told her to keep away from his restaurant, and he
asked me to try to keep her away, too."

"Mr. Xiang? But why was he involved? Did she owe him money?
And why you?"

"*Me*, because I was once as bad as Eileen. I haven't picked up a
card or a chip in twenty years but back then we all played friendly
games in Mr. Xiang's back room after work. Then we started gambling more heavily. We were all pretty good, so we decided to make
a little extra cash by inviting other players and, well, playing them
for our own benefit."

"You rigged the games?" I asked.

"Sometimes, when money was tight, but mostly it was just fun to
play with new people. One day we played the wrong people, and
they figured out we were working together. They came back and
roughed up Mr. Xiang to get him to tell them how to find the rest of
us. But he wouldn't tell them anything."

"Did he go to the police?"

"Of course not. We were running an illegal game and he didn't want the kids he hires to know he was skirting the law. He tries to set a good example. He finds at-risk kids, employs them for a few years, and then sends them to college. Great schools, like UCLA, Berkeley, Smith, MIT, Stanford, and Northwestern. He'd do anything for those kids." She shook her head. "I have no idea what will happen to them now. I hope he left provisions for them in a will or something. And that the funds won't be tied up for long."

"Was Rafi one of those kids?"

"Rafi Maldonado? Great kid. Mr. Xiang saw something in him. We all did. He helps me with inventory every year." Liz had answered my question, but then returned to the main thread of her story about Eileen's role in the neighborhood's latest crisis.

"They sent goons one day to destroy the inside of the restaurant. Threatening Mr. Xiang hadn't worked, so they started in on the kids who worked there. Almost broke someone's arm before Mr. Xiang said he'd do what they wanted."

"Which was?"

"They run the games now in the back of the store and have for twenty years. The day they took over was the day I quit gambling. Mr. Xiang did too. We pay the goons a hundred dollars a month not to play, and they let us. It's worth it."

I was speechless and flabbergasted. I came from a town that was rough around the edges, but I'd never expected to uncover something like this in Orchard View or Mountain View. Both towns seemed so tame. I couldn't figure out why Liz was telling me all this either. Had the mess someone had made of the dumpster been the last straw? Did she want something from me? Or was she spinning a story to cover up what had really happened to Mr. Xiang? I didn't know and wasn't sure how to find out. Instead, I plowed forward with my questions, planning to follow wherever the answers led.

"But who are they? And why does Eileen still play?"

"I don't know who *they* are, except that they're bad news. They have no ethnic mobster identity, they don't wear gang colors, and I'm not about to ask them for IDs. As for Eileen?" Liz shrugged. "An addiction is an addiction. Until she decides she needs to change, she'll go on gambling until it kills her or someone else does her in."

"But why would they target Mr. Xiang now if he was cooperating and they were still successfully running the games out of his place?"

"I'm not sure. Maybe they found out he was trying to get Eileen to stop. Maybe they were trying to expand or were 'under new management.' It could be anything. They don't think like we do. And I've avoided any mention of them for years. If Mr. Xiang had gotten in deeper with them or they were delving into other rackets, I'd have no way of knowing."

"But, Liz, who is behind all this?"

"I have no idea. Maybe Mr. Xiang found out. The goons they send are different every time. It keeps them from becoming too sympathetic, I think. But they're just hired hands. I doubt even they know who is behind it." She leaned her elbows on the table and buried her head in her hands. "If they're the ones who killed Mr. Xiang and made this attempt with the dumpster to destroy Eileen's store and inventory, who knows what they'll do next. I'm afraid for Eileen. And for all of us, since these guys are apparently too stupid to even get the store right."

"Do the police know? Why don't they stop it?"

"I'm sure they have some idea. But you've got to understand, Maggie—the person behind all this, that kind of person doesn't make mistakes. And it's mistakes that get crooks and killers caught."

"So, did Mr. Xiang have gold at the restaurant?"

"Gold? Where'd you hear that? Because it's called the Golden Dragon?" She shook her head and traced a line in the grain of the table with her finger. "No, if he had any gold, or even any significant wealth, he would have spent it on the kids who worked for him or paid off the goons long ago."

Liz's front door chimed, and I let her go to her customers, a young mom and two little girls. One had a pink cast on her leg, which explained why they weren't skiing.

I left quietly out the back and ran to the car. Partly, I felt guilty for leaving the dogs alone for so long. But I was also victim to a surge of adrenaline that kicked my fight-or-flight response into overdrive. I chose flight, hoping to outrun what I'd learned from Liz.

By the time I reached the car and realized the dogs were fine, I'd half convinced myself that Liz was a compulsive storyteller who'd gotten a kick out of the fact that I was so gullible. I speed-dialed Paolo anyway.

Chapter 12

If your children's rooms are cluttered and they have
trouble letting go of items they no longer play with, get
some large cardboard boxes. Label each one with the
child's name and the year and have them put in it the
belongings that no longer interest them but that they
aren't ready to part with. Place the box with your
off-season or longer-term storage items. If they haven't
sorted the boxes by the time they are married or have a
mortgage, ship the package to their new home. It's a
time capsule from their childhood.

From the Notebook of Maggie McDonald,
Simplicity Itself Organizing Services

Presidents' Day, Monday, February 20, Afternoon

Paolo's phone went to voice mail, so I told him I'd discovered a key
that could unlock clues to the mysteries surrounding the Golden
Dragon. I suggested he come to dinner again or call me back soon.

I headed home and was nearly halfway up our long driveway before I realized the car wasn't lurching from side to side and the dogs
weren't scrambling to keep their footing. Max and the boys had done
an amazing job filling in the pot holes. It was a job that had been on
our to-do lists since we'd moved in, but that I'd despaired of ever
getting around to. I hoped we could get it paved before the pot holes
formed again.

I entered the house, hung up my coat, backpack, and the dogs' leashes, then called out loudly enough to reach the upstairs den where I assumed my spouse and offspring would be ensconced in cut-throat video games. "Great job on the driveway, guys. No danger of breaking an axle out there anymore."

I turned to grab a cup of coffee, planning on a few contemplative moments enjoying a dose of caffeine—my version of Sherlock Holmes's clay pipe. My family sat at the table, trying unsuccessfully to stifle their laughter over my gaff.

"Sorry, I assumed you were all upstairs." I blushed, lowered my voice, and grabbed my own seat at the table where Max and the boys were consuming our family's version of afternoon tea.

"We figured," said David, passing me a mug, and the teapot. From the remains of cracker boxes, cheese rinds, grape stems and tangerine peels, they'd had a relatively healthy snack, and there was no rush to plan or cook a meal.

"Looks like you all did a good job cleaning out the fridge." I poured myself some well-stewed black tea and added milk. I nodded to David and Brian. "Can you two please grab the grocery bags from the car and unpack them?"

They frowned, but before they could protest, I reminded them what I'd bought. "I can't make cookies until you do."

They took off for the car.

Max gave me a kiss and put his hand on mine. "It seems like I haven't seen you for ages," he said. "Want to tell me what's wrong? You look shaken. Did one of those homeless people bother you?"

"No, not at all."

"But something happened."

I sighed and the boys clattered in with the groceries and began unpacking the bags, putting the cookie ingredients next to the mixer and adding baby carrots, hummus, apples, and peanut butter to the mixture of food on the table. They were about to sit down, but I asked them to get the refrigerator and freezer items put away first.

Brian looked from me to Max and his forehead wrinkled. "What's going on in here?" he asked. "Something's up."

David stopped in the process of putting away a carton of milk, closed the refrigerator door, returned to the table, refilled his cup, and sat. "Did you get Stephen out of jail?"

"I was just about to tell Dad, but you two might as well hear." I filled them in on everything that Liz had told me, including how dangerous she considered the people who ran the gambling racket out of the Golden Dragon.

"But why did she tell you if she was so frightened?" David asked. "Are you sure she isn't still in business with them and was just trying to scare you off? Or pinning the blame on this Eileen person to deflect your attention?"

"I'd half convinced myself that she was a part-time screenwriter fleshing out the plot for a new nighttime drama," I said, grabbing a piece of cold cinnamon toast. "But that was just wishful thinking. Unless she's an award-winning actress when she's not selling wool, she was truly afraid."

Max, the shameless punster, muttered something about her pulling the wool over my eyes, and the boys cracked up. The break in the tension helped me relax. I was glad to be back with my family and wondered why I fancied myself a detective anyway. There was nothing in the world more wonderful than having all four of us at the table with dogs and cats underfoot.

Then Brian reminded me. "I get that there is something bad going on in Mountain View and you want it to stop, but what does it have to do with getting Stephen out of jail or finding out who hurt Munchkin?"

"Good question. I'm not sure it does help get Stephen out of jail. Nor does it help me find his friend Rafi. But part of convincing the police that Stephen did not kill Mr. Xiang is finding a motive for someone else to have done it. And Liz has certainly provided enough information to establish a motive for someone."

"But who?" Max asked.

"That's the problem. No one seems to know who is behind any of this. Just that someone is pulling the strings. I wonder what it would take to bring them out of the shadows."

Max stood up and started clearing the table of empty boxes and cartons. "No way. This is really not safe. You're talking about someone who solves problems with guns and knives, Maggie. Leave it to the police. They're trained. They're armed. They wear Kevlar. And most important, they approach dangerous people and situations with backup. Munchkin and Belle are great, but Munchkin almost got killed protecting Stephen, and neither dog is going to stop a bullet, no matter how hard they might try to defend you. You might not care about deliberately putting yourself at risk, but what about Belle? And what about us? We'd be devastated if anything happened to you. And what's to stop the bad guys, whoever they are, from coming after the boys?"

I grabbed his hand, held it tight, and urged him to sit back down. "I'm taking everyone's safety very seriously," I said, making eye contact with each of the boys. "After some of the other things that have happened here, I've learned my lesson. I won't put anyone's health or welfare at risk. I don't have a death wish. I'm only going to public spaces where there are lots of people. And none of them have any idea where we live."

"But what about the stores?" Max asked. "It doesn't sound like any of them were teeming with customers when you visited."

"But anyone could have walked in at any moment," I said. "And you and Paolo always knew exactly where I was. Mr. Xiang was killed in the dead of night. This killer or killers—or whoever is the architect behind this scheme—is someone who has dodged the police with his illegal activities for nearly twenty years. He's not about to make a mistake now by attacking me during business hours."

Max didn't look convinced, but he sat down. I looked at the boys.

David spoke first. "Mom, the Internet. Anyone can learn where you live in three seconds. No one is anonymous anymore."

"He's right, Mom," Brian added, but then he looked around the table and his expression turned grave. "But what about Stephen? The bad guys went after him, someone who'd never hurt anyone. And they hurt Munchkin. Mom has no choice. Neither do we. We have to get Stephen out of jail and the crooks need to be caught." He stopped talking, scanned our faces, then left the table. He sighed and made a noise filled with the sounds of frustration. Then he rejoined us and leaned on the table. "No matter what Mom does, are any of us really safe if we live in a town where a murderer walks free? Where cruelty to animals goes unpunished?" He tilted his head and raised his eyebrows as if waiting for a response from us. But I was too full of emotion to speak. I'd never been so proud of him.

Max grabbed Brian's hand. "You're right. And your mom and I will figure this out. But now . . ." He smiled and paused for effect, then spoke with false cheerfulness. "Vacation's almost over. You have school tomorrow. Is everything ready to go? Homework, forms, clothes laid out, PE clothes washed, lunches made, instruments and backpacks by the door?"

Both kids moaned dramatically for appearances' sake but left the table to begin getting ready for a busy week. The dogs followed them.

I glanced at my watch. Max covered it with one hand, and touched my face with the other. "Be careful, Maggie. Just be careful. And let the police take care of tracking down Mr. Xiang's killer. I love you and would be lost if anything happened to you. We all would."

"I will," I promised. "But I'm not in much danger tonight. I've got a list of Maldonado families to call in my search for Rafi and his grandmother. Do you want to help with that? Or with Mrs. Bostwick's file folders? I've got the labels all made up, but I still need to attach them to the new folders and make the tabs for her hanging files."

"I'll suffer the risk of paper cuts to spend time with you."

I grinned and patted his hand. "Mrs. Bostwick will be thrilled."

We cleared the kitchen table and got to work in assembly-line fashion on the labels. Peeling and sticking in companionable silence, I got to thinking about what Stephen had reported about Rafi. Rafi was sure he'd heard one of the thugs say something about finding Mr. Xiang's gold. I still needed to talk to the boy, but in the meantime, I needed more information about Mr. Xiang. Liz had scoffed at the idea that Mr. Xiang had any hidden riches. Stephen, on the other hand, had included the information in the note he'd given me, which meant there must be something to it.

I pulled out my phone and called our friend April Chen, who was now the principal at Orchard View Middle School.

"Hey, April. It's Maggie McDonald." We made polite small talk and caught each other up on our activities and the kids' news before I got around to asking my questions.

"April, did you know Mr. Xiang, the man who ran the Golden Dragon?"

"Because I'm Chinese and we all know each other?" she said.

"Don't be ridiculous; you know that's not what I meant. I'm working with Stephen Laird to help a boy who worked there. I can't go into all the details, of course, because Stephen has sworn me to secrecy, but I wanted to check with you on a rumor that has to do with real gold being hidden at the Golden Dragon."

"I'd heard that rumor, too, from the kids at school."

"Could there be any truth to it? I know that people give out those red money envelopes for Chinese New Year. Could Mr. Xiang have had a lot of money on hand for that?"

April laughed. "I don't think so. Besides the fact that the New Year began in January and any lucky money would be long gone by now, no one gives gold for New Year. It's all symbolic and metaphorical. The idea is to give one another luck, and the red envelopes are called lucky money. But it's the gift, the good wishes, and the red envelopes that are important, not the money inside. Restaurants will often give away tangerines. In a sense you could say they symbolize gold, but the Mandarin word for tangerine is very similar to the word for luck, so they're doubly symbolic.

"I *have* heard about counterfeiters cashing in by printing fake bills with lucky serial numbers and selling them at a premium. Could this Mr. Xiang have been involved in something like that?" Before I could answer, April began speaking again.

"The odd thing is that, at Chinese New Year, newly printed phony money with auspicious numbers might be considered as lucky as the real thing."

"From what everyone's told me, he was a very quiet, sweet, honest man."

"Mr. Xiang? That's what all the neighbors say about serial killers, you know."

April's consistently irreverent attitude took some getting used to, but she had integrity down to her bone marrow, and her love for middle schoolers was authentic. Her students adored her, but more important, they trusted her implicitly, which was something most young adolescents found very hard to do with adults. "Tell me about business customs for Chinese New Year. What kind of connection would you assume two business owners had if one gave the other a money plant for the New Year—several years running?"

April was silent for a moment. I was about to prompt her when she said, "I'm not sure, Maggie. Like my mom would tell you, I'm not really as up on all this as I should be. A lot would depend upon how traditional the two businesspeople were. It could represent anything from friendship to flirting, deference or degradation—since typically it is elders who give lucky money to children who can't support themselves. The most you could say is that it meant they knew one another or wanted to know one another. Often a gift can be given as an introduction." She paused. "What's with all the questions? Maybe it would help if you told me what it is you're really after."

"I don't know what I'm looking for. I was trying to find out if there was any truth to the rumor about there being gold stashed at the restaurant. But, like you said, maybe it's just the name Golden Dragon that started it all. Do you know a boy named Rafi or Rafael Maldonado? From downtown Mountain View? He would have been in middle school maybe four or five years ago?"

"That would have been before my time, and he would probably have attended the other middle school, unless he's only recently moved from this part of town. The name doesn't sound familiar. Sorry I couldn't help more. If I hear anything, I'll let you know. And when you get this all wrapped up, we'll have to have lunch."

I thanked April again and we ended the call.

Max shrugged. "I heard most of that. Too bad. It was worth a try."

I nodded and turned back to Mrs. Bostwick's files. Max straightened the stack he'd been working on and stood up. "My hands are getting stiff. I'm going to get a glass of wine. Would you like some?"

"Please. And Max?"

Max poked his head around the edge of the door between the pantry and the dining room.

"Thanks for all your help."

His face softened, and he came back into the dining room to give me a hug. "Always."

We decided to skip the wine and go straight to bed. Upstairs, we said good night to the boys, reminding them to set their alarms for the morning.

"Mom," said Brian, "you're going to keep working to help Stephen and this Rafi kid, right? It sounds like they don't have anyone else."

I started to reassure him, but then looked at Max. I suspected that Brian really needed to hear that Max wasn't worried about my safety. Max's thinking must have been along those same lines.

"We'll make sure she's safe, Brian. Even if I have to sew her up a set of Kevlar jeans myself. Do you think Yelp! rates local shops that sell spy gear? Is there a Kevlar bunny-suit pattern on the web?"

Brian laughed, but I tucked him in a little bit, trying to give comfort without treating him too much like a small boy. "Is there enough room in that bed for both you and Munchkin, or is he stealing all the covers?" I arranged the blankets around him.

"I'll be fine," he said.

"Me too," I said. "Me too."

Chapter 13

You'll have more luck adapting your storage system to
your family's needs than forcing your family to adapt to
the needs of your organizational schemes. For example,
if no one in your family will rehang a towel on a towel
bar, replace the bars with hooks. If that doesn't help, a
hamper or laundry basket in the bathroom may be your
best bet.

From the Notebook of Maggie McDonald,
Simplicity Itself Organizing Services

Tuesday, February 21, Evening

After dinner on Tuesday, while the kids got their things ready for
school, Max and the dogs and I drove to the Y. I felt a tad guilty
to be so close to the gym without planning a workout. But that's not
what we were here for.

"I'll take Belle and walk the path around the outer edges of the
park," Max said. "Give a shout if you need me. I should be able to
see you most of the time."

I took a chilly seat on a hard metal bench near the Y entrance and
marveled at how pretty the park looked. Thanks to the recent rain, the
air held more moisture than usual.

Streetlights lit up the water particles, and the scene looked a bit
like Hollywood's version of Sherlock Holmes's London or the world
of Jack the Ripper—but friendlier and cleaner.

Small children and their parents came and went to swimming lessons. Packs of nattering teens came for exercise classes, and older adults in business attire carried heavy bags that almost certainly contained both workout and casual wear to change into later. Dog owners chatted while waiting to walk home with spouses or offspring. I kept an eye out for Harry Franklin, who'd promised to meet me here. I didn't see him.

Before long, I began to notice fewer people walking on the paths. Instead, slumped figures appeared one by one with overloaded backpacks. They surreptitiously entered the park, staking their claim on a bench or under a dense bit of shrubbery. I was stunned. Here was a whole aspect of life in Silicon Valley that I knew nothing about—an underclass that existed amid one of the wealthiest areas of the country. It made me sad to realize that some of the best minds in the country studied at our local universities, but no one had yet been able to solve this growing problem. My conscience sent sheepish messages to the rest of my brain and fell silent, but I knew it would be back. Consciences are like that.

A laughing woman with gray braids exited the Y, bantering with others from what must have been a swim class, because everyone's hair was wet. Their faces were flushed with health, and they all looked happy. The woman I'd guessed was Annie hung back from the others. It seemed she wasn't ready to enter the park while her classmates headed to their BMWs and Teslas. I admired her colorful knitted gloves and embroidered skirts, worn in layers. She carried a paper cup of steaming liquid in one hand, while a plastic bag weighed heavily in the other.

She stooped to greet Munchkin, winning a sloppy kiss. He sniffed her hair and her clothing, probably getting more information about who she was and what she knew than the police or I could ever glean by questioning her.

She looked up. "But you're not Stephen." She raised her eyebrows in question.

I held out my hand. "Maggie McDonald. Friend of both Stephen and Munchkin."

She shook my hand, looked me up and down, and then peered into my face. "Forgive me," she said, "but do I know you? When I left the building, you seemed to recognize me and now you appear to have been waiting for me. Have I forgotten that we met? Is there something I can do for you?"

I suggested we move to the side of the path, to keep from blocking the entrance.

I gave her the rundown on Stephen and Rafi and Mr. Xiang, not bothering to edit my remarks at all. Annie seemed capable of spotting any attempt on my part to skirt the truth, and I saw no way that she could be a threat to Stephen or to Rafi.

"O . . . kay," she answered. "That was a lot. Would you like to walk with me to my bench before someone snags it?"

"Can I carry something for you? Or take your clothes to a Laundromat?"

"No, no. I'm fine. I don't own more than I can carry. I'm funny that way." She giggled. "I'm funny a lot of ways, actually."

A cloud covered the moon and darkened the parking lot. A gust of wind created a dust devil, and I squinted to protect my eyes. "Will it rain tonight?" I asked. "Will you be able to stay dry if it does?"

Annie peered at the sky. "There's no ring around the moon. I've always heard that's a sure sign of rain." She shrugged. "I don't know, though. I've got a tarp for the rain and if it comes down hard, I move to the parking garage and stay warm enough." She laughed again. "We homeless people are probably the only California residents who've appreciated the drought and will be sorry to see it end."

Annie settled on a bench near the public bathrooms, explaining that if she ever felt unsafe she ran to the restrooms and locked herself in a stall. "This is a premium spot," she said. "With a reading lamp, even." She nodded to the lamppost that cast a ring of light around the bench. "I've got seniority." She sipped at her hot drink and glanced at the grocery bags I held. "Watcha got there?"

I unpacked some of the sandwiches and cookies and asked if she wanted any. I peered into the bag and told her I also had clean dry socks and fresh fruit. She looked at me and then at the bags. "Is it a bribe?"

I tilted my head and pursed my lips. "Kind of."

She slapped her leg and laughed, nearly spilling her drink. "I like your honesty, Maggie. You're a girl I can trust. Unless you're one of those people who needs the warm fuzzy feeling of handing out your treasures in person, leave those bags with me. I'll distribute them to the shyest among us. The ones that find it hard to line up to accept a handout." She held out her hand. "I'm Marjorie. We have almost the same name."

My mouth fell open and I closed it quickly to avoid looking like a dying fish. "But . . . I was told your name was Annie. Do I have the wrong person?"

"Annie's my street name, I guess you'd say. I used to wear a cowboy hat and folks started calling me Annie Oakley. Now hardly anyone calls me Marjorie anymore, but I like you. You were honest, even when you didn't want to be. I thought I should share something authentic about me in exchange."

"I have a few other questions I'm hoping you can help me with."

"Shoot!" she said, pointing her fingers like they were six-guns she'd pulled from a holster.

"Stephen told me to find Rafi's grandmother, but I haven't been able to pinpoint an address for her. Do you by any chance know Rafi? Know where they live?"

Marjorie shook her head, and my heart sank. She was my last hope of finding Rafi's family.

"Now, don't panic. You people give up so easily. You aren't used to any kind of hardship, are you?" She *tsk*ed, but went on without waiting for an answer. "I don't know the address, but I can tell you where she lives. You got one of those fancy phones? I'll show you on the map."

I handed her my phone without thinking, but she beamed. Her eyes twinkled and she made a motion as if she was going to stuff it in her pack. But I knew her well enough now not to fall for her jokes. I liked her. She typed away on the phone faster than I could, as if she'd spent her whole life with the latest model of this electronic toy. "Here," she said. "I saved it as a bookmark." She held out a gnarled hand and pointed to the screen. "They're on Cedar Street, south of Hope. Three houses in on the right if you're coming from Hope Street. If no one's home, knock on the door of the fourth house. I don't know the woman's name, but they are good friends."

Munchkin hopped onto the bench on the other side of Marjorie and put his head in her lap. She patted him and rubbed his ears. He sighed. She was being so open with me, I hesitated to ask her any questions I didn't absolutely need the answers to, but I was dying to know her backstory. With her sense of humor, bearing, and sparkling intelligence, why was she living on the street? I couldn't resist asking how she knew the details of Rafi's family's life.

"Rafi's abuela used to walk here every day and sometimes brought me tamales. She would offer to let me sleep on her couch on rainy days, but I don't like to be beholden and I don't like to be indoors. I'm funny that way."

"Do you think it would be reasonable if I were to call on her tonight?"

Marjorie cackled. "You're asking me? The homeless witch in the park? You want my etiquette expertise? That's a hoot. I can't wait to tell the others."

I frowned. It wasn't that I minded being the butt of the woman's joke. Or even that I felt it wasn't well deserved. But it was urgent that I connect with the grandmother, and I was running low on patience. I was also freezing, which didn't help.

Marjorie stopped laughing and put a hand on my shoulder. "I'm sorry, hon. I really am. This is a serious emergency. I don't think anyone would mind if you talked to her tonight, but she'd probably feel safer letting you in and talking to you in daylight." She looked up at the moon and seemed to consider what she said. "Wait until morning. Everything is better in the morning. And now, if you don't mind—or even if you do—it is past my bedtime. If you've got more questions, you can come back tomorrow."

"But I wondered if you saw Stephen that night? The night Mr. Xiang died?" I stood as it became obvious that Marjorie was preparing to lie down on the bench and would be asleep on my lap in an instant unless I moved.

Munchkin sniffed at her blanket, as if tucking her in and saying good night. She took his big head in her two gloved hands and kissed him on his ample forehead. "Good night, Mr. Munchkin. You'll get your Stephen out of jail soon. I know it. Maggie, you come ask me your questions tomorrow. Good night."

She closed her eyes and began snoring. I suspected her of faking, but as I tucked the bags of food and socks under the bench, her breathing became deep and even and I was sure she was asleep. She coughed, but did not wake up, and I made a little wish, or prayer, for her continued good health. Munchkin and I set off to find Max and Belle.

After I caught up with Max and we were settling the dogs in the car, Harry Franklin ran toward us, breathless. While he recovered, I introduced him to Max and offered him a water bottle from the stash I kept in the car for the kids.

"I'm sorry I'm late," he said. "Did you get in touch with Annie?"

"I did, but by the time we got around to talking about what she might have seen at the Golden Dragon, she wanted to sleep." I frowned. "Maybe I'll come back tomorrow night. But you were going to introduce me to Freddie, the man from the intersection. Have you seen him?"

Harry shook his head. "That's why I was late."

I furrowed my brow and waited for him to explain.

"I was at the hospital. Freddie was hit by a car earlier this evening."

"That's terrible," said Max. "Is he okay?"

I could tell by Harry's expression that he wasn't.

"I'm afraid he didn't make it."

"The poor man!" I said, and after a moment added, "I don't suppose he said anything about Stephen or the Golden Dragon?"

Harry shook his head. "The only thing he said was 'Munch.'"

Max gasped and I covered my mouth with my hand, shaking my head. I felt guilty, as if I'd caused his accident. When I'd first seen him at the intersection, I'd noted that it was a dangerous corner, but I'd said nothing. Not to Freddie and not to anyone who might have known how to help him, like Paolo, or the people at either the Day Worker's Center or a homeless shelter.

"That's terrible . . ." I could think of nothing to say that didn't sound trite or insincere given the fact that I didn't really know Freddie and had been dismissive of him when he'd approached the car. Both David and Brian had suggested I talk to Freddie, but now I'd never be able to do that. And if he knew something about what had happened at the Golden Dragon, that knowledge had died with him.

"Was it an accident? Or do the police suspect someone hit him deliberately?" Max asked.

Harry and I stared at Max. Although I'd been about to ask a similar question, it was a shock to hear the eternally positive Max immediately suspect foul play.

"What?" Max said in response to our unspoken question. "You weren't thinking the same thing? That someone killed Freddie, making it look like an accident, to keep him from telling anyone about what he saw at the restaurant?"

"Yes," I admitted. "But it's a bit of a jump at this point. We don't know for sure that Freddie saw anything at all that night, or that he had anything to tell us. All we know is that at some point, he'd met Munchkin and Stephen. He could have met them anywhere."

"But now we'll never know," said Max, glumly. "Poor old guy."

Harry bowed his head. "You've got that right. As far as we know, he has no one to mourn him. No family and no friends."

"Will there be a service?" I asked, promising myself I'd go, if only to thank Freddie for the friendship I assumed he shared with Stephen and Munchkin, and show respect for the passing of a human life.

But Harry shook his head. "There isn't anyone to plan it. And Freddie probably wouldn't have wanted one anyway. He avoided any kind of gathering and kept to himself except when he needed money and was panhandling."

Max grabbed my hand. "We can make a donation to the homeless shelter in his honor. Unless Harry knows of another cause that would have been special to Freddie, that is."

Harry shook his head again. "I'm afraid I can't help. I just don't know."

"Munchkin obviously knew and liked him. I'll ask Stephen to recommend something," I said. Munchkin's ears perked up at the mention of Stephen's name but my spirits drooped lower. Everything, it seemed, hinged on getting Stephen out of jail. But I felt no closer to that goal than I'd been days earlier.

Freddie's violent and tragic death brought Mr. Xiang's freshly to mind. How similar they were in that both men had no family and no one to plan a service and help the rest of the world say good-bye. At my stage of life I hadn't been to very many funerals or memorial services, and I took them largely for granted. Everyone I knew who had died left people behind to mourn their loss—family or friends close enough to organize a traditional ceremony to honor their life, along with a host of people who would attend. Freddie and Mr. Xiang may not have had family, but even Max and Harry and I, who didn't know them well, felt the need to mark their passing. I wished now that I had some way to reach Becca Hsu, the young woman who hoped to plan a service for Mr. Xiang and create a memorial scholarship for him. I'd told her to contact the funeral home and given her my card. Perhaps, if I didn't hear from her later, I could get her contact information from the funeral director myself.

The following morning, I decided I needed to go back and press Marjorie for information about the night of the murder, especially since there would be no evidence from Freddie. But first, I needed to see Rafi's grandmother, Mrs. Maldonado.

I found the neighborhood easily following Marjorie's instructions, but parking was another matter.

The small houses, close to downtown and the train station, had been built in the 1920s with either very small garages or no garage at all. Residents parked on the street, as did commuters catching either the train or the private buses that shuttled workers to various high-tech headquarters. I found what was almost big enough to be called a parking spot a few blocks away, and parked my car so the front bumper infringed only a tiny bit on the driveway of one of the homes.

I made my way back to the Maldonados' bungalow, admiring early-blooming flowers in the tidy gardens I walked passed. But when I knocked on the door at the address Marjorie had described to me, no one answered.

I was about to move on to the neighbor's house when the door creaked open, just a crack.

"Hello," I said. "My name is Maggie McDonald. My friend Stephen Laird asked me to come see you. He needs your help. He thinks your grandson may need a hand, too. Maybe we can pool our resources?"

The door inched open, and I lowered my gaze. Mrs. Maldonado was wrapped in a pink striped comforter and held a cloth handkerchief to her nose.

"Hola . . ." she said, tilting her head to look up at me. Then she coughed. It was the type of nasty, bone-rattling raspy noise that terrifies parents in the middle of the night. I frowned and introduced myself again, more slowly this time.

Mrs. Maldonado smiled when she heard Stephen's name. She opened the door wider and welcomed me in. "Please, sit," she said, pointing to a worn but spotless sofa in an extremely tidy and comfortable living room. Before she could join me, she coughed again, leaning forward from the waist, covering her mouth with the handkerchief, and leaning against the wall.

"Have you seen a doctor?" I asked. "El médico?"

She stood up straighter and walked slowly to a small upholstered chair that swiveled slightly and rocked as she sat down. She took a moment to collect herself after she was seated, almost as though she'd entered a small boat and was hoping it wouldn't tip. The woman was very sick, with the flushed skin of the feverish.

But then she smiled. Her face, while still looking ill, erupted in wrinkle-enhanced laugh lines. "La médica," she said.

"Sí? La médica? I thought it was masculine. But it's been a while since I've taken a Spanish class."

"Sí," she said. "It must have been many years ago if you learned that all doctors are men. My doctor is most certainly a woman."

I laughed and she joined me until her laugh turned into a cough. "I am sorry for teasing you," she said. "Your Spanish is not too bad."

"But not too good, either, I think."

"Sí," she said, making an artificially sad face.

I looked her over with the eyes of a mother who has spent too many sleepless nights treating coughs. Brian has asthma and can rattle the rafters when he's ill.

"Can I get you anything?" I asked. "Tea or soup? I'd like to ask you some questions, but you're not going to be able to answer them with that cough."

She shook her head, leaning forward to catch her breath. I headed into the kitchen without asking permission. I wanted to give her time to recover and she needed someone to bring her tea. And probably someone to make dinner for her grandchildren so she could rest. I wondered how much she might allow me, a perfect stranger, to do for her.

The kitchen, like the living room, was spotless. Antiseptically clean. Gleaming like a commercial for some new and improved kitchen cleaner. Either this woman had been working much harder than she should have for someone so ill, or she had her grandchildren trained well.

I glanced in the cupboards. They were nearly empty, with none of the staples and canned goods that many people keep on hand. I found a tea bag, dunked it into a mug full of water, and heated it in the microwave. While it spun on the turntable, I hunted for sugar or honey or something to add calories. If I could find bread for toast, I'd make that too, and heavily butter it. I located the sugar bowl before the microwave beeped, but the refrigerator was empty save for some tired Chinese leftovers and about a quarter cup of milk in a gallon jug. Mrs. Maldonado was long overdue for a trip to the store.

I took the tea to the living room. Mrs. Maldonado took a grateful sip, but waved at me to place it on the side table when she began coughing again.

I needed to get bossy. Or neighborly. Or both. "Mrs. Maldonado, I know we've just met and it probably makes you feel a little strange to have me bringing you tea. No, don't answer. Every time you open your mouth you cough, and that's not going to get us anywhere. I'm going to go to the store and get you some things to help you with your cough and some other food that I can cook up for your grandchildren so you can rest. No, please. Don't answer."

I smiled then. "Look, you need help. I need answers if I'm going to assist my friend Stephen and your grandson. We're in this together. Nod yes, or I'm going to have to get tough and mean and I don't want to do that."

Mrs. Maldonado frowned. But then she sighed and dropped her hands in her lap in resignation.

"I take it that's a yes?"

She nodded.

"Let me help you get into bed and maybe you can sleep while I shop." I checked my watch. "I have hours before I need to pick up my own children."

She pointed to the sofa and said, "Bed is for nighttime." I got her settled and she was asleep before I could leave. There was no point in making a list. They needed everything.

At the store, I put every item I could think of in the cart. Liquids that would be good for a cold, fresh fruit that might be helpful in preventing colds in the little girls, and soup and frozen meals that would be easy for the girls to make. I bought some canned chicken soup, but also picked up a rotisserie chicken, a premade salad, plenty of vegetables, and some broth for making chicken soup that could simmer on the stove. Eggs, milk, bread for toast and lunches, sandwich fixings, cold cereal, and other basics. I threw in a package of cookies to cheer everyone up, and several varieties of tea.

In my freezer at home I had frozen quarts of homemade soups that would do for my own family for an easy dinner tonight. On a whim, I grabbed a spiral-bound notebook and a pen. The girls could help make a grocery list for tomorrow, and if Mrs. Maldonado still couldn't speak without coughing, she and I could write notes to one another.

As I waited at the cash register, I had time to think about all the people I'd spoken to so far and how little useful information I'd gleaned. I grew discouraged and feared I wouldn't be able to spring Stephen from jail before he was tried, convicted, and sentenced to death. I took a deep breath and let it out, loudly enough for the checker to look at me strangely.

"Sorry," I said. "Pilates breathing practice. How much did you say it was?"

After I paid, I tried to focus on one tiny piece of the puzzle at a time. In this case, getting Mrs. Maldonado taken care of so that she'd be able to answer my questions.

When I returned to the house with the groceries, there was a note on Mrs. Maldonado's door telling me to knock at the neighbor's. An arrow pointed to the left.

I knocked as instructed, and a tall woman with long, dark straight hair answered the door and introduced herself as Alejandra.

"I work nights as a nurse," she said. "I often check on Señora Maldonado y las niñas during the day. I saw Gabriela earlier and she mentioned you'd be coming back. I wanted her to sleep, so I told her to lock the door and I'd let you in when you got back. Just a moment."

She grabbed a key with a red ribbon on it from a table in the little front hall, but took a key ring from her pocket to lock her own door. She took one of the bags of groceries from me and we walked together across the front lawn to the Maldonados's.

She thanked me for helping her friend, but I suspected she didn't trust me quite as much as Mrs. Maldonado had. She unlocked the door and asked me to wait outside for a moment. I could hear her inside speaking in Spanish that flew past too quickly for me to translate, but I got the gist. Alejandra didn't want me to bring more trouble to the Maldonado family.

I must have received the proper endorsement, because Alejandra returned to the door, let me in, and glided past me on her way out with the ease and poise of a dancer.

"Alejandra, wait. Is there any chance that you could stay for a bit and ask Mrs. Maldonado some questions for me? I sense that speaking Spanish might be less tiring for her, and I know she's ill."

Alejandra frowned. "I'm sorry, but I can't. We've been swamped at work and I'm working extra shifts. You're right to avoid overtaxing her, though." She started to leave, then leaned her head back in before she closed the door. "Maggie, I have my phone." She held it up to prove it. "We have a police lieutenant who lives on our street and the patrol officers respond quickly. You take good care of my friend, sí?" She spoke seriously but winked before closing the door. I got the message. She mostly trusted me, but wanted me to know two things. First, that Señora Maldonado had friends in the neighborhood who loved and cared for her. Second, that if I hurt her friend, there would be swift and serious consequences. I had no problem with either message. Feeling loved, protected, and cared for was what neighbors, friends, and family were all about. And, as Marjorie had shown me when she offered to pass out the food and socks I'd brought, neighborliness wasn't restricted to streets with single-family homes and gardens. Apartment buildings, parks, and anywhere that people came together could provide community too.

Chapter 14

Store things where you use them. For example, place
plastic garbage bags in the bottom of the bin before you
line it with a new bag. This method prevents the need for
additional storage, makes it easy to replace the bag when
the bin is full, and you'll always know when you need to
put more bags on your grocery list.

*From the Notebook of Maggie McDonald,
Simplicity Itself Organizing Services*

Tuesday, February 21, Afternoon

Once I was back inside her home, Mrs. Maldonado insisted I call
her Gabriela. I made her another cup of tea and some toast and
she supervised while I put away the groceries, started some soup, and
packed up lunches for the little girls, whose names I'd learned were
Sofia and Isabella.

Gabriela's cough had quieted, but I handed her the packages of
over-the-counter pain reliever, decongestant, and expectorant that I'd
bought. She examined the package of cough drops I'd purchased,
nodded, and set them aside.

I unpacked the spiral notebook and pen. "I thought if you were
still having trouble talking, I could ask you questions and you could
write down the answers."

She pulled a small tablet from the pocket of her skirt and held it up.
"I had the same idea. I wrote down everything I knew that I thought

might help, and I pulled out a box I've used to store pictures and papers connected with Rafi's parents."

"Where is Rafi?" I asked before I looked at her notes. "Is he safe?"

"Yes. He is visiting his uncle, my little brother Julio, outside Sacramento. The phone number is in the little book."

"Would you like me to call?"

She nodded. "I don't want to start coughing again."

While she sipped at her tea, I called the number. It was answered by a man speaking Spanish and my high school skills weren't up to the task of explaining who I was or what I needed. I said what I thought was "Please ask him to phone his sister Gabriela, thank you." But it could have been "Your squash has feet like a rose bud" for all I knew. Languages can be tricky.

Gabriela held out her hand for the phone, an old-fashioned avocado-colored landline with buttons in the handset. She punched in the numbers, cleared her throat, and asked politely for Julio. She waited a moment, and then started speaking so sharply and loudly that I was glad I wasn't on the other end of the phone. I heard my name before she slammed down the receiver and muttered some words under her breath that she wouldn't have wanted her grandchildren to overhear.

"My brother has moved and did not tell me," she said. "The phone number I have for him is old. But the man who answered the phone will get a message to Julio." She made a *tsk*ing sound and sipped her tea. "He should be ashamed of himself. His English is fine. He was making trouble for you. Idiot."

"But if your brother's phone number has changed, how will Rafi find him?" I asked.

"Rafi is a teenager. He has my brother's e-mail address, his Twitter handle, and his Facebook account. And he has e-mailed me to say he arrived safely. He does not make his old abuela worry. If I do not hear from my brother later this evening, I will e-mail him."

I blushed, smiled, and apologized.

Gabriela patted my hand. "Pobrecita, do not worry. I see your heart. Let me tell you as much as I can about my family. You have the notes I made in case I forget anything."

I opened the small notebook. Gabriela's handwriting was gorgeous: small, uniform, and easy to read, but I closed the book so that I could pay close attention to what she was saying.

"Rafi, my grandson, is a legal American citizen," Gabriela said. "He was born right here in this house. And his father, my son Rafael Ernesto Maldonado, is also a citizen, as am I. The problem is that we have no proof that Rafi was born here. No birth certificate. Years ago, it wasn't a problem. Everyone knew our family had lived here for generations—since before California was even a state. But now there are so many new people here and there is so much suspicion of anyone with a name that sounds too Latin. As Rafi has grown older, we've been asked to provide documentation more often for him. Documentation we don't have." Gabriela began to cough again and stopped talking to take a few more sips of her tea. I got up and put the kettle on for more hot water. "He can't get a job or a driver's license and could only register for high school because I could prove I owned this house and he had records that showed he'd gone to school here since he started kindergarten." She stared into her tea cup as though she'd become lost in her memories or was reading nonexistent tea leaves.

I was about to prompt her when she resumed speaking. "Stephen was helping us with the paperwork and procedures, but then poor Mr. Xiang was killed. Rafi came home that night with Stephen's car. He packed some clothes and said Stephen had told him to go away for a while. As Rafi explained it, Stephen feared that the evidence would point toward Rafi. With no documentation, he thought there was a chance Rafi could be turned over to immigration authorities and disappear into the system before anyone could prove he was born here and had nothing to do with Mr. Xiang's death."

"Is that legal? I thought only noncitizens convicted of a felony were removed or deported."

Gabriela shook her head. "I am not sure. Rafi came through here in a rush that night. He was very upset about Mr. Xiang. And I was trying to get him to go to the hospital." She sucked air in through her teeth and muttered a word I didn't know. "He had been badly beaten."

I patted her hand. She took a sip of her tea and continued talking. "I've thought about it a lot since that night, wondering why Stephen wanted Rafi to leave and why he has not been in touch with us to follow up. I have to believe that he meant well. I think he was afraid the legal system might move too quickly. An ambitious assistant district attorney might be tempted to scare Rafi with a charge of first-degree murder. Then my dear sweet grandson could have been tricked into confessing to a lesser charge if he were told he would not go to jail. But what they might not tell Rafi was that if he confessed to a felony, he'd be fast-tracked for deportation without any chance to plead his case or prove he was a citizen."

I was scribbling notes as fast as I could, but stopped writing as soon as she finished talking. I looked up. Her face was lined with age, strain, and worry.

"Could that be it, do you think?" she asked. "Could that be the reason Stephen told Rafi to go away? But why would Stephen not call to check on Rafi? I've tried his number but he doesn't answer and doesn't call back."

I took her hands in mine. "I'm absolutely sure Stephen will call as soon as he can," I told her. And then I took a deep breath. I had to tell Gabriela about Stephen's arrest, but she wouldn't like the news any more than I'd enjoy telling it. I spoke quickly, trying to get the dreadful news out into the open all at once, like ripping off a Band-Aid. "Stephen is in jail. He's been charged with Mr. Xiang's murder."

Gabriela clutched her chest. Her skin blanched and she began coughing again. I feared she was having a heart attack and I stood up quickly, but she patted the air and quickly got her breathing back under control. "I'm sorry," she said. "I'm fine. I'm just so surprised. Stephen could not have killed Mr. Xiang. He wouldn't kill anyone."

"I know. And we're going to prove it. But first we have to document that Rafi is a citizen. If we can do that, Rafi can talk to the police about what happened that night and then they'll release Stephen."

The tea kettle boiled and I made us both more tea. I let Gabriela sip quietly for a few moments while I opened the difficult seals on the cold medicine packets for her. "Why don't you continue your story about your family," I said as I handed her the tablets.

"Rafael Ernesto told me that he and Rafi's mother were married but I have never seen a marriage certificate from a church or from the government. My son disappeared before Rafi was born. His mother, Dani Moreno, was afraid of doctors and hospitals and refused all prenatal care. She went into premature labor here. Rafi was born too quickly to get her to a hospital and she recovered quickly, so I didn't force her to go. She let me take the baby to the pediatrician for all his shots and checkups. The only reason Rafi does not have a birth certificate is because we never thought to request one. I do have his baptismal certificate, but the priest who signed it died many years ago. I have a photo of Rafi with Dani taken shortly after he was born. I sent the photo to my son at the last address we had for him, but it came back marked undeliverable."

"Do you have a birth certificate for your son? For Rafael Ernesto?"

"I think so, in here." Gabriela opened the top of a shoebox overflowing with photographs and documents. "But how will that help, if we can't prove Rafi is his son?"

"That's for the lawyers to decide," I told her. "But locating your birth certificate and Rafael's couldn't hurt."

"That picture of Rafi and his mother is in here, too, somewhere." Gabriela began flipping through the pictures, pausing, smiling, and stroking the faces of each one, distracted and lost in time.

I put my hand on her arm and nodded to the photos. "May I?"

She pushed the box toward me and I quickly sorted the photos into four piles: photos with no people in them, photos with children and babies, photos of animals, and those with only adults.

We were left with a pile of about ten photos of children and babies that might contain the picture of Rafi with his mother at the time of his birth. I returned the other three piles to the box and continued sorting the infant photos. One contained a young, proud, exhausted mother and an infant. I turned it over. On the back was inscribed *Rafaelito y Dani, Mayo 25, 1999. ¡Enhorabuena por el bebé nuevo!*

"Where is Rafi's mother now?" I asked, handing Gabriela the picture.

"She was deported when Isabella was six months old. We stayed in touch for years but recently the letters have gone unanswered and no one that I know in Mexico has heard from her or knows where she has gone. It was painful for her to be separated from her children, especially when she was still nursing Isabella. How a mother can handle that, I do not know. Perhaps she couldn't. The children do not ask anymore."

"Is Isabella and Sofía's father still in the picture?"

"'In the picture'?"

"Sorry. Is he still a part of their lives?"

"Yes, of course. And he treats Rafi like his own son. But he is in the navy and is now deployed, so the children stay with me. He is a good man. I do not know why he and Dani did not marry. The girls are both citizens. They were born at El Camino Hospital and we made sure their paperwork was complete. When immigration started the process to deport Dani, the girls' father was serving in the Middle East. He tried to get the navy to help with the paperwork, but everything happened so fast." She tilted her head. "It is also possible that Dani and the father were not so happy anymore. I do not know. I did not live with them then. The girls and Rafi moved in with me after their mother was forced to leave. They all still feel the loss. I want to finish our talk before the little girls come home from school."

We both glanced at the clock. "May I make a copy of this photograph with my phone?" I asked.

"Sí," said Gabriela, resting her head on her hand and closing her eyes. "Whatever will help. Take the original if you need it. As long as I get it back." She opened them again. "Can you help Rafi?"

"I think so," I said, as I centered the photograph in the frame of my camera app and snapped several pictures of the front and the back. I put away my phone and pulled one of my business cards from my wallet. I handed it to Gabriela. "Can you ask Rafi to phone me? Or he can e-mail or text if that's easier. I'll call the lawyer as soon as I get home and come see you tomorrow. Please tell the girls to make a list of anything they need from the store or anything they need me to do."

"You are too kind, Margarita. Too kind."

"I'll let myself out. Would you like me to help you move to the couch before I go?"

She shook her head and smiled, stifling a cough. I still thought she should go to the doctor, but I knew I wouldn't be able to convince her to go if she didn't want to.

After I left, I scribbled a note to Alejandra asking her to check in on Gabriela when she returned from work. No matter what the time. I told her I thought Gabriela needed to see a doctor and seemed to have increasing trouble breathing.

I dashed across the lawn and tucked the note into the frame of Alejandra's screen door. It would have to suffice, for now.

As I drove back across town, I spotted clusters of children wearing backpacks standing and waiting at various intersections, and I was glad that the Orchard View school day began and ended about half an hour later than the Mountain View district's did.

I picked up Brian at the middle school and we chatted in the car while we waited at the curb for the high school to get out. Brian spotted his brother first, coming toward us in a cluster of kids, staring at the ground and shuffling his feet. He glanced up and saw the car, then waved to his friends, one of whom patted him on the back as he headed our way.

"What's wrong with David, Mom?"

"I'm not sure anything is wrong," I answered, though I knew Brian was right. "Maybe he had a bad day. We'll let him tell us when he's ready, okay?"

David tossed his backpack and trumpet onto the back seat and climbed in after them.

"Dude, what's wrong?" Brian said. "You look like someone killed your best friend."

I was tempted to glare at Brian but instead I looked carefully over my shoulder and pulled away from the curb. Some adolescents seem to find automobiles invisible, and I wanted to be sure I could see and avoid anyone in close proximity.

David grunted and kicked the back of the front seat. I wrinkled my forehead and scowled at him in the rearview mirror.

"Sorry, but can we talk about it later?" he said before plugging in his earbuds and staring out the car window.

The lag between *now* and *later* turned out to be the time it took to drive three blocks. "A group of idiots stopped me when I was coming out of PE this afternoon," David said in a barely audible grumble. "They said they'd make trouble if my mom didn't back off."

I stared at David in the mirror, and without realizing it, jerked the steering wheel to the right. The car ran onto the rumble strip of noisy concrete separating the road from the unpaved shoulder. "Say what?"

"You heard me."

"Dude," said Brian in a voice mixed with awe and fear.

"Hang on, I'm pulling over at the next corner."

"Don't," David said. "Just drive. Let's go home. I'll tell you everything there."

I chewed my lip, wanting nothing more than to wrap my six-foot-tall son in a pale blue blanket, pull him onto my lap, and snuggle him until he felt better. But that wasn't going to happen. Not now, and not at home. No matter what I did. So I looked at him in the mirror, made eye contact, nodded, and drove on.

Brian seemed to sense that David wouldn't say another word until we were back in our own space. He turned to look at David, but said nothing and turned away.

After what seemed like more than an hour, we'd traveled the twenty minutes it took to get home.

Munchkin and Belle greeted the boys with enthusiasm, which was probably exactly what David needed. He rubbed their ears to return their greeting, tossed his backpack and hoodie near the hooks we'd installed to hold their school things, and placed his trumpet gently on the floor next to them.

He sat at the table with his head in his hands, refusing all offers of snacks made by an uncharacteristically helpful little brother.

I made myself some coffee to give David time to collect himself. While it brewed and filled the kitchen with its comforting fragrance, I pulled tubs of frozen soup, rolls, and cookie dough from the freezer. Then I turned on the oven and filled a cookie sheet with lumps of chocolate-chip dough. The oven wasn't completely up to temperature when I popped them in, but I'd had enough experience trying to speed up cookie baking that I knew it wouldn't matter in the least.

Brian held up a carton of milk. I nodded. He put it on the table next to my coffee cup and got out two glasses, filled them, and placed one in front of David. David, to his credit, took a sip and muttered, "Thanks," to his brother.

"Look," Brian said. "I can go upstairs if you need to talk to Mom alone."

"You should hear this." David sighed heavily and then repeated the words he'd said in the car. "I was coming out of PE and these jerks stopped me. Stood too close, you know? They told me . . . They said . . . Well, they used a whole bunch of words that no one should ever use for someone's mom and told me that there'd be trouble unless I got you to back off."

"I'm so sorry, David." I reached for his hand. He yanked it away, not ready for comfort, at least not from me.

The coffee had finished brewing, so I filled my cup, added milk, then pulled the cookies from the oven, transferred them from pan to plate, and set it on a table in front of the boys.

David grabbed one, dunked it in his milk, and took a large bite. He leaned back in the chair and relaxed his shoulders. "I wasn't sure

I should tell you about it. I thought you might, you know, lose it and lock me in my room forever, like Rapunzel or something."

He looked up and smiled, so I laughed. Brian looked worried, but David seemed relieved.

"Of course not," I told him. "Though I'll have to come to school with you from now on. To every class—unless Dad thinks he should do it."

David panicked for a nanosecond before he realized I was kidding.

"Did you tell anyone?" I asked.

"My friends. There are band kids in almost all of my classes, and they'll make sure I don't have to go anywhere alone for a while. You saw they all walked me to the car."

I nodded. "Good idea. What about any teachers or someone in the office?"

"I told the band teacher 'cause I had class right after and everyone wanted to know what happened. She said I shouldn't worry and she'd take it from there. But I might have to talk to the principal or even the police tomorrow. She had me sit in her office and write down everything I could remember."

"Sounds like you did a great job," I said. "And—"

"And now we can forget about it, right? You're not going to let those jerks keep you from helping Stephen, are you? I asked around about Rafi a bit, by the way. No one has seen him in a while."

"Whoa!" I said. "One question at a time." The boys rolled their eyes. "I know, it sounds weird coming from me. What's the record number of questions I've packed into one breath?"

They laughed, which broke the tension and was all I could ask for. It also gave me a chance to do some quick thinking about how an adult should handle the situation.

"I don't think we should forget about it," I said. "I'm going to let Paolo know what's going on so he can have a chat with the police liaison officer for your school. The more people who know the better. Dad should know, too. Do you want to call him at work or should I? We can wait until he comes home tonight if you want, but no later."

"Let's tell him together at dinner," David said.

"Perfect. I'm also going to call the principal now. If I can't reach anyone, I'll call again in the morning. I'm sure your band teacher followed through on her promise to you, but I need to call. It's a mom thing," I said, when David frowned.

"Not worth fighting you on, you mean?" David said.

"Right. Definitely not worth fighting me. Okay, I've got a ton of calls to make on Stephen's behalf in addition to following up on this. Scoot upstairs and get your homework done. We're supposed to get fresh snow in the mountains tonight and Dad said something about taking you boys skiing this weekend if the new product is launched by the end of the week."

The promise of a ski trip was enough to propel both boys to grab their backpacks in one hand, more cookies in the other, and head upstairs, followed by the dogs hoping for dropped crumbs.

Of course I didn't like the idea of anyone threatening either one of my kids. But I was proud of the way David had handled himself. I couldn't remember if I'd told him that, but knew it wouldn't hurt to tell him again. I promised myself I'd remember at dinner, but then I decided to be sure I told him before I forgot. I poked my head in his room and shouted his name until he heard me despite the music playing on his headphones. How anyone could study like that was beyond me, but it worked for David.

"I'm proud of you," I told him.

"Thanks, Mom. I know," he said. He sat a little taller in his chair and smiled before turning back to his keyboard. And that was worth it.

The dogs followed me downstairs and I let them out to run in the field while I sat on the back steps with my phone.

I called the principal and left a message saying that I'd like to talk to him as soon as possible, but that if I didn't hear from him earlier, I'd drop by his office in the morning.

Then I called Forrest Doucett, making notes while I waited to connect with his office. After he answered, I caught him up on the progress we'd made and told him that Nell Bevans, the immigration lawyer he'd referred me to, had not yet returned my call. He put me on hold, or meant to, but I could hear him calling her name.

"Hang on," he said. "She's right here."

Following some quick introductions, Nell asked me what information we had about Rafi. I told her about the photograph and said there was a baptismal certificate, but that the priest who'd signed it had died. I added that Rafi's grandmother, Gabriela Maldonado, had birth certificates for herself and for Rafi's father.

"That should be enough to get what's called a birth affidavit, and with that, we can get a birth certificate, which will open all the other doors for us," she said.

"What's the first step?"

"We need to go to the county clerk recorder's office and ask them to do a search for a birth certificate. Then we wait a month for them to issue a 'certificate of no record.' Once we have that, we can go to the California Department of Public Health with a variety of secondary documents and ask them to issue the birth certificate."

"And how long does that take?" I tried to tamp down my panic, but my voice squeaked as I asked the question.

"The schedule for appointments is pretty backed up, but once they issue the certificate, it shouldn't take more than a month or two to get the paperwork."

"A month or two? But that means we won't have proof of Rafi's citizenship until April or May. That's way too late. You know that Stephen's in jail, right? We need to get him out of there, but he won't say anything until he's sure Rafi won't be deported. He doesn't want Rafi going anywhere near the police until he can prove he's a legal citizen. Is there any way to speed up this process?"

Nell was silent for a few moments. Just as I became sure she was thinking of a way to tell me that there was nothing she could do, she spoke. "We could get a court order for a certificate. We'd need to complete four or five different legal forms and provide notarized statements from two people present at the birth . . ."

"We can get hold of only one, Gabriela. The mother was deported years ago and is either missing or deceased."

"Okay," Nell said slowly. "Forrest told me this would be a tricky one. What other documentation do they have? Dated family photos? Marriage records for the parents? Infant immunization records? Baptismal records? A family bible? Because we don't have the typically accepted records, we'll need to overwhelm the court with evidence."

"Gabriela was at the birth and would be willing to swear an oath to that effect. She said something about taking him for his baby shots, so it sounds like she'd have his immunization records."

"That will work. It would be stronger with two witnesses, but we can get her statement notarized and submit that. What else?"

"The priest who married the parents and baptized Rafi as a baby has died, but the church would still have the records, wouldn't they?"

"I should think so. Is Mrs. Maldonado a regular churchgoer who knows the parish priest and office workers? If so, it shouldn't be too much trouble to get copies of those documents. I'll do some research on what we need to do to assure the court they can be accepted as evidence. I'm not sure a notarized statement would help or if a copy will do. Maybe all it will take is a letter from the current parish priest. I'll find out."

"Will that take long?"

"I shouldn't think so. Please ask Mrs. Maldonado if there is anyone else still living who was present at the baptism or birth. Maybe a neighbor, relative, or friend who stopped by after Rafi was born. An official statement from them could help. Look, probably the easiest thing is if I send you a list of documentation that courts have accepted in the past. The more we can provide, the better."

"We found a photo of the mother and baby in their living room shortly after the birth. It's dated on the back with one of those codes they used to put on photos during processing, and with a note handwritten by Gabriela."

"Can you get a video or photo of the same room today? And bring a deed or utility billing record that shows Mrs. Maldonado has lived there all this time?"

"I think so, but wouldn't it be easier to do a paternity test since Gabriela can prove Rafi's father was an American citizen?"

"Maybe, but it would take too long. We won't need all of the materials I mentioned, but gather up everything you can, as quickly as you can. I'll talk to Forrest to see if he knows a family court judge who'd be willing to review the case immediately. Are both Rafi and his grandmother local and available? If I pull strings to get a judge to hear this case, I'll want to be sure everyone can show up at a moment's notice."

"I'm told that Rafi is in Sacramento. Which means we'd need a lead time of at least a few hours to get him back here for a court appearance." I thought of another snag and it took me a moment to catch my breath before I could explain it. "Nell, could any of this be done in Sacramento? Stephen won't like Rafi being anywhere near the Mountain View Police Department unless Rafi can prove he's a citizen."

I could hear a tapping through the phone and assumed it was a nervous habit Nell had, drumming a pencil against a table or something like that.

"It would be easier to ask a judge to hear the case locally, where Forrest and the other partners know the judges," she said. "I could ask . . ." Her voice trailed off and the tapping sped up. "No, I don't think there's any way around that particular problem. Even if we could get a court order in Sacramento, and I don't think we could possibly get one on an accelerated schedule, we'd still need the Santa Clara County clerk recorder to issue the birth certificate."

"How soon do you think you'll need Rafi here?"

"As quickly as possible," Nell said. "Does he drive? Can someone bring him down here? Or can we get him on a train or send someone to fetch him?"

"Probably," I said. "We'll work something out."

"Great. I've got another idea, but I want to run it by Forrest first. Can you get the documentation in order on your end and see what the options are for getting Rafi back here? If that works for you, I should have more information in an hour or two that will help us pin down our plans."

This puzzle had so many moving pieces and people, I was getting a headache trying to keep it all straight.

We wrapped up the call, and I focused my attention on getting in touch with Rafi. I wasn't yet sure how much he knew about what was going on with Stephen and the plans to finally get him a birth certificate.

I phoned the number Gabriela had given me, but the call went to voice mail, again.

"Rafi, I'm a friend of Stephen Laird's, and I'm working to get him out of jail and to finish his project to get you a birth certificate to prove your citizenship. I've talked to your grandmother. I think we have the paperwork we need, but I need your help with the next step. Can you call me please, as soon as possible? I don't want Stephen to be in ja—" The voice mail system cut me off.

Chapter 15

Refrigerated storage.

One day a week, toss UFOs (unidentified or unloved
food objects) from your fridge. UFOs include leftovers
that are still good but that no one is interested in. I tackle
this task on Sundays because that's my farmers' market
day and I like to make room for all the fresh fruits and
vegetables. Pick a day that works for you. (If all else
fails, do it when you can't sleep. The prospect of cleaning your fridge may be all you need to suddenly feel
ready for bed.)

From the Notebook of Maggie McDonald,
Simplicity Itself Organizing Services

Tuesday, February 21, Evening

I hadn't wanted to tell Rafi in the message I'd left that I needed him
to come back to the Bay Area. I knew he'd be afraid to do that because Stephen had urged him to stay away. I suspected the best way
to handle the issue would be to have Gabriela explain the situation to
her grandson. Or to have her vouch for me or for Nell before we gave
him the details.

Or . . . maybe we all needed to hop in the car and head to Sacramento to explain it to Rafi and his uncle in person. While electronic
communications are great for efficiency purposes, any emotional or
dicey situation is so much better handled face-to-face.

In the meantime, I set an alarm on my phone to remind me to dial Rafi every two hours. He couldn't dodge my calls forever.

While I waited to hear back from Nell, I decided to phone Gabriela despite my earlier reservations. I hoped the good news from Nell would lift Gabriela's spirits. She'd also need to make arrangements for her granddaughters' care so she could go to court with Rafi when the time came.

"It is *milagro*," she said when I filled her in on all that Nell had said. "A miracle. Thank you so much for doing this for Rafi and for me. It is such a load off my heart."

"Don't count your chickens before they hatch. Are you sure you're well enough to go to court? You should be in bed."

"I am sure that no one is strong enough to stop me. We say, *No hay que vender la piel del oso antes de cazarlo*. Don't sell the bear's hide before you catch him. With a birth certificate for Rafi, he can come home and we can release *pobre* Stephen from his cage. I am cured of everything that ails me."

"Get some sleep. I'll call you in the morning with an update."

"First I will phone Rafi and tell him to call you back immediately."

The dogs, tired from chasing one another through the grass, had literally collapsed at my feet. The air outside was the perfect temperature, with a gentle breeze that held a hint of rain. I thought of Stephen locked up in a small cell and decided to enjoy the outdoors on his behalf.

By the time Max came home, it was getting chilly on the back porch. Belle had curled up in one of the cushioned rocking chairs. Munchkin had pulled a blanket from my lap and was lying on it, asleep with his nose dangerously close to Belle's rocker. An outsider would have said we looked relaxed and content, though that assessment was far from the truth.

I still hadn't heard a word from Rafi.

Max ran up from the car, beaming. He gave me a big hug and kiss. "We finished the project and I'm taking vacation days for the rest of the week. Happy virtual weekend!"

I returned his greeting, but I was distracted. And still worried about David and the threats from the guys at the high school. I wondered what connection they might have to the thugs who'd killed Mr. Xiang or to the strange undercurrent of secrecy, tension, and fear I'd felt among the shop owners. Was Liz's description of the illegal gambling club at the center of everything, or was something even more dangerous occurring or in the works?

I wondered if David knew the names of the boys who had threatened him, though I wasn't sure it mattered. From his description of his encounter with them, both he and the music teacher and probably the administrators would be able to identify them. If we could get Rafi's situation settled, he could confirm the identity of the felons who'd broken into the restaurant and fatally wounded Mr. Xiang. David could identify the boys who'd threatened him. And the police could pull together the case, let Stephen out of jail, and put pressure on the shop owners to reveal what they were so afraid of. But there was still so much to do.

Max put his hand on my shoulder. "Maggie? What's going on? Your brain seems to have taken up residence on another planet."

I covered his hand with mine. "Sorry. David has something he wants to talk to us about. He's asked me not to tell you about it until he can be there."

David was already waiting in the kitchen when we went inside. He set out wine glasses for Max and me and pulled a bottle of chardonnay from the fridge. He uncorked it and poured.

"Thanks," Max said, sitting at the table. "But what's so bad that we need wine to choke it down?" Max listened intently as David retold the story about the threats he'd received. When David was done, Max shook his head. "I don't like this. Not at all. Have you called the police?"

I nodded. "Paolo hasn't gotten back to us."

"I'll call him now," Max said, "but I'm thinking it might be a good idea to take the kids out of school for the rest of the week and head up to go skiing. What do you think, Mags?"

I pursed my lips. It wasn't like Max to dangle a treat like two days off school and a ski trip in front of the boys without discussing it with me first. I cut him some slack because I knew he was exhausted from his hectic schedule, craved more family time, and was terrified by threats to those he loved.

"We'll all go," Max said. "I wonder if Tess would let us stay at their place near Squaw Valley?" I pushed my chair back from the table, still mentally reviewing everything I had to do. David looked at me with pleading eyes that would have done a hungry golden retriever proud.

"Uh-uh," I told him. "Dad and I have to talk first and get some pesky adulting out of the way. Let us see what we can do to juggle schedules, and we'll let you know at dinner."

David looked hopeful, excited, worried, and an adolescent soup of other emotions I couldn't identify. He probably couldn't either. I pointed toward the stairs. "Homework, trumpet practice, or reading. We'll see you at dinner."

"But if we're not going to school tomorrow . . ."

"Then you'll want to have all your homework done so you don't have to worry about it during the trip."

He grabbed his trumpet and flew up the stairs. "Bri, find your ski stuff," he called to his brother.

I turned toward Max. "Looks like you successfully changed the mood around here from fearful to celebratory, but what are we teaching the kids?"

"When the going gets tough, the McDonalds go skiing?"

"Yup, that's what I was afraid of."

"Look at it from the school's point of view. According to those boys who threatened him yesterday, David's safety is at risk. The school is going to have to spend the next few days working with the police to defuse that danger and deal with the scumbags. We'll make sure the principal knows that David was intimidated to stop you from learning more about the murder at the Golden Dragon." Max leaned forward on his elbows. "As a manager trying to keep my employees safe, if anyone on my team didn't feel safe, I'd prefer they stayed home until I was sure we had all of our security issues ironed out. Surely the school will feel the same way."

I considered Max's point. "David handled everything exactly right from his end of things. The school is probably already working on an investigation that ties these bullies back to the murder in some way. David is in real danger, as are any kids in his classes, if those jerks decide to prove they were serious. If we can get the administrators on board with this plan to keep David out of harm's way, then I'm okay with it. Especially if they keep David looped in so that he can be part of the solution." I bit my lip. "I think."

Max threw his hands up in a "touchdown" gesture and beamed. "I know this trip idea sounds capricious and extreme, but if you think about all the incidents on school campuses, I expect the administrators will be relieved to know that David will be safely out of their jurisdiction for a few days. We'll make sure the boys know this is a once-in-a-lifetime deal and that they'll need to get all their work done and keep their grades up. I'll talk to them."

"I'll take care of calling Tess and the schools. If I can't reach them tonight, I'll send them e-mails outlining our plan and ask them to phone as soon as they get in tomorrow."

The music teacher had given me her home number when I worked with her months earlier on a volunteer project. I felt justified in using it now. Not because planning a ski trip and skipping school were urgent, but because the threat to David and to me constituted an emergency.

While the phone rang, I thought about all the other calls I needed to make: the lawyers, Rafi, Paolo, Jason, my clients, and probably seven, eight, or ninety-three other people I'd forgotten all about.

I hung up the phone after talking to David's music teacher and filled Max in on our conversation.

"Kathryn spoke to the vice principal this afternoon, and they both had a meeting with the police. It sounds like all the school needs from David is for him to call the police and confirm the names of the two boys who intimidated him. We can do that through Paolo. We also need to check in with the principal in the morning, and you'll need to be available for phone conversations and e-mails during the ski trip."

"Wait. *I* need to be available? You aren't coming with us?" Max's shoulders sank. "I wanted us all to have some family time. To celebrate the end of the project together. And those jerks at school told David they'd hurt you. We need to get *you* out of here just as much as we need to protect David."

"I get that. I do. But Munchkin's not up for the trip and someone needs to stay with him. We could put him in a kennel, I guess, but Stephen's still in jail and I'm hoping to rectify that situation very soon. I haven't had a chance to tell you that I've spoken to Nell Bevans, a lawyer who works with Forrest. I've been leaving messages for Rafi all day. Nell thinks that if we get him down here tomorrow or the next day, she can schedule some time with a judge who will issue a court order to create Rafi's birth certificate. If everything goes smoothly, we'll have Stephen out of jail before the weekend."

Max sighed, and then looked guilty. "I'm sorry, Maggie. It's great that you've worked so hard and it's paying off for Rafi and Stephen. They're lucky to have you on their side and I'm happy for them. But I'd be lying if I said I was thrilled that you're staying behind while we head up to the snow."

"Maybe we can consider this an emergency trip and plan another jaunt for all of us?" I offered. "I know at least two people who'd approve that plan immediately." I pointed upstairs, where we could hear drawers opening and closing, and Brian and David calling out to each other from their rooms.

While they all packed up their gear, I tried to reach Rafi and asked him yet again to get in touch. I was growing increasingly annoyed and worried because he hadn't responded to my messages. Had he lost his phone? Let the battery die? Had the bad guys found him? Or had Stephen completely misjudged him? That last possibility terrified me the most—the idea that Stephen's noble gesture might have been wasted on someone who ignored common courtesies.

I was about to call Nell to tell her we needed to make other plans when my phone rang. I didn't recognize the number but was relieved to hear a young man's voice on the line.

"Mrs. McDonald? This is Rafi Maldonado. My grandmother Gabriela said that I needed to talk to you tonight because you had good news about my birth certificate and Stephen Laird. I hope I'm not calling too late."

"I'm happy to hear from you. I hope your grandmother explained that I'm a friend of Stephen's and acting under his instructions."

"She did tell me that, and said I could trust you . . ."

"You don't sound convinced, and you're right to be wary. What can I tell you that might reassure you?"

"I've thought about that. Stephen has a friend who spends a lot of time with him at night. Can you tell me the friend's name?"

"There are two friends who fit that description, Jason and Munchkin."

I heard a sigh of relief from Rafi's end. "Is Munchkin okay? And Stephen? My grandmother says Stephen's in jail. It's my fault, Mrs. McDonald. We have to get him out of there."

"Which is why I'm calling. Stephen had been working to get you the citizenship papers you need and the lawyer thinks that we can do that as early as tomorrow if you can get down here to the Bay Area."

"Stephen told me to stay away until I heard from him."

"I know he did. But according to the lawyer, Nell Bevans, your birth certificate has to be issued in the county where you were born. That's Santa Clara County, so we need to work with a judge in San Jose. As soon as I can assure Nell that you'll be here, she'll make an appointment with the court." I went on to explain the rest of the steps that would culminate in a happy outcome for Rafi and free Stephen.

"I drove up here in Stephen's car in the middle of the night, so there was no traffic," Rafi told me. "I don't have a driver's license and I was terrified that I'd get pulled over or get into an accident."

"Is there someone who can drive you back down here? Or I could look at the bus schedules along with trains or even a shuttle flight. We need you back in the Bay Area as quickly as possible."

"Would you mind holding on for just a moment?" Rafi asked. I agreed and the muffled sounds of discussion followed. "My uncle says he'll drive me down tonight. We can stay with my grandmother if you think that's safe and visit you in the morning."

I looked at my watch. If they left right now, assuming there were no major tie-ups, they could be in Orchard View before it grew too late. "Rafi, may I speak to your uncle? I think it might be better for you to stay with my family. We've never met, but that means anyone who might be searching for you won't expect to find you here."

Rafi passed the phone to his Uncle Julio, and I explained again my connection to Stephen Laird and our plan to solve Rafi's problem and Stephen's in one fell swoop. uncle Julio was understandably wary until I heard Rafi remind him that we had Munchkin. He said, "If he's staying with her, she's okay. Stephen would never allow Munchkin to stay with anyone he didn't trust."

Uncle Julio told Rafi to pack a few clothes, but explained to me that he wanted to check in with Gabriela before he agreed to anything. I approved of his caution. While he phoned Gabriela, I called Nell, hoping we still had time to pull our plan together, get on the court calendar, and release Stephen from jail before the weekend.

Chapter 16

Everyone has clothing they seldom wear but must hang
on to. In our area, both formal wear and ski clothing are
worn only a few times a year.

I store ski clothing in well-marked bins in the garage,
one bin for each family member. At the start of the sea-
son, we make sure everything fits and we're not missing
anything. The clothes remain in their bins and can be
quickly packed for each trip.

Max and the boys each have one black suit they wear
with black shoes and socks and a narrow assortment of
ties and dress shirts. After each wearing, we make sure
all the elements of the ensemble are clean and pressed
and hang them carefully in a garment bag at the back of
the closet where they're ready for the next occasion.

From the Notebook of Maggie McDonald,
Simplicity Itself Organizing Services

Thursday, February 23, Morning

Rafi and his uncle Julio arrived in the early hours of Thursday
morning.

We had a few awkward moments as we all faced up to the fact
that we'd made unusual plans on the spur of the moment with virtual
strangers. Rafi's safety and my family's, along with Rafi's future and

Stephen's, hung in the balance. I suspect we all had misgivings similar to those Max had voiced when I told him earlier that we'd be welcoming unexpected house guests.

"Have you met these people?" he'd asked, stopping in the process of packing a duffel with clothes for the ski trip.

"No, but talked to them over the phone. And Stephen trusts them. He went to jail for them, for Pete's sake. You don't do that for just anyone."

"But you don't have any way of verifying that the people you've spoken to on the phone are the same people Stephen told you about."

I thought about that for a moment as Max went on. "In fact, your connection to them came through a homeless person."

I sat down on the side of our bed. Not once had I thought that Gabriela or Rafi or Julio or Annie were anyone other than who I'd expected them to be. I trusted that they would help me solve Stephen's problems and I'd counted on them to have the same confidence in me. But why? None of us were naive. Everyone except Rafi was a cautious, responsible adult with a family they needed to keep safe. Annie had more street smarts than I would ever acquire. So why did we automatically trust each other?

I shook my head in answer to Max's question and his concern. "I hear what you're saying. I agree that this whole situation is a little unconventional and it all happened very quickly. But it's not Stephen and Annie who have vouched for these people; it's Munchkin."

Max looked at me as though I'd gone stark raving mad. "Seriously, Maggie? You want me to leave you here with strangers while I go skiing, even though you've been threatened? You're telling me it's safe because the world's biggest dog has told you it's going to be fine?"

I laughed quietly. "I admit it sounds nuts, but let me explain."

I must have sounded sane enough, because Max sat on the bed across from me and listened as I outlined why I felt confident in my decision to invite Rafi and his uncle to our home.

"Stephen told me about Rafi and went to jail to protect

him. I located Gabriela and Rafi through Annie, that's true, but Annie knew Munchkin immediately. He's a huge dog and often terrifies people, but Annie was completely comfortable with him. He can be a bit of a scaredy-cat in unfamiliar surroundings, but he was completely comfortable with Annie. He practically crawled into her lap. And Gabriela was horrified when she learned that Stephen was in jail. I don't think the most brilliant actress could have played the role as convincingly as she did. They're friends. And when Rafi wanted reassurance about me, he wanted to make sure I knew Munchkin."

Max still looked skeptical and began unpacking his duffel bag. "The boys and I will stay. Just to make sure. We'll keep them out of school, but we won't go skiing."

"Max, listen. The ski trip is the perfect plan. You need it and the boys need it. I would go with you if I possibly could. But I'll be safe, I promise. Look, you'll be here when Julio and Rafi arrive. They're coming in Stephen's car. He gave Rafi the keys without any qualms. And Julio asked all sorts of responsible questions before he agreed to bring Rafi down here. The same questions you or I would have asked. They're good people and I'm confident they are who they say they are."

"I'm not sure I completely agree with your logic, but I trust your judgment. I'd feel better if we had Stephen here. Or Jason."

"I can call Paolo and ask him to join us for breakfast, or if he can come over now . . . "

Paolo hadn't been able to join us, but he pulled some strings and sent us a DMV photo of a Julio Maldonado from Sacramento who had no police record and was the same age as Gabriela's brother.

But by the time Max watched Julio and Rafi pull up to our front door in Stephen's car, and heard Munchkin's exuberant greeting of Rafi, he was ready to laugh along with Rafi and Julio when Munchkin nearly knocked Rafi over.

We still had those few awkward moments as we introduced ourselves, laid out the plans for the morning, and showed our guests to their suite in our remodeled attic. But the three boys became acquainted quickly. Rafi was visibly relieved to see Munchkin had healed so quickly from his injuries. And Julio gently grilled Max over the qualifications of the lawyer in whom he was entrusting his nephew's future.

By the time we were all yawning our agreement that it was time for bed, we'd come to an unspoken understanding that while the situation was undoubtedly strange, we shared a concern for Rafi, Stephen, and Munchkin that bound us to one another for the time being, at least.

In the morning, Julio and Rafi helped Max and the boys pack their car, while I cleared the big dining room table to make room for everyone at breakfast.

It was easier for Max to follow through with the plans for the trip when we heard from Paolo that he'd picked up the boys who'd threatened David. They were spending the morning at the Orchard View Police Department where they couldn't hurt any of us.

Max kissed me before he left. "You are going to feel so much better once you've got Stephen out of jail. Call or text me to let me know what happens."

An overwhelming number of dominos were lined up in front of me. If any one of them were to fall in an unexpected manner, the whole series of events would fail to play out as planned. I reminded myself that the most I could control was the job right in front of me. I wished the guys a safe trip and waved them off, promising myself that we'd plan another getaway for an upcoming weekend.

Julio left shortly after Max and the boys to pick up Gabriela and all the documentation she'd pulled together for Rafi's case.

Nell's GPS system had let her down, and she called from a local Starbucks for directions. She pulled up about fifteen minutes later driving a tiny red Fiat, and climbed out of the car carrying a voluminous briefcase, the largest cup of coffee I'd ever seen, and a white paper bag of what I hoped were bakery treats to share.

Nell's light brown hair streaked with blond highlights was up in a no-nonsense ponytail. She carried what she referred to as her "lawyer costume" in a dry-cleaner bag. "This casual gear won't work for court," she explained, referring to the pale-pink cotton sweater she wore over a collared shirt and black corduroy slacks. "Judges are more sympathetic to lawyers in suits."

Nell knew dogs and greeted Munchkin appropriately, which won Rafi's immediate trust. "What a gorgeous guy you are," she told the dog. "If your manners are as beautiful as the rest of you, we'll do fine. But I've got work to do if we're going to get your buddy out of jail. Mess up my papers and you're toast."

"Sorry," she said, standing to address me. "Let me start over. I'm Nell Bevans. You must be Mrs. McDonald and Rafi Maldonado." We shook hands, leaning over Munchkin to do so. "Now that we've taken care of the formalities, let's get going." She handed Rafi the white paper bag. "Croissants," she said. "For you to share and keep far away from me. I've already had two, which is probably two too many." As Rafi thanked her, she turned to me and asked, "Where can I set up?"

I led her to the dining room, where I'd begun clearing the remains of our breakfast. Nell unpacked her computer and busied herself with detangling power cords. "Would you mind plugging this in, Rafi? Is there a printer I can connect to? Mrs. McDonald, do you have a Wi-Fi password you wouldn't mind me using?"

Gabriela and Julio returned just as we'd finished reconfiguring the dining room from a breakfast area to a conference room. Following brief introductions, Nell stood at the table with her legs shoulder-length apart, hands clasped behind her back with the demeanor of a wartime general.

"We have until 9:00 a.m. tomorrow morning to finish preparing our case. Our goal is to get Rafi a court order for the birth certificate he should have been awarded as a matter of course as an infant. It's not fair. It shouldn't be this difficult. But we don't have time to change the world today. Most of the work will be mine. I'll need each of you to help streamline the process and make sure that we have all the supporting documents in order. It will be slow and boring, but I need everyone to stay focused. After we get Rafi taken care of, we'll attend to getting Mr. Stephen Laird out of jail. But first things first."

Julio interrupted. "Ms. Bevans, I'm appreciate what you are trying to do, but my first priority is my nephew's safety. Mr. Laird urged Rafi to stay away from the Bay Area to prevent him from being harassed, arrested, or deported. What assurances do we have that he'll be safe here or at the courthouse?"

I was eager to hear Nell's reassurances. She took a deep breath and her posture changed. Suddenly she looked more comforting than domineering. She directed her answer to Rafi, speaking softly but firmly. "Stephen advised you well. Part of the reason we want to do this quickly is to protect you. But whoever killed Mr. Xiang is still out there and we don't know who those men were. They have no reason to look for you here, however. By tomorrow morning, you'll be able to talk freely to the police and that will help them find the murderers and bring them in."

"But what about the police?" Julio asked. "My nephew tells me that Mr. Laird feared that overzealous officers might move very quickly from questioning Julio to deporting him."

"After he has his birth certificate, he can't be *removed*, which is what we're calling deportation these days. But Rafi's case is on the court docket for 9:00 a.m. tomorrow. Even if the police tried to pick him up on the courthouse steps, they wouldn't be able to take him in until after he sees the judge. An appointment with a judge always takes precedence."

"But what if you can't get the court order?"

"I'll get the court order," Nell said. "That's my job. I love my job and I'm exceptionally good at it." She looked around the room, making eye contact with each of us.

"But Rafi tells me that Stephen's husband is a cop," Julio said. "Will that be a problem?"

Rafi fed Munchkin bits of croissant under the table, but we all pretended not to notice. He turned his head from his uncle at one end of the table to Nell at the other like a fan at a tennis match.

"Jason is out of town at the moment and isn't aware that Stephen is in jail," I said. "Stephen has asked us to keep that news from him for now."

"But why would he go to jail for Rafi?" Julio asked. "I love my nephew. He's a good boy. I would go to jail for him, but I am his uncle."

"You've not met Stephen Laird. He's a fine man unlike any other. But I can't speak for him. You'll have to ask him yourself when you meet him."

Julio nodded and put his hand over his heart. "And thank him."

I smiled, momentarily overcome with emotion, realizing the impact of Stephen's sacrifice.

"You need to know one more thing," I said. "There is another police officer, Paolo Bianchi, who is a good friend to Stephen and to my family. You may not meet him while you're with us, but I don't want you to panic if he shows up or calls, or if his name is mentioned in conversation. You can trust him."

Julio and Rafi exchanged a look. "Can we hear him say that?" Rafi asked.

"Of course." I speed-dialed Paolo and put him on speaker. I outlined our plan and asked if it would create any conflicts for him.

"Not at all," Paolo answered, speaking formally. "The Orchard View Police Department is not working any current cases with Mr. Maldonado. I understand Mountain View may be interested in him as a witness, but as far as I'm concerned, he's committed no crime.

"Rafi, are you there?" he added.

"Hello, Officer Bianchi. This is Rafi."

"Okay, buddy. Look, I get that you're scared. That was a terrible night for all of you. Are you worried that the guys who killed Mr. Xiang will come after you?"

Rafi blushed and looked around the room before lowering his voice and whispering, "Yeah, I am."

"Okay, that's cool. You're right to be scared. They're nasty guys. But you'll be safe at Maggie's and as soon as Nell has set things up with the judge, you'll head straight to the courthouse. That place is super secure, with guards and metal detectors everywhere you look and some places you wouldn't think to look. And it's not like anyone wants to arrest you anyway. The detective from Mountain View just wants to interview you. Stephen would like you to talk to them too, so you can get him out of jail. That's always been the play, right?"

Rafi relaxed and spoke in a normal voice. "Yes, that's right."

"Okay then, any other questions?"

Rafi shook his head as though Paolo could see him through the phone.

Julio smiled and said, "Thanks, officer. This is Rafi's uncle Julio Maldonado. I think we have everything we need."

I took my phone off speaker. "We'll let you go, Paolo. Thanks. You handled that just like Jason would have."

Paolo was silent at first and when he finally answered, the confident young officer I'd heard reassure Rafi moments before was gone. I'd flustered him with my compliment. "Ah. Hm. Thanks, Maggie. See ya later, okay?"

I ended the call and Nell cleared her throat. "If there are no more questions, let's get back to work. Maggie, can you check the clothes Rafi brought and make sure they're appropriate for court?"

Rafi looked a little insulted, so I jumped in. "That's code for 'Get out of here, you can't help us with the documentation.' Come on upstairs. We'll take Munchkin with us. I need to make sure my own clothes are pressed and ready."

While I waited for Rafi to get up from the table and convince Munchkin to wake up from a deep snooze, Gabriela rummaged in her bag and pulled out a file folder with the papers and photos she'd collected documenting Rafi's birth and childhood in Mountain View.

"Thanks for bringing those; that's perfect," Nell said, taking the folder. "I want to go through it all in order. That way, I won't forget anything and we'll have it all in the same sequence the court will request them. We want to make it easy for the judge to give us the paperwork Rafi needs. And difficult to find a reason to delay or send us away."

Chapter 17

Pantry storage.

I tackle pantry storage in the fall when there are food
donation boxes in the library, gym, schools, and grocery
stores.

1) Toss healthy food that tastes terrible. If no one eats it,
it doesn't matter that it's healthy; it's just gathering dust
(or worse, critters you don't want in your cupboards).

2) Toss or donate everything your family once liked but
stopped eating as soon as you bought it in bulk.

3) Donate duplicates you don't need.

*From the Notebook of Maggie McDonald,
Simplicity Itself Organizing Services*

Thursday, February 23, Morning

"You left Sacramento in a bit of a rush," I told Rafi as we left the
room. "I've got two boys of my own and between them we
can probably outfit you with whatever you need."

"Do you really think she'll be able to get Stephen out of jail?"
Rafi asked. His face was furrowed with worry and he had deep circles under his eyes as though he'd had very little sleep for weeks.

"It was Stephen's choice to avoid answering the police officers' questions," I reminded Rafi. "Don't feel guilty. There was nothing you could have done to prevent it."

"I *do* feel guilty. If I'd stayed . . ."

"We can only look forward, Rafi. Trying to change the past is a waste of time. According to Nell and another lawyer we've been working with, Forrest Doucett, Stephen will likely be released tomorrow. You'll meet with the judge and get the court order. Then you'll go to the county clerk recorder's office to get your actual birth certificate. After that, we'll focus on Stephen, and Forrest has a team working on scheduling the interviews, meetings, and whatever else is needed to set Stephen free. Have you thought about what you're going to tell the police?"

"The truth, I guess. Why?"

"I've done some snooping around the other businesses near the Golden Dragon while I was waiting to get in touch with you. All the shop owners seemed to like Mr. Xiang, but I got the sense that they were tense and afraid of something or someone they didn't want to tell me about. They were definitely keeping something from me. Do you know why those men attacked you and Stephen, or who they were?"

"I can describe them pretty well, I think," Rafi said. "That night wasn't the first time they'd come to the restaurant. Those jerks were after money, like before, but they were angry that last time. They said things like they were going to make Mr. X pay, one way or another."

"Was there any pattern to the time of day or day of the week that you'd see them?"

"Not really, except that I saw them only on the nights that I was working late and most of the other staff had gone home. They'd meet with Mr. X and some other people I didn't recognize in one of the small private dining rooms. Mr. X took them food and drinks but he wanted me to stay away from them."

"Was he afraid of them?"

"I think so. At least, he treated them differently from any of the other customers."

"How so?"

"He liked his job and his customers. He had regulars that he'd tell me about. There was one couple that was finally getting married after having dinner at the restaurant every Tuesday evening for two years.

He gave them a bottle of really good champagne. And there were other people he'd known since they were babies coming to dinner with their parents. Now they're bringing their own children. He loved that and had their pictures on a wall in the kitchen. There really aren't that many restaurants successful enough to stay in business for long, but the Golden Dragon is one of them."

I thought Rafi had finished, but he went on. "There was a man who picked up the same take-out order every Sunday at 5:30 p.m. so his wife wouldn't have to cook dinner. Every Sunday. Mr. X loved that, and would toss in extra fortune cookies and coupons. But the bad guys? He never talked about them and seldom smiled when they came in. I could tell he didn't enjoy serving them the way he did the other customers. Most people, even if it was their first time in the restaurant, he'd treat 'em as if he'd known 'em for years. It was his way of saying he hoped they'd come back."

"Do you know why he didn't like the bad guys?"

Rafi paused, sighed, and pushed his hair off his forehead. "Mostly, I just did my job. I cleaned up and got things ready for the next day. Vacuumed, wiped down the chairs and tables, put new tablecloths on and bagged up the old ones to go to the laundry. I swept in front of the restaurant and in the back. That kind of thing. I had a lot to do and didn't pay too much attention to anything else. Sometimes Mr. Xiang would get done early and tell me stories while he helped me finish up."

"But if you had to guess?" I pressed Rafi a little harder than I'd originally planned, believing that he knew more than he thought he did.

"I think they were forcing Mr. X to do something he didn't want to do. Maybe something illegal. I know he'd want to put a stop to that sort of thing. That's the kind of guy he was." Rafi swallowed hard and cleared his throat. " 'It ends with me,' I heard him tell them once."

"That fits what I heard from some of the shop owners."

"Maybe the store people knew what was going on with Mr. X and were afraid they'd get pulled into it," Rafi said. "I saw the bigger of the two guys coming out of the back of one of the stores one night last week. Er, not last week. I mean . . . the week before Mr. X got shot."

"Do you know which store?"

Rafi shook his head. "They all look the same from the alley. And they all have old signs that don't match up with the stores that are there now. It wasn't the Pet Wash on the corner though. It was maybe the second, third, or fourth."

That meant the flower shop, the quilt store, or the yarn shop, I thought. But I still wasn't sure what it could mean. Had Rafi seen the thug coming away from helping to plan a crime or committing one? Was one of the shop owners the mastermind behind all the violence, or were they all victims? Was the landlord involved? And who was he? I thought back. They'd all mentioned the landlord, but I'd never met him. Could he be one of the crooks, or the ringleader, hiding in plain sight?

"Did you ever see anyone vandalizing the stores?" I asked Rafi.

"No, I heard about it though. Mr. X had his front window broken. It happened before I started working there."

I knew that Mr. Xiang had been reluctant to share any of his problems with the police, but I wondered if he'd called the landlord about installing a security system or replacing the front window. And that thought brought me to another question. Why was there no video surveillance anywhere on that block? Did the landlord or the store owners have a special need for privacy, or was the lack of security another way to pinch pennies and maximize the skimpy profit margins inherent to running a small local business? I wish I'd thought to ask that question when I was talking to the store owners. Were there surveillance cameras I hadn't noticed? If there were, surely the police would have picked up the video recordings following any of the break-ins that were reported.

Or had any of them been reported? Eileen, Liz, and Ed had all told me they'd phoned the police, but I wondered if they really had. I was beginning to question everyone's honesty, but certainly no one from the police department had arrived the morning I'd helped Liz clean up, even though she'd said she'd called the station to report the problem. I'd been in her shop for quite a while, and hadn't seen any officers or even a patrol car.

I'd started to feel as though I was getting close to solving the puzzle, but now I felt I was further away than ever.

And then I remembered the health inspector, another person who had been mentioned frequently but whom I'd never met.

Rafi had reported to Stephen that he'd heard the thugs threatening Mr. Xiang. With the tight profit margins most restaurants were experiencing in the slowly recovering economy, Mr. Xiang would likely be bankrupted by blackmail demands. Paying the bad guys off would eat into his profits, but so would ever-expanding bills for repairs if they made good on their threats to plague the restaurant with unexpected "accidents." But who was the inspector? A corrupt public official or someone pretending to be a county employee? I had no way of knowing. Not yet, anyway.

Nell called from downstairs, "Rafi, can you come down as soon as you've finished? I want to type up a statement for you to give to the police."

"Go ahead," I told him. "I'll get some clothes together and you can try them on later."

Rafi hesitated. "Can you come back down with me? She scares me a little."

I laughed, but started down the stairs. "I know what you mean, but she's super smart and I think she's harmless. Hopefully, she'll scare the court into acting quickly on your behalf."

Nell's new questions were about Rafi's dad, Rafael Senior. "I don't want to upset you," Nell said. "But we can try to locate him for you. If he has a reasonable job, he could be liable for back child support. And if, as your grandmother fears, he hasn't been in touch because he's deceased, we can obtain a death certificate or have him declared dead so that you and your sisters are eligible for Social Security benefits and veterans benefits if he was honorably discharged."

"I don't know where I would find those documents," Rafi said slowly, looking uncomfortable talking about the possibility that his father had abandoned his family or was deceased. "Can I think about it?"

"Of course," said Nell. "When you're ready, let us know and we can file all the forms for you."

Just then, my phone rang. I glanced at the screen. It was Jason.

I gulped, squared my shoulders, and walked into the kitchen so I wouldn't disturb the legal proceedings.

Jason didn't know anything about what had happened to Stephen or Munchkin. All he knew was what I'd last told him—that everyone was fine. I cleared my throat, leaned against the kitchen counter, and answered the call.

"Maggie, I'm so glad I caught you. What's going on up there? I can't get a text through to Stephen and haven't spoken to him in days.

He hasn't answered my e-mails. I know that communications have been sketchy, but e-mails should be getting through."

I paused before responding, delaying the inevitable.

"Maggie, you're scaring me. You texted that everything and everyone was fine. What aren't you saying?"

"I'm sorry, Jason. You're right. There's more to the story. How much time do you have?"

"As much as it takes. No more stalling. What's happened?" Jason, normally the coolest man in a crisis, couldn't prevent the hint of panic I heard in his voice. I thought for a moment about how to ease him into the news I'd been keeping from him, but there was no gentle way.

"Stephen's in jail. We hope he'll be released tomorrow."

"Did you say *jail*? How long? What's happened? Is he okay? He can't be cooped up. You know that. I'll make some calls. Pull some strings."

"Jason—"

"I can't believe you kept this from me. Did Paolo know? Why didn't he say something? This is *Stephen* we're talking about. I thought we were friends."

"It's a very long story and it's probably best if you hear it directly from Stephen. He asked us explicitly not to tell you. Not until he was released. He didn't want to disrupt your trip."

"But what happened to him? And what happened to Munchkin? You said you took him to the vet. If Munchkin was hurt, that means . . . Oh, Maggie, how bad is it? How badly is Stephen injured?"

"I don't blame you for being angry. I've been uncomfortable with this whole thing myself. But Stephen's my friend, and he asked me to trust him. We've been working as hard as we can to get him out, I promise." My heart hurt in sympathy with the tumult of emotions Jason must be feeling. Hurt because Stephen had turned to me for help instead of to Jason. Frustration and confusion because Jason was the one person who could have pressed to have Stephen's arrest delayed until more witnesses had been questioned and more of the facts were established. And that could have meant that Stephen wouldn't have spent a single day in jail. Jason was the one person, other than Stephen and Munchkin, who knew how tormented by PTSD Stephen was, and I knew he must be aching in sympathy for his husband's pain.

"Do you really have time to talk? I can give you a little of the background . . ."

"Never mind. I'm coming straight home. I'll text you with the details as soon as I have them."

"I'll send you an e-mail with the background. And updates on our progress. There's a good explanation, Jason."

He laughed, but I could tell he found nothing about the situation at all funny. "There better be." He paused. "Okay, I changed my mind. Is there a short version of the story? If I don't get some solid facts, I'll go nuts. My brain is already creating a horror story. Stephen in jail. I don't want to imagine it."

"We're taking care of that. I've got a lawyer here at the house writing up the paperwork. We'll go to the DA. Stephen's been charged with murder, but we have a witness who was there. He knows that Stephen tried to save the man who was killed. The forensic evidence will back up his statement. Stephen's release will be a formality—"

"Murder? Not Stephen. Never." Jason's voice broke. "And the DA? There's no way they're going to admit they made a mistake. No way."

"Forrest Doucett says there won't be a trial. The DA will submit a motion for *nolle prosequi* and have the case dismissed. . . . Stephen's record will show the arrest, but also the dismissal. If you want to pursue it further, you could ask Forrest to file a motion requesting that Stephen be declared factually innocent. That's a little more complicated and probably unnecessary, but Forrest can explain all that."

"Who is this Forrest person?"

"Max's roommate from college. He helped us earlier—"

"I remember now. He's sure the DA won't throw up roadblocks?"

"I asked the same question, but Forrest says everyone in the justice system likes it when situations like this happen. I mean, they don't like prosecuting innocent people, but it happens so seldom that they won't waste any time telling everyone about it. And the judge? In a case like this, most of them will drop whatever they are doing to sign the release order."

"So . . . what happens now?"

"We continue working here, and you get on a plane as soon as you can. I'll keep you updated while you're in flight. I'll get someone to meet you at the airport."

"I still don't understand what happened, why he had to go to jail, and why he trusted you but not me." I heard the hurt in his voice.

"It's best you get all that from Stephen. But the short version is that he was in jail to protect someone else. He knew you'd move heaven and earth to get him released if you knew, and he couldn't let that happen. Whether he was right, wrong, or making bad decisions in a bad situation is something you'll have to decide for yourself when you get all the facts—from Stephen, not from me."

"You'll let me know if anything changes?"

"Absolutely. If you can get Wi-Fi on the plane, do that. I will bury you in updates."

I ended the call and hid my face in my hands, exhausted. I didn't know if Jason would ever trust or forgive me, but I couldn't worry about that now. The only thing that was important was helping Nell and Forrest sort out all the legal matters that stood between Rafi and Stephen and the freedom they deserved.

Nell entered the kitchen through the pantry. "I heard the end of that call," she said. "Jason sounds like one extremely annoyed Marine Corps officer," she said. "I take it he's the husband?"

I nodded. "He's in Texas helping out with the storm damage and flooding. Stephen asked us to keep him out of the loop. He's not happy. He'll be here later today or tomorrow."

"All the more reason for us to finish our job."

I agreed. Admitting I'd misled Jason was hard enough over the phone. The best way to deflect his anger and hurt was to succeed in our mission to free Stephen as soon as possible so that Stephen could explain the situation to Jason himself.

"Maggie, if it's any comfort, I want to tell you how important your contribution was. I had all the legal details hammered out, but I couldn't do a thing until we found Rafi. And with Stephen in jail refusing to talk to anyone, I had no hope of finding him. I can't believe the key to locating him was essentially stalking a homeless woman none of us had met."

"I didn't see that one coming, either." I could only hope that finding Annie had marked the end of any surprises. I wasn't sure we could take any more.

Chapter 18

Let there be light. No one wants to store things in the dark. No one can find things they can't see. For example, when we first moved to Orchard View, I always left my clean socks in the laundry basket. When I stopped to ask myself why, I realized the lighting over my dresser was so limited that I couldn't tell black from brown or navy. When I added a lamp, I was able to put the socks away and select them with ease.

From the Notebook of Maggie McDonald,
Simplicity Itself Organizing Services

Thursday, February 23, Late evening

By the time Nell pronounced the paperwork complete, we were all exhausted, mentally and physically. The dining room looked like a bomb had hit it, with empty plates, glasses, and cups intermingled with crumpled papers and edited drafts of the final legal documents.

I handed Rafi a garbage bag and gave Julio a paper grocery sack to gather up the recycling. I loaded the dishes onto a tray and Gabriela wiped down the table.

"What do you think you'll do with your new birth certificate first, Rafi?" Nell asked.

Julio cleared his throat. Rafi laughed. "I've already promised my uncle that I will take driving lessons. But I also want to get a better-paying job so I can help the family out more."

"I have some ideas about that," said Gabriela. "We've asked so much of you in the last few years. You need to concentrate on school and I'd like you to go to college. Julio and I were talking last night. If I were to sell my house, I could buy another small one near Julio, where it is not so expensive to live. We would have more money and it would be nice to live near family again. There's time to decide. You will want to finish up this school year before we go anywhere else."

"I think there's more we can do to improve your situation," Nell said. "Let's look into getting government benefits for all of your grandchildren. They qualify and it would take some of the financial pressure off your family. We can talk about it more when you're not quite so exhausted." Nell yawned, launching a contagion that soon had everyone thinking of bed.

"Thanks again, Maggie," Julio said. "I'm going to take Gabriela home. She wants to pick up the girls from Alejandra's house and bring them to court tomorrow. I don't want them to be alone. I know there's no question of those thugs coming back, but it wouldn't feel right to leave my sister unprotected. Do you think Stephen would mind if I held on to his car?"

"Not at all. Please drive carefully. Are you sure you both don't want to stay? It's been such a long day for everyone."

"Gabriela will sleep better in her own bed, knowing that the girls are safe."

After we'd walked them to the car and seen them off, Nell and I returned to the living room to find Rafi sound asleep on the couch with Munchkin snoring at his feet and Holmes settled on his chest. They all looked so comfortable we decided to leave them undisturbed.

I showed Nell to David's room, where I'd cleaned up, changed the sheets, and laid out fresh towels, a toothbrush, and other essential toiletry items. I stumbled to bed myself with Watson for company. I missed Belle, the boys, and Max, not necessarily in that order, and hoped they were having a great time in the mountains. I pulled out my phone to check for messages, but fell asleep before I could enter the code to unlock it.

I heard Nell up early, making phone calls, and dragged myself out of bed, trying to be a good hostess. It was difficult. She'd already fed the animals, started the coffee, mixed up a jug of orange juice from some concentrate I had in the freezer, and taken all the available fruit to make a gorgeous salad.

I sniffed the air, smelling cinnamon and butter. "Did you hire elves to cater breakfast, Nell, or have you been up all night?"

Nell was wearing a bathrobe that my mother had given David, but which he never wore. She'd rolled back the sleeves, pinned up her hair, and wore thick socks on her feet. She was ironing and did indeed have an elfin look to her face as she struggled to press the collar of her suit jacket. She scrunched up her nose and pressed hard on the iron. She must have been satisfied with the result, because she nodded, shook out the jacket, inserted a hanger into the sleeves, and hung it on the back of the kitchen door.

"Morning, Maggie," she said. "I was up early and made a French toast casserole. It should be finished in a few minutes. I hope you don't mind that I took over your kitchen. Forrest and I had a few legal details to go over before he left San Francisco. After we got them all sorted out, I was too wired to go back to bed."

"You can get up early and take over my kitchen any time you want. Coffee?" I held up the pot and she nodded enthusiastically, causing her pinned-up hair to tumble around her shoulders. She looked about twelve years old, but I was convinced Forrest had found us the best possible lawyer for the job.

Rafi stumbled in from the living room at the same moment the timer went off for the French toast. While Nell tested her creation and transferred it to a plate, I pulled out a chair for Rafi, poured a glass of orange juice, and invited him to help himself to the fruit.

"Thank you," he said.

"Don't thank me. Your lawyer apparently provides an array of essential services. I just woke up myself. This is all her doing."

Nell proclaimed herself too wired to eat and left to take a shower and get dressed for court. "Rafi," she said, "help yourself to the iron if you've got any clothes that became rumpled in transit. You want to be sharply dressed to show respect to the law, the court, and the judge. No jeans. Dress shoes. A tie." She turned to me. "You said you could outfit him with any clothes he needs? A jacket, I think, rather than a suit. This is still California, and he's still a teenager. We want the judge impressed, but not fainting from shock."

She dashed up the stairs and was gone before Rafi turned to me. "A tie? Dress shoes? Seriously?"

"Oh, I think she was pretty serious. Leave all this and come with me. I'd forgotten we were supposed to lay out your clothes yesterday, but don't tell Nell."

Rafi pulled a wrinkled pair of khakis and a button-down shirt from his bulging backpack and we headed upstairs to Brian's room. Most of Brian's dress clothes were uniforms for his various concert bands, including a tuxedo that he was outgrowing, a black suit, and a navy blue jacket he wore for jazz band. I pulled that out of the closet and checked it carefully before handing it to Rafi.

"No stains. No dreadful smells. I think we're good. Want to try it on?"

Rafi dropped his khakis and shirt on the floor and then pulled the jacket on over his T-shirt. The sleeves were a little long, but it was a good emergency fit.

I reached down to pick up the clothes he'd brought with him. He frowned. "I'm sorry. They look pretty bad, don't they?"

I looked at my watch. "Nell's on a tight schedule. Why don't you head into the shower? I'll take these downstairs and iron them for you. They'll be fine. I'll have them back up here before you're ready to get dressed. I'll hang them from the hook on the back of the bedroom door so your new friend Holmes doesn't take a nap on them before you've had a chance to wear them. There is nothing as bad for the look of a navy blue jacket as the hair of a marmalade cat."

Rafi's face reflected his delight over getting out of the ironing chore mixed with fear of what his powerhouse lawyer might do if she found out he'd disobeyed her instructions and let me press his clothes for him. It was a look I had no trouble reading.

I winked. "If you don't tell her, I won't."

"Great," he said, and bounded toward the shower at the end of the hall.

"Everything should be in there somewhere, right where Brian and David left them. Feel free to rummage around until you find what you need."

We were due at court at 9:00 a.m., which put us in the thick of the morning traffic, but I dropped Nell and Rafi off with moments to spare. Julio, Rafi's sisters, and Gabriela waited for us on the courthouse steps.

Not having a role in the proceedings, I found parking, went through security, and asked for directions to the judge's chambers. His clerk pointed to a bench where I could wait. I could hear Nell's muffled voice from the other side of the closed door, but couldn't make out the words or even whether things were going well. After what seemed like hours but was only twenty minutes, I heard laughter and congratulatory sounds. The door opened to reveal a beaming Rafi, who was already loosening his tie and shrugging off the jacket. Before I could give him a hug or high-five, he handed me the jacket, pulled his sneakers out of his backpack, and exchanged them for Brian's dress shoes.

"Ah," he said, looking up, smiling, and handing me the shoes. "That's *much* better."

I laughed and finally had the sense that I was seeing the genuine Rafi. A great kid, but a real kid. The teenager that Stephen had gone to jail for. I liked him.

"How'd it go?" I asked, scanning the room and trying to read the faces of Rafi's family.

"Great," said Nell. "The judge was impressed with both Rafi and his paperwork. He signed the papers right away."

"He was cool," Rafi said. "He reminded me that Abe Lincoln, George Washington, and scores of other great Americans were born at home and no one doubted their citizenship."

Nell looked at her watch. "He also didn't want to let us leave until he was convinced all the other procedures would go smoothly. If we hurry we can get to the county clerk recorder's office before it opens. The judge even waived the fee for an expedited birth certificate."

I laughed with joy and handed a tissue to Julio, who was crying. The little girls, Isabella and Sofía, hung back behind their grandmother.

"And what about the DA?" I asked.

"The judge called him, too," Nell said. "They made arrangements for Rafi to meet with the police detective and the DA in Mountain View after school one day next week."

"If Rafi's not being interviewed until next week, that means . . ." I said, disappointed that Stephen would spend another weekend in jail.

I didn't want to put a damper on the festivities, though, so I looked up and tried to smile.

Nell shook her head. "Stephen's release was out of our hands and the judge's, I'm afraid. It's not within his sphere of influence. He did, however, recommend a lawyer to represent Rafi's interests when he meets with the police."

Rafi looked at me, and nodded toward the jacket and dress shoes I held in my arms. "I'm sorry. I can carry those. I didn't mean to foist them off on you. Thank Brian for me too."

Julio and Gabriela and the girls pressed forward to hug Rafi. But Nell gave them only a moment. "We need to go to the clerk recorder's office and then Forrest wants to meet us on the steps of the Superior Court building. He's been talking to another judge and the DA about Stephen's case. I'm giving him a lift back to San Francisco. You all don't mind going over there, do you? He asked to meet Rafi."

I nodded. "I'm happy to do that. I want to thank Forrest in person for all that he's done."

For reasons known only to San Jose city planners, the old county court buildings were located downtown while other courts and county offices were located a mile north on Hedding Street. Out of respect for Gabriela's age and the fact that she was still recovering from a nasty cold, we took our cars and were able to find parking quickly since the clerk recorder's office wasn't open to the general public until 10:00 a.m.

We followed Nell into the building like a line of ducklings following their mother and were ushered with great formality through a side door even though the main office was not yet open. The clerk had the paperwork filled out as much as possible when we arrived, and we were in and out in less than ten minutes. The young women staffing the office charmed Rafi and embarrassed him by handing him his birth certificate along with a Mylar balloon saying IT'S A BOY! I think Rafi would have stashed it in the nearest trash bin, but his sisters were delighted and insisted on carrying it for him.

Nell texted Forrest to tell him we were on our way. She instructed me to pull up right in front of the courthouse, in an area used solely for dignitaries since September 11 had put heightened security measures in place. Forrest waited for us at the curb.

I turned off the car and jumped out, eager to stretch and to offer Forrest my thanks. I was certain that stopping or parking here wasn't truly allowed, but right at this moment, Homeland Security rules weren't my primary concern.

"When I'm arrested for murder, I want you to represent me," I gushed to Forrest, hugging him and crushing his perfectly tailored suit. I stepped back, looking up at his face. "I mean . . . Oh, that didn't come out right, but thank you."

"It's been a long week for all of us," he said. "But especially for . . ." He turned slightly and waved to someone we couldn't see inside the building. Moments later, the door opened, and Stephen walked out with his arm in a sling and a bandage on his forehead. He looked thin, exhausted, and pale, but free.

"Everyone, please give me a moment," I said. I ran forward, up the wide stairs, took Stephen's hand, and hugged him with tears running down my face. Neither one of us spoke until Stephen whispered, "Thank you, Maggie. For everything."

I wiped my face and looked up. "I was happy to do it, Stephen. But please don't ask me to keep secrets from Jason again. He's very angry with me for not keeping him up to date. He wanted to be here for you."

"You told him? But I wanted to do that." Stephen wrinkled his brow and his face took on the sorrowful expression I'd seen so often on Munchkin over the last week.

"It's a long story," I told him. "And all those people want to thank you and congratulate you." I indicated Rafi and his family waiting on the sidewalk below.

We were saved from any more uncomfortable emotional exchanges by the arrival of Munchkin himself. Stephen was nearly knocked to the ground by the exuberant dog who leaped to lick his face and sniff all of him, all at once.

As if by magic, Jason caught Stephen before he fell. Confused, I looked to the street and saw Paolo's car, with a ski rack attached to the roof, parallel parking behind mine. Paolo must have picked Jason up at the airport. Jason and I had texted back and forth about his flights the day before, and I'd understood he wasn't due in until much later in the day.

I was confused, until I saw Nell exchange a smile and wink with Forrest. They both beamed. They must have arranged for Jason to get on an earlier flight, orchestrating a dramatic scene worthy of the great epic film directors.

Jason hugged and kissed Stephen, then aimed a friendly punch at his good arm.

"I'm sorry," Stephen said.

"And you should be. But you can grovel and explain later. I had time to think and cool my temper on the plane. I decided that the bottom line is that I love you and trust you. If you didn't tell me any of this, you must have had an unshakable conviction that it was the right thing to do. You were wrong, of course, but I forgive you. It was a terrible, cruel mistake, but I forgive you."

Jason smoothed the front of the uniform he'd traveled in and waved everyone else forward. "We're going straight to Stephen's favorite restaurant to celebrate." Munchkin barked and glued himself to Stephen's side, licking his knee.

Jason looked down at the dog. "It has an outdoor patio and a dog menu."

He turned to the rest of us. "Lunch is on me, and we'll use the people menu. I'm not sure what all has gone on here in the few days I've been gone, but I'm sure it's worth celebrating. You can start to fill me in over the meal, but it sounds like it will take weeks or months or years to tell it all."

I could only agree. But we'd sort it out eventually. That's what friends do.

"I'm really sorry, everyone," Stephen said, hugging Rafi. "But thank you from the bottom of my heart for getting me out of that place. It was a once-in-a-lifetime experience. I wouldn't mind if I never go anywhere near this courthouse again."

"That should be easy," I said. "Outside of jury duty, of course. What are the chances that you and I would ever get involved in another murder?"

We trooped off to lunch, laughing as we all tried to update Stephen and Jason about the steps leading to this moment. Lunch was a loud confusion of toasts, thanks, and interruptions. Munchkin licked Stephen repeatedly as if he needed reassurance that they'd finally been reunited.

"How did Munchkin get here?" I asked.

Paolo explained that Jason had insisted he stop at the house for Munchkin before driving to the airport.

"But how did you get in?" I asked.

"I have a few recommendations to improve your security," Paolo said, blushing. "But that's for another time. I need to get back to work." He said his goodbyes and was soon followed by Gabriela, Julio, Rafi, and the girls. Julio planned to stay a few days until Gabriela had completely recovered from her cold. Then he'd take the train back to Sacramento. Later we learned that Julio had paid the entire lunch bill as he left, leaving a note for me and Stephen saying that he would always be in our debt.

The rest of us needed to get moving, too, but I had one last question for Forrest.

"What about the thugs who beat up Stephen and Rafi and killed Mr. Xiang? They hired some stupid kids to threaten my son at his school. Are we safe now?"

Forrest wiped his mouth with a napkin and nodded. "Absolutely. The Orchard View Police picked up the kids who threatened David. They started talking right away in exchange for suspended sentences and community service. They described the men who'd hired them and Mountain View Police brought them in yesterday. They aren't talking, but when the cops found them, the smaller one still had all of Stephen's credit cards and, I kid you not, a stack of discount cards from the restaurant with traces of Mr. Xiang's blood on them. The bigger crook wasn't much smarter. He'd stashed a gun in his refrigerator that matched the caliber of the bullet that shot Mr. Xiang. When the ballistics specialists are finished with it, they expect it will prove to be the gun used at the Golden Dragon."

"What about the puppet master?" I asked. "We need to get the guy who's pulling the strings." No one seemed to have any idea what I was talking about, so I laid it out for them: the pattern of violence, the shop owners' fear, and the strange comings and goings in the alley.

"What do you think was going on?" Jason asked.

"I'm not sure," I said. "Other than the illegal gambling ring. I'm certain about that part. But it could be almost anything. The store owners are terrified and they aren't the sort of people who are easily cowed. You have to be brave to run a small business, don't you? It could be drug distribution, money laundering, or a plot to clear out the block for redevelopment." I told Jason about the damage to each of the stores, the story Liz had told me about Eileen's ongoing gambling, and the persistence of the rumor about there being gold hidden in Mr. Xiang's restaurant.

Jason reached for his phone and excused himself from the table to make a call.

"I can't tell you much because it's an ongoing investigation," he said when he returned. "But, Maggie, your hunch was right. Mountain View Police have been watching the downtown businesses for months but somehow they'd missed the mess that was made of Ed Bloom's shop. There was no police report," Jason continued.

"I was involved in another investigation in Orchard View with a very similar pattern of activity that centered around the flower shop managed by Ed's brother. We suspected they were moving either drugs or money through the stores, distributing the stuff at night to crooks dressed up like homeless people, figuring no one pays attention to the homeless. If we see them, we look away. It was a perfect disguise." Jason took a sip of his water, wiped his mouth with his napkin, and continued.

"We had no idea how they were bringing the drugs into the shop. I called Mountain View PD just now to follow up on your story about the destruction of all the flowerpots and figurines. Claiming theft or destruction of more inventory than you actually have is a common form of fraud, but the insurance company would require a police report. That tells us something else was going on. MVPD had a report of a disturbance in the alley that night, but found it quiet when their patrol car showed up. None of the shop owners seemed to know anything about it."

He took a sip of water and paused. The rest of us waited impatiently for him to continue. "We'll go back to interview the businesses that surround both of Ed Bloom's stores. I'm guessing we'll be able to prove that at least some of his deliveries and all those gnomes and spaceships and other kitschy pots aren't exactly what they seem." He leaned forward. "My gut tells me that it may have been Mr. Xiang who destroyed Bloom's inventory in an effort to put a stop to his drug trade. The attack could have been retribution or an attempt to recoup their losses if Mr. Xiang confiscated any of the drugs he found."

I was skeptical. "That's an awful lot of dangling threads you've knitted up there, Jason. It sounds more like a television plot than anything you'll be able to prove."

Forrest laughed. "You'd be surprised, Maggie. Crooks watch television too. Many of the cases that the DA prosecutes and that I defend end up looking like badly written screenplays performed by actors who've forgotten their lines. The crimes are clichés and the words the bad guys use to describe them are trite. If we wrote them down word for word, no one would believe they were real."

Jason nodded enthusiastically. "The trick is pulling together enough of the story to make the suspects believe you've connected all the dots. Once you bring them in and do that, they get nervous. They become eager to tell their stories to end the suspense or to brag about their crimes. It doesn't make sense, but I guess they don't watch the parts of the programs where crooks are warned to get lawyers. I don't think we'll have any problem wrapping this up."

He looked at his watch. "Thanks to you, Maggie, Mountain View and Orchard View Police are now requesting warrants to conduct a coordinated search of both flower shops, along with the financial records, computers, and phones." He smiled at me as what he was saying slowly sunk in. "And the gold? It's street slang for high-quality drugs. I've heard it used for cocaine, crack, marijuana, and heroin, so there's no telling what Ed Bloom was up to. But I'll give you odds it was something nasty that we don't want in Orchard View. Because of you, we'll shut that down."

I smiled. I'd helped with that. And helped the Mountain View Police solve the murder of poor Mr. Xiang.

No wonder I was so exhausted.

Chapter 19

Finishing a project doesn't mean we're done. I schedule
a follow-up visit with clients to review how their new
system is working for them. Some customers find that
while the systems make life much easier, maintaining
them requires more time, energy, or skill than they are
able to commit. Often they're frustrated. If finances and
temperament allow, I suggest they hire a housekeeper or
cleaners. In other cases, we'll schedule monthly or quar-
terly "tune-ups," during which I'll work with them to
help maintain long-term order in their home.

From the Notebook of Maggie McDonald,
Simplicity Itself Organizing Services

Saturday, February 24, Morning

With Max and the boys still skiing in Tahoe, and my other guests,
including Munchkin, back in their own homes, I slept in on
Saturday morning, sandwiched between Holmes and Watson. Lulled
to sleep by their purring, I was awakened as soon as they decided it
was time for breakfast. They told me so by batting at my eyelids until
I opened them.

We had a delightfully slow day, but by afternoon I was at loose
ends. I thought about going to the gym and got as far as putting my
bag in the car. Instead, I decided to pay Annie/Marjorie a visit, update her on all that had happened, and try to learn more about her history.

I saw her long before she saw me. I watched as she fed peanuts to the squirrels with the same kindness she'd demonstrated when she offered to distribute the food and other items I'd brought earlier in the week.

I'd stopped to buy two large coffees on my way to the park, and I offered her one. She took it from me with a little bow of thanks, but with a presence and dignity that suggested it was her due.

I asked Marjorie her last name, but providing it was too intimate a gesture for our short friendship. "Maybe I'll tell you next year," she said. "It's Czech and unpronounceable, although my family has lived in California for five generations."

We fed the squirrels in silence and drank our coffee, watching the shadows change as the sun sunk lower in the sky. As daylight moved on toward dusk, Marjorie told me her story.

First she smoothed her skirts, fluffing and straightening each layer, one by one. She flicked both braids behind her back, where the sun made them glint silver.

"I was a nurse in the navy," she said. "During Vietnam. So many of the homeless are here because of damage they sustained during that war and others, but that's not why I'm here." She tossed a peanut to a tiny squirrel that had approached slowly but stopped beyond the circle of braver animals.

"I had a master's degree and a doctorate. I worked in the VA hospital in orthopedics. I liked watching physicians squirm when I insisted they refer to me as *Doctor* Nurse Marjorie." She giggled then, like a little girl, and hid her smile behind the coffee cup.

"I lost my job because my hips couldn't take all the standing and I couldn't afford hip replacement surgery. My insurance would pay some, but not enough to cover the bills and the time off work. My time in Vietnam made it hard for me to develop close friendships, so I didn't have anyone I trusted to look after me while I recuperated."

She kept speaking, but took frequent sips of coffee between her sentences, cleared her throat, and looked away. "I was living in my RV to save money, but someone reported it as abandoned, so the police had it towed to an impound lot. With the parking fine, the towing fee, storage costs, and taxes, the towing company wanted one thousand dollars in cash to get it back. I didn't have the money. And every day I waited, trying to scrape up the fees, it cost more, because the storage charges went up. Everything I owned was inside it. Eventually, the towing company held an unclaimed vehicles auction and someone bought my RV for less than it would have cost me to get my own belongings back." She shook her head, but she recounted the story matter-of-factly, as if it had happened to someone else. She cast no blame and didn't ask for or want pity.

"And I've been here, ever since," she told me, without specifying how long that time had been. "I saw what happened the night Mr. Xiang was killed, when those thugs beat poor Rafi, Stephen, and Munchkin. It was horrible. They kept asking Mr. Xiang where he kept the gold."

She shuddered. I shifted on the hard bench, about to ask a question, but then I froze because I'd startled the squirrels and was afraid I'd spooked Marjorie. I wasn't sure why she'd decided to be so forthcoming, and I didn't want to do anything that would alter the circumstances.

"I had been working on getting signed up for new medical insurance and veterans benefits and retirement—things I worked hard for all my life. But I lost my paperwork, my records, my phone, and my computer when my RV was towed. I didn't have the money to request duplicate identification. Truth be told, I was in pain because of my hip and that made everything more difficult. I got depressed, and it all seemed like such an uphill battle."

"What about the library?" I asked.

She sighed. "The library computers time out after thirty minutes and the government web sites are painfully slow to load. Thirty minutes wasn't long enough to sort out anything. I gave up."

I cleared my throat, scaring off the squirrels for good. "May I give your name to the detective investigating Mr. Xiang's death? They have Rafi's testimony as well as Stephen Laird's, but your statement would make the case against them that much stronger."

Marjorie thought for a moment, and I was sure she would decline my request. But she surprised me. "Give me the detective's number. If I have a good day, I'll phone. There's a lady in the Y who lets some of us use her phone while she works out."

I scribbled the number on a scrap of paper and handed it to Marjorie. It disappeared into the folds of her skirts. I could see she was tired, so I took her empty cup from her and helped her get settled. "You bring that Munchkin back to see me," she said. "I miss him."

I agreed and was about to walk away when I turned back. "Marjorie, did you know Freddie?"

She sighed. "I told him that intersection wasn't safe."

"He tried to tell me something last week when I was stopped at his corner. It was something about Munchkin. I wondered if he saw anything the night Mr. Xiang was killed."

"Did you have Munchkin with you in the car?"

I nodded.

"Then he probably just wanted to say hello. Poor Freddie never said much to anyone, but he loved that dog and would whisper secrets to him whenever he could. He called him Munch. Just Munch."

"So he wasn't in the alley that night?"

"No. At least I didn't see him there. He never traveled far from that blasted intersection—the one that finally killed him. Even if he had been at the Golden Dragon that night, he wouldn't have been a helpful witness."

"How so?"

"'Munch' was about all anyone ever heard him say."

I wished her good night. As soon as I was out of earshot, I phoned Detective Smith at the Mountain View Police Department. I told her that a homeless woman named Annie or Marjorie would likely be calling her with an eyewitness account of what happened the night Mr. Xiang was killed, but that she had no reliable way to phone back. When she called, the detective would have to talk to her immediately, because she probably wouldn't have the courage or the ability to phone twice.

A few weeks later, the DA called to thank me for locking down the information that would put the thugs away. With the evidence that Rafi, Stephen, and Marjorie provided, he was confident their case would succeed in convicting a number of very bad people, including the Bloom brothers and the thugs who'd killed Mr. Xiang and hurt Rafi, Stephen, and Munchkin. Undercover cops were working to shut down the illegal gambling operation and bring those behind it to justice.

Ed Bloom, who turned out to own the entire block, had confessed to making life miserable for the other shop owners by causing problems with their heat, air conditioning, electricity, and plumbing and then dragging his feet when it came to repairs. A friend of his had posed as the landlord whenever Ed needed a real person to make an appearance. He'd also been behind the vandalism, hiring local kids to do his dirty work for him.

Local laws stipulated that leases couldn't be terminated for any reason other than lack of payment or destroying property. But Bloom was already working with a developer on a plan to level the block and build shops with high-density housing above them. An architectural model was displayed in his apartment over the store, which also contained expensive antiques, artwork, and high-end electronic devices that Ed Bloom could never have afforded based on the sales from his shop.

"We did get one thing wrong," the DA said, laughing. "We'd been keeping an eye on the owner of the comic book store, thinking he wasn't open enough hours to be earning any kind of a living selling only comic books. And the age of his customers was in the range we'd expect for people distributing illegal drugs. It turned out his only crime was falling in love with a woman who lived out of town. He's moved to Santa Cruz to be with her and opened a store there. He'd planned to run both stores, but he couldn't find anyone to manage the Mountain View shop, so he's closing it."

"I never had a chance to talk to him about the Golden Dragon issues, but I'm glad he's happy. I liked him."

But none of that information answered one annoying lingering question.

"Why on earth would Ed suggest I look for Annie, er . . . Marjorie? She provided the information that tidied up most of the loose ends in this case."

"It's hard to say. He may have been completely confident that he'd covered his tracks and got a thrill from appearing to help your investigation. The police in Mountain View tell me Annie seldom ventures more than half a mile from Cuesta Park. Bloom probably thought she knew nothing about what was going on in the business district, and he was creating a distraction by suggesting you speak to her. But Annie knows all the local homeless people. She listens, and she's smarter than he gave her credit for."

"Have you seen Annie?" I asked the DA. "I haven't seen her for days and I'm worried about her."

"We're looking after her," he said. "Helping her with her paperwork and finding veterans housing. Part of that is self-serving. She'll make a more reliable witness if she has a stable address. She's scheduled for hip surgery and in the meantime is getting physical therapy and anti-inflammatories so she's in less pain. Without the pain and worry, she's a fireball. She's been talking to a friend of mine on the Orchard View city council who has wanted to address some of the city's homeless issues. She wants to find a way to register them all to vote to give them a little more clout. They're working on plans to form a county task force to get homeless people the services they need."

He cleared his throat. "I'd like to tell you more, but it has to remain in the strictest confidence."

I'd had enough of keeping other people's secrets. "No, thanks," I said. "No more secrets. I only want to know things that I can announce on Facebook or shout to the media."

"Well, let's just say that the health inspector who was making it difficult for the shop owners to feed the homeless has taken early retirement. He was acquainted with Mr. Xiang's killers. We may or may not be looking at trying him for extortion." He coughed and continued.

"We may not be able to prove any wrongdoing on his part. But we're patient, and the Mountain View Police Department is working hard. Since the health inspector is a county position, we're looking at other communities within Santa Clara County to see if we can find a bigger pattern of crimes.

"Mountain View and Orchard View are also launching a joint effort to strengthen connections in the business districts so that shop owners and others like them will be able to act against similar pressures should they reoccur."

"That will help," I said. "Mr. Xiang didn't want to contact the police because he didn't trust them."

I was about to thank the DA and end the call when I remembered the rumors about the gold. "Do you have any idea why Mr. Xiang's attackers kept talking about gold?" I asked. "It was a rumor that wouldn't die, and it was all over town."

"Piecing together what we've learned from Ed Bloom, evidence in his store, and some things the homeless have reported, we think that it referred to a premium strain of heroin Bloom was smuggling inside his figurines and potting supplies. I think that Mr. Xiang discovered what Bloom was doing, destroyed the figurines and confiscated the heroin. We haven't found it anywhere, but one of the street people saw Mr. Xiang toss some garbage in a dumpster the same night as the burglary. It could have been garbage from the store, or the heroin, or both."

"So it was probably picked up and is now deeply buried in a land-fill?"

"We hope so."

"There was an incident outside the yarn shop," I said. "Someone flooded a dumpster . . ."

"We think that could have been a dual-purpose disaster—an effort to destroy any remaining evidence of the drugs and put pressure on the other store owners to close."

"Did any of your people get information from the café owner?" I hadn't had any luck getting her to talk to me, and hadn't been able to figure out whether she was busy, guilty, or both.

"We looked into her and she has no record whatsoever."

I was relieved to know there were shop owners in Mountain View that were neither part of a crime ring nor threatened by it.

"And the evidence against Bloom and the thugs," I said, "it's solid? You're confident of a conviction."

"As much as we can be. The thugs confessed, as you know, and thanks to you and Dr. Davidson, the UC Davis animal lab confirmed that Munchkin's fur was caked with blood belonging to the larger bad guy. We have his fingerprints on the knife that the Davis experts say matches Munchkin's wounds. He claims they were ordered to threaten Mr. Xiang and get him to return the heroin. If he didn't, they were told to kill him."

"By Mr. Bloom?"

"Yes. Bloom denies it, but money in the attacker's possession bore evidence of heroin and of potting soil from Bloom's shop. We're continuing to test some of the evidence from the shop and the murderer's apartment, but the connection is solid."

We wrapped up the call, and I leaned back in my chair, fully sat-isfied that Orchard View was back on an even keel. Annie was thriv-ing and contributing to the community and the people she loved and cared for. Freeing Stephen had worn me out and dragged me down. Every day that I worked to do as he'd asked, I was keeping secrets I didn't want to keep and uncovering a side of Orchard View I didn't want to see. But I couldn't un-see it, and I couldn't forget.

But while working to free Stephen I'd made new connections in the community with good people who were fighting an uphill battle to do the right thing. For a while, I'd lost sight of the good that was happening and could only focus on the cruelty of the people who'd injured my friends and kept the homeless and the shop owners under such a dreadful shadow.

The students who had worked for Mr. Xiang had held a beautiful service followed by a park clean-up day, and had established two scholarships in his honor at the high school. Jason, looking over the volunteers working on the park, had said he recognized several of them as once troubled kids who'd turned their lives around when they began working for Mr. Xiang. They were now on their way to becoming engineers, doctors, accountants, teachers, and other professionals who would have positive impacts on the community. Max and I had donated to the scholarship fund and to the homeless shelter to honor the lives of both Mr. Xiang and Freddie, whose last name I never was able to learn.

I was happy to live here and might add volunteering with the homeless agencies to my list of things to do, which included finally helping Jason and Stephen prepare for their remodel and delivering Mrs. Bostwick's long-awaited files.

As it so often does, good had won out and those doing the right thing had overcome those bent on doing evil.

If you enjoyed *Dead Storage*, be sure not to miss Mary Feliz's

SCHEDULED TO DEATH

Professional organizer Maggie McDonald has a knack for cleaning up other people's messes. So when the fiancée of her latest client turns up dead, it's up to her to sort through the untidy list of suspects and identify the real killer.

Maggie McDonald is hoping to raise the profile of her new Orchard View organizing business via her first high-profile client. Professor Lincoln Sinclair may be up for a Nobel Prize, but he's hopeless when it comes to organizing anything other than his thoughts. For an academic, he's also amassed more than his share of enemies. When Sinclair's fiancée is found dead on the floor of his home laboratory—electrocuted in a puddle of water—Maggie takes on the added task of finding the woman's murderer. To do so, she'll have to outmaneuver the suspicious, obnoxious police investigator she's nicknamed "Detective Awful" before a shadowy figure can check off the first item on their personal to-do list—*kill Maggie McDonald.*

Keep reading for a special look!

A Lyrical Underground e-book on sale now.

MARY FELIZ

SCHEDULED
TO DEATH

A MAGGIE McDONALD MYSTERY

Chapter 1

We don't use the word *hoarder* in my business. It holds
negative connotations, few of which are true of the
chronically disorganized.

From the Notebook of Maggie McDonald,
Simplicity Itself Organizing Services

Monday, November 3, 9:00 a.m.

I couldn't be sure where the line was between a mansion and a really
big house, but I knew that I was straddling it, standing on the front
porch of the gracious Victorian home of Stanford Professor Lincoln
"Linc" Sinclair. The future of my career here in Orchard View strad-
dled a similar line—the one between success and failure.

I rang the doorbell a second time and glanced at my best friend,
Tess Olmos. She was dressed in what I called her dominatrix outfit—
red and black designer business clothes and expensive black stilettos
with red soles. I wore jeans, sneakers, and a long-sleeved white T-shirt,
over which I wore a canvas fisherman's vest filled with the tools of my
trade. I'm a Certified Professional Organizer and my job today was to
finish helping the professor sort through three generations of furniture
and a lifetime's collection of "stuff" he was emotionally attached to.

The professor was a brilliant man on the short list for the Nobel
Prize in a field I didn't understand, but his brain wasn't programmed
for organization and never would be.

And that's where I came in. Organization is my superpower.

I glanced at my watch. It was 9:10 a.m. We had arrived promptly for our appointment at nine. Tess had arranged to use the house for her annual holiday showcase to thank her clients and promote her business, but she wanted to double-check our progress on clearing things out before she finalized her own schedule. All but one of the rooms was empty, but Tess had a sharp eye and might well spot something I'd missed. If she had questions about anything Linc and I had done, I wanted to be on hand to answer them immediately.

Participating in Tess's holiday event would give my fledgling business a huge boost. Endorsements from Tess Olmos and Linc Sinclair were likely to bring me as much—if not more—business than I could handle.

"We did say nine o'clock, didn't we?" I asked Tess. "I wonder if he overslept after that storm last night?" A rare electrical storm had coursed across the San Francisco Bay Area the previous evening, bringing buckets of much-needed rain. With it came winds that downed trees and power lines. Thunder shook my house to its foundation.

"What did the weather folks predict? *Isolated storm cells with a chance of lightning.* The morning news was showing footage of funnel clouds in Palo Alto. My dog whined all night." Tess bent to peek through one of the front windows. "Wow, you've really made a lot of progress in there," she said. "I can see clear through to the dining room."

I smiled as I stepped off the porch and onto the fieldstone path running across the grass and past the chrysanthemums and snapdragons that edged the front garden.

"Linc's been working hard," I said. "All that's left, beyond a few boxes, is his upstairs workroom with all that electronic equipment and research papers. I'm hoping to organize most of that today and take it to his freshly cleaned and cataloged storage unit. If it goes well, we'll tackle his office at Stanford."

I looked up and down the street. No professor.

"Where is he?" asked Tess, echoing the question I'd already asked myself.

"I'll take a look 'round back," I said. "He may be working in the garden or kitchen with his headphones on and can't hear the bell."

I followed the flagstone walk around to the side of the house and let out a yelp. My hand flew to my throat and my heart rate soared.

"Oh my! Sorry—I'm so sorry," I said to the woman blocking my way. I fought to regain my balance after my abrupt stop. "You startled me. Can I help you?"

"Humph!" said the woman, straightening as if to maximize her height. "I could ask you the same question. Does Professor Sinclair know you're here? He appreciates neither visitors nor interruptions." Her face was overshadowed by a gardening hat the size of a small umbrella. Green rubber boots with white polka dots swallowed her feet and lower legs, which vanished beneath a voluminous fuchsia skirt splattered with potting soil. A purple flannel shirt completed her outfit.

Tess's stilettos clicked on the path behind me. With one hand on my shoulder, she reached in front of me, holding out her hand to greet the woman.

"Tess Olmos," she said. "I'm Linc's Realtor and this is Maggie McDonald, his professional organizer. We're here for an appointment."

I scrambled in my cargo vest for a business card as the woman picked up the business end of a coiled garden hose. I had the distinct impression she was waiting for an excuse to turn the nozzle on us. I found a card, plucked it from my pocket, and handed it to her.

"I was checking the professor's house for damage after that storm last night," the woman said as she took my card and put it in her pocket without looking at it. "My nana would have called it a *gully-womper*. Nice to meet you ladies, but I need to get to work. For twenty years, the Sinclairs have allowed me to use their water in my community garden." She waved her arm toward an overgrown hedge at the back of the half-acre property. "In exchange, I provide them with fresh vegetables."

"Of course," Tess said as if she knew all about the arrangement. "And you are?"

"Oh, sorry." The woman wiped her grubby hands on her pink skirt before shaking Tess's outstretched hand. "I'm Claire Domingo, but I go by Boots. I'm the president of the Orchard View Plotters Garden Club. We run the community garden in back of the house."

Before any of us could say anything more, I heard the screeching of bicycle brakes. Linc careened around the corner with his legs outstretched and his jacket flapping behind him. His Irish wolfhound, Newton, loped beside him and made the turn easily.

Out of breath, the professor jumped from the bike and let it fall to the ground beside him as if he were an eight-year-old who was late for lunch.

"Sorry. Sorry. Sorry," he said, scurrying toward us. "I had an idea for a new project in the middle of the night and I rode over to the university. Time got away from me. Sorry to keep you waiting."

Newton barked in greeting and lunged toward me.

Linc unhooked the dog from the bicycle leash he'd invented ten years earlier but had never sought a patent for. Once he'd created it and proved it worked, he'd lost interest.

Newton barreled in my direction. I stepped back and knelt to give him more room to slow down before he plowed into me. Linc had trained him well, but his exuberance sometimes got the better of him. I scratched him behind the ears in a proper doggy greeting before turning my attention to Linc, who picked up the bicycle and leaned it against the fence.

"No problem, Linc," I said. "You're here now. Shall we get started?"

Linc patted the pockets of his jacket, his jeans, and his sweatshirt and looked up, chagrined. "I'm afraid I've forgotten my key again."

Tess, Boots, and I each reached into our own pockets and plucked out keys labeled with varying shades of fluorescent tags. I laughed awkwardly and headed toward the back porch, knowing that the lock on the kitchen door was less fussy than some of the other old locks on the house.

"Let's add installing new locks to the list of jobs," I told Tess.

Boots followed us. We stepped carefully around some of the boxes of discarded clothing and housewares that awaited pickup by a local charity resale shop. I unlocked the door and we trooped in.

Linc shifted from one foot to another, took off his glasses, and cleaned them with his shirttail. He looked around the room, blinking as if surprised to find he was no longer in his Stanford University lab. I flicked the light switch, but the room remained dim. Last week I'd brought over a supply of bulbs to replace several that I'd found burned out. I must have missed this one.

"Did you lose power in the storm?" I asked Linc.

He answered with a shrug. "I'm not sure. Maybe? I was at my lab working on my project."

Boots pulled open the refrigerator door and plucked a bag of lettuce from the darkness within. It had turned soggy in the bag.

"I'll take this for compost and bring you back some fresh spinach this afternoon," she said. "The kale's coming along nicely too."

"Can I get you all a cup of tea?" Linc asked. It was a delaying tactic I recognized from experience. Sorting and organizing were nearly painful for this man, who was said to have several ideas that could reverse the effects of climate change.

"Let's get started upstairs," I said. "I want to show Tess how much progress you've made."

Boots rummaged in the refrigerator. "I'll see what else needs to be tossed, Linc. Go on. I'll let myself out."

"I can't withstand pressure from all three of you." Linc shrugged and turned toward the staircase that divided the kitchen and living room. I started up the steps behind him, then stopped and called over my shoulder. "Tess, I'm going to show you Linc's workroom first. He's been working in there while I've been tackling the other rooms." I mouthed the words *praise him* to her. Linc hadn't, actually, made all that much progress, but he *had* agreed on broad-based guidelines for culling the equipment and organizing some of his papers.

Newton nudged past us to lead the way up the stairs. When I reached the hall landing, it was dark. *Right,* I thought. *The storm. No electricity.*

Newton growled, low in his throat, then whimpered. Linc moved down the hall toward his office and workroom. In the doorway, he gasped and froze. His mouth dropped open. His eyes grew wide. He stepped back, but leaned forward with his arm outstretched.

"Whatever it is, we can fix it," I said, rushing toward him, terrified I'd tossed out something of great value. "Everything we moved out of here is still in the garage."

Peering over Linc's shaking shoulders, I bit my lip, swallowed hard, and grasped his arm as he tried to move forward into the room. We couldn't fix it. Not this.

"No, don't," I said, pulling him back. "Tess, get the police. An ambulance."

Tess moved forward in the narrow hall, apparently trying to get a look at whatever had shocked Linc and me. I shook my head and whispered, "It's Sarah. Just dial. Quickly."

I hoped my voice would carry to the kitchen. "Boots, do you know where there's a fuse box or electrical panel? Can you make triple sure the power is out all through the house?"

"What's going on?" shouted Boots.

I couldn't think of an appropriate answer, but I gave it a shot. "We've got a problem up here, Boots. Can you make sure the power is off, *now*? Please? Right now?"

"'Kay," said Boots, though I could hear her grumbling that she wasn't our servant to command. Her voice was followed by the creak of old door hinges and the sound of her rubber boots galumphing down the basement stairs.

I forced myself to look at Linc's workroom again. Nothing had changed. Sarah Palmer, Linc's fiancée, lay sprawled on the floor in a puddle of water. Sarah, one of my dearest friends, whose caramel-colored skin normally shone with warmth and health, lay facedown with her hand outstretched, clutching a frayed electrical cord.

Worst of all, the body that had once been Sarah's looked very, very dead.

Mary Feliz writes the Maggie McDonald Mysteries featuring a Silicon Valley professional organizer and her sidekick golden retriever. She's worked for Fortune 500 firms and mom and pop enterprises, competed in whale boat races and done synchronized swimming. She attends organizing conferences in her character's stead, but Maggie's skills leave her in the dust.

For professional organizer Maggie McDonald, moving her family into a new home should be the perfect organizational challenge. But murder was definitely not on the to-do list . . .

Maggie McDonald has a penchant for order that isn't confined to her clients' closets, kitchens, and sock drawers. As she lays out her plan to transfer her family to the hundred-year-old house her husband, Max, has inherited in the hills above Silicon Valley, she has every expectation for their new life to fall neatly into place. But as the family bounces up the driveway of their new home, she's shocked to discover the house's dilapidated condition. When her husband finds the caretaker face-down in their new basement, it's the detectives who end up moving in. What a mess! While the investigation unravels and the family camps out in a barn, a killer remains at large—exactly the sort of loose end Maggie can't help but clean up . . .

MARY FELIZ

ADDRESS TO DIE FOR

A MAGGIE MCDONALD MYSTERY